SHE DANCED

Fiona Howe

Published by Scenario, London 2019
52 Avenue Gardens
London W3 8HB

ISBN: 9781096766865

For my family

1.

The glitterati spilled into the crisp, nightlit square with a swelling hum of self-congratulation. Film-lovers, illustrious academy members, industry heavyweights, actors, all rubbed shoulders with the febrile, hushed intent of bees in a hive. Seen closer, they might have been opera-goers in their dinner suits and evening gowns, clustered like so many gorgeous jewels at a dancer's throat, lovely in every shade and nuance, flanked by the press and public waiting for the winners to appear. Here and there, the flashes began, tentatively.

Mia smiled for the cameras as she emerged into the Royal Opera House lobby on Stephen's arm. He held aloft their trophy for best documentary, awarded for *Lovergirls*, a much-admired study of female juvenile obsession filmed on a London council estate, released in the cinemas a few months earlier. Elegant in sea-green, having ditched her customary jeans and jacket for the ceremony, Mia detailed to the journalists their two years of research, how Stephen had painstakingly gained the trust of the teenage girls they'd interviewed, her own child-protection role as producer, bowling them the soundbites she wanted to read in the papers the following morning.

The fêted couple, accompanied by their young subject Dalila and their artist daughter Charlotte, posed for one final photo call for the late evening editions, then headed for the doors. Ignoring the continuing press calls of *Mr Chancery? Over here..?* Stephen leant to murmur in his wife's ear, as he ushered her toward the cars waiting to take VIPs to the official dinner. 'What a bloody night! Be glad to get home to bed with you.'

Elated, Mia steered Stephen away from the crush. Beyond the hubbub of the piazza, a late guitarist was playing.

'Let's have a drink together before the dinner? Just the four of us, away from the journos.'

'We could give it a miss couldn't we? No one would notice.' He kissed his woman on the cheek, still besotted with her after twenty years and God knows how many temptations, as they waited for the girls to catch up, Dalila with her black-eyed broodiness, so compelling on screen yet somehow eclipsed by their fair daughter with her dancing step and sparkling quickness.

'I think they might.' Mia laughed. Hassles with production funding faded into insignificance. The award would have an immediate impact on the business. She'd be fielding the press for the next month but it would be worth it.

She embraced Dalila a touch proprietorially, 'Excited?' but the girl's response betrayed something closer to agoraphobia. Mia turned to Lottie with a touch of compunction. 'Quick one to celebrate?'

Lottie laughed, dismissive. 'We'll leave you to your media love-in.' Their star had already turned down the dinner and afterparty. She was out of her comfort zone and Lottie was rescuing the situation of course. Mia waved them off with a fistful of notes and effusive thanks.

'No stamina, the young,' chuckled Stephen. They watched the crowd close around the girls, not before he had clocked the way his daughter placed her hand very delicately on the small of Dalila's back as they climbed into the back of a waiting black cab. 'Did you see that, Mia?'

'She was very clever to get that taxi. Born to be a producer.'

'No, I mean…' He eyed his wife meaningfully. She glanced back, but the cab was already driving away, the girls concealed within. All at once she felt herself stupid, blind.

They were passing the singer-guitarist, stationed near the warm air vent of the tube station, a bearded, bedraggled individual in tattered jeans and sweater, nothing remarkable about him but the sweetness of his voice, the passion of his playing and the fact that his bare feet were bloodied from long exposure.

'Oh look…' Mia's stomach gave a lurch. She could never bear the idea of people sufferering on the streets. 'Stephen, look at his feet.'

She retrieved a twenty pound note from her clutch bag and walked over to the young man.

'Please take this,' she said. 'It might buy you a bed

3

for the night or a pair of sneakers or something?'

He broke off playing for a moment and squinted at her. She shivered in the night air, but there was something else as he reached out and took the money, his dry fingers brushing hers with the scratch of autumn leaves, something like a bomb dropping on the seafloor of his mind. The money was in his pocket in a fraction of a second, although it was not exactly that he had snatched it from her. He looked away, abashed.

'Thank you. You're amazing, thank you.'

Self-conscious in her finery, she retreated into the protective embrace of her husband and they moved across the square towards the bright lights of a local wine bar. Mia's heart was racing, she didn't understand why she was so flustered, it was knowing all that she had and seeing all that others – this other – did not, that floored her, shamed her.

'It's too much, Mia, he'll just put it straight in the pocket of his dealer.'

'Don't, Stephen.'

'If you're going to dispense charity, at least pick a good cause. Or our children, they'll appreciate it more.'

Mia bridled at his disapproval but her voice was quiet. 'How can you know *he* won't?

From behind, she heard the start of a rocking, upbeat song whose chords stabbed at the night in defiance, though she couldn't quite make out the lyrics.

> *Can't see can't breathe can't die can't live*
> *You're onto me*
> *You're onto me*

You're sweet hard dark light
Know how to feel right
Into me

They entered the bar and were enveloped by the warm air and the gentle undulation of voices bent on recreation, in counterpoint with the innocuous soft jazz-rock piping through the interior in the same uniform way as underfloor heating.

They sat together at a window table and Stephen ordered a bottle of Montepulciano.

'And some breadsticks. Christ, I'm starving… Mia, d'you want to pick up something here?'

'Hm?'

Mia fingered the menu without interest. She could still see the figure of the young busker across the way. He was *dancing* now for God's sake, like some crazy Mr Tambourine Man lost in his own otherworldly ecstasy. He could die. The balance of the planet would scarcely be disturbed. She shifted in her seat so that she was looking at the dumbshow inside, at her husband.

'Some olives?'

The trophy was on the table between them. Mia suddenly found this at once absurd and alarming. She thrust it across the table as the waitress scribbled on her pad. 'Yes, if you put that somewhere safe darling. Please.'

Stephen looked at her strangely as he wrapped it in his raincoat and placed it on the windowsill out of sight, but he was happy to tell the waitress all about it. Yes, he was well-known but he wasn't going to tell her his name. Yes he would like a bottle of water as well.

When they left the bar-restaurant half-an-hour later to join the stragglers departing for the awards dinner, the busker had dematerialised, leaving behind only a bloodstained patch on the pavement. Mia saw it and looked away, heart quailing.

It was past two o'clock when they got back to the house in darkness, the roar of the afterparty still ringing loudly in their ears. The street off Ladbroke Grove was quiet except for a drunk kicking over the traces further down towards the public gardens and the cab ticking over as Mia paid the driver.

'Still not back.' Stephen was more curious than concerned. Mia shivered, tired from the evening's exertions. She took out her key as they descended the steps to the lower ground entrance. 'She's nineteen. She's at college, you just have to behave as if she were away from home. You wouldn't have a clue what she was up to then would you?'

She knew it wasn't the same. She couldn't pretend that ignorance was bliss when the girl still lived in their pockets, in all the spaces she'd lived with them since a child.

The child was only a memory, had been slowly, inexorably modified by time into the quirky, penetrating, at times strangely guarded young woman who now cohabited with them. In her mind's eye, she glimpsed for a moment her five-year-old eco-warrior in full-throated declamation, prancing half-naked across the room, flapping silver foil like a badly wrapped Christmas turkey, oblivious to the family laughter. Lottie's defiant inspiration owed nothing to anyone, she'd always been in charge of her own drama.

Stephen and Mia moved naked around each other in the marble bathroom, their habitual wind-down merging with half-remembered fragments of an extraordinary day, faces and speeches, handshakes and kisses, tears and trophies. Bent over the wash-basin, Mia carefully removed eye make-up, unpinned her hair. Stephen was already beneath the scalding shower, sending steam clouds out into her space and obscuring the mirror.

'Still as just as beautiful.'

He gazed out at her, the sweep of her hips, the way she arched her neck as she looked back at him over her shoulder, and his flesh rose at the splendour of her. 'Come in and join me?'

She lowered her eyes with that half-smile which made her so desirable to him. She reached out for his hand and stepped under the shower.

At three-thirty a.m. she lay naked in the big bed, enjoying the muted half-light of their bedroom, letting her thoughts travel far and wide, while Stephen's soft breaths played against her shoulder. She had long passed the time when she would automatically fall asleep afterwards. It wasn't that her climax was less intense, if anything it had matured like a good wine into a deeply satisfying draft of the eternal. She took her pleasure slowly, but the afterglow was fertile, life-affirming, mysterious. She felt distantly amazed that her hunger could be so durable, that she still felt the swooning into desire when her man gathered her to him and kissed her hard; she delighted that he knew the secret of her body and mind, what made her spark.

She heard the gentle thud of the front door closing and light footsteps on the stair. It was now three-fifty according to the clock alarm that winked its green LED display at the edge of her vision. An obscure sense of relief washed over her: whatever her daughter had been up to, she had returned. She was safe within the bosom of her family, had chosen this haven in which to spend the remainder of her night. Mia knew she wouldn't see her at breakfast. They were keeping opposing hours presently. Mia would be out of the house and on her way to the office at nine without making the slightest impact on those heady, youthful dreams.

There was a time when all her endeavour, all her creative and professional striving, all the borders of her life, were circumscribed and intimately bound up with her identity as mother. She danced to the tune of that imperious infant voice. She took her daughter wherever she was, until she could no longer justify it to the local education authority. Then for three years she took only London-based line producing jobs, commercials, corporate shoots, rubbing many backs up the wrong way when she disappeared at five to pick up her kid. No matter how perfectly she delivered her work from home, there were plenty to call her flaky and not to employ her if there was anyone else to choose from. But by dint of her personal charm and a faster turnover in the executive producing grade than her own, not to mention a clutch of powerful friends who would recommend her despite the will o' the wisp she was enslaved to, she managed to keep working – as often as decency and independence would permit with Stephen – so that they could build up their company and she would have to suffer less often the slings and arrows of outrageous fortune.

Lottie's door closed quietly. There was nothing in this to disturb Mia's equilibrium and she finally began to drift, lulled by the insomniac blackbird that sang outside her window. The city was too warm, too light, haemorrhaging energy, but the throaty warble was like liquid music, something holy. As she fell asleep, another sound, a girlish giggle, resolved into a sigh in the farthest reaches of her consciousness.

The phone hadn't stopped since Mia had clattered up the narrow staircase at nine-thirty into the bright but chaotic office overlooking Monmouth Street. It was a broad, open-plan space, frequently hectic, this morning occupied only by their P.A. Ally fielding interviews, and Stephen trawling through the post-awards press, while Mia made the phone rounds of their current film backers, making sure they knew exactly what kind of a hot property they were investing in. The acceleration of events was abrupt, but it wasn't that unsettling her, there was something flaring yellow at the edges of her vision. She knew her daughter had had a lover with her in the night. She'd gleaned this from the unzipped pair of high leather boots littering the upper hallway alongside Lottie's own, the jackets slung together on the bench like debauchees. The boots belonged to a girl she knew very well, someone she'd worked with intensively over the previous nine months. Clearly another kind of relationship had been gestating while Lottie had worked on the set logging shots and checking the digital rushes. She'd had plenty of time to get acquainted with Dalila, now Mia thought it over, but she'd never given any sign.

How did she know they'd been doing anything other than sleeping together as friends caught out late together and using the nearest refuge? That was more elusive to define. Lottie could easily have dropped the girl home and stayed with her if that had been the intention, but they had clearly wanted to have fun together. All kinds of fun. And they wanted Mia to know about it. She thought about the body language the previous evening but it was oblique. In retrospect they'd both been out of their depth at the awards ceremony, Dalila a bit arrogant, Lottie a bit wired, too much bubbly and smirking behind the backs of the great and good. Maybe it was their first taste of going public together. Maybe the first time they'd even realised? But she knew in that half-waking moment before dawn that she had heard the sigh. And she knew it wasn't her daughter's.

It made her restless. Once Stephen's first interview was underway with Pamela Joliffe, a freelance arts journalist who would pitch her feature to a handful of the broadsheets and Sunday magazines, Mia excused herself to get stronger coffee for them all from the café a few doors along. She clattered down the steel rimmed staircase in her own high boots and felt the frosted air climb to her knees in chill greeting. Her face was flushed and her newly highlighted hair seemed to have an angry life of its own. And was she angry? Did a child have to share its parents' erotic definition? Of course not. It was just another example of how one's offspring failed to become the reflection of oneself that one expected when they were in the womb. Just another instance of the tyranny of the genes that misled one to expect a chip off the old block. She knew she should be proud of her girl's independent spirit, the confidence, the passion which was not so far removed from her own, but yes, she was angry, and it fuelled her long past the usual espresso bar.

At Seven Dials the mêlée of street sounds began to drag her back into consciousness of the material world, and the smell of fresh pastries made her hungry. She'd take those almond croissants Stephen liked back to the office along with the coffee, make a proper fuss of him and Pam. She stepped forward toward the doorway of an Italian café and a hand landed lightly on her arm. She wanted to believe it was a mistake, someone jostling her in the crowd, someone anonymous, not a pickpocket, please not that, she had so much to do, but the instant she thought this and shrugged off the unwelcome touch she found herself looking into the eyes of someone she knew, not well.

He was a step further from death's door than the previous evening but only just. She found herself looking at his feet. He had on a pair of monstrous walking boots that showed their tongues of fleece to the chill air like children catching mouthfuls of snow.

'You saved my life last night.'

Dark green eyes scrutinised her. Probing. Hers flicked across his face in brief discomfort, she was *blushing* for God's sake. She let herself take in his mood. He was ok. Better than she'd left him. She'd done some good.

'I'm glad,' she said, but she was nervous, what did he want from her, more money? She didn't want to walk around her neighbourhood in the fear she'd be accosted by someone who wasn't a stranger. By this time she'd already let her barrier down. Something in his look drew her and she knew he wasn't the same as those she passed a hundred times in a week and threw her small change to.

'I'm getting coffee, can I buy you one?' she offered, baulking at herself, confounded. He broke into a smile as pale as the sun. A first fleeting sense of who he was.

'Sounds good.'

Mia hustled her order across the counter at the startled coffee shop owner, who winced at her tone. She got out her cash, oblivious, remembering a literary friend who'd once told her that when the poet Byron had smiled it was said to be like the gates of heaven opening. She'd always laughed at that as a piece of high Romantic hyperbole. But now as she watched him out of the corner of her eye though the plate glass window laden with confectionery, she feared and longed to see that smile again. Anyone who could smile like that would not die. It was a smile that meant salvation. And it meant a whole lot besides: this was someone who knew their main chance. Most of all it meant a disruption to her schedule if she got any further involved. To her relief, he waited at a distance until she came out, tray of coffee in one hand, bag of pastries in the other. 'Here…' she nodded at him to take one of the espresso cups and perched the tray on one of the outside tables, handing him a croissant. He took it from her, eyeing her with what seemed a fathomless hunger, crushing the fragile pastry in his jaws with animal haste. In an instant it was gone, and he was brushing the crumbs clumsily from his matted beard.

'Another?' she ventured. He nodded, unsmiling,

holding out his hand for it, the urgency of appetite awakened. She made her decision and pulled him into the warm shop.

'Could you please serve this man a full English breakfast?'

'Anything for you madam?'

Mia met the shop owner's frosty look. The implication was clear. If she was there to accompany him they wouldn't turn him out.

'A pot of tea for two. Please.'

She slumped into the seat opposite him and contemplated her rapidly cooling consignment of espressos. She drank one off and handed him another, feeling the need to fix the world up, an instinct that had pulled her through countless years and bleaknesses before, the acquired strength that never really failed her. 'How long have you been on the streets?'

'I'm not sure.'

'Weeks? Months?'

'Couple months probably.'

'What happened?'

His mouth did a strange twist. Something raw. He didn't want to talk about it. He played with the coffee cup but didn't drink.

'Sorry.' She looked at his fingers, calloused, dirt-engrained, but still the fingers of a musician, not a down-and-out. 'You're not going to be able to play for long like this are you?'

He exhaled, defiant. 'Spring's coming.'

'You'll wreck your hands. What about your voice? You'll get pneumonia out there.'

'It's a kind of freedom.'

'It's not freedom. What if you get beaten up.

Robbed. Raped. You won't be so bloody cheerful then.'

He was laughing at her quietly.

'What's free about that?'

'I don't think I'm in any danger.'

She raised her eyebrows, she really wasn't interested in his naïveté. She did not wish to get involved but she had the bit between her teeth now.

'So you're not really homeless. Just pretending.'

His look darkened. 'I'm offline.'

'Pretty radical way of jacking it in.'

Now he was staring at her. She was nearer the truth than she knew and he was angry with her. Angry that his secret was so easy to guess.

2.

I jerked awake to the sound of her song, the ringtone on my phone I should have changed but for a terrible inertia that held me pinned to the earth like Gulliver. I'd taken to falling asleep in odd places since we'd split. I found myself staring blearily into the eyes of a fellow bus passenger as Tarzan's voice ground into my brain.

'If you're not here in four minutes I'm dead. And I'm gonna have your balls you stupid fucker.'

My scalp tingled. 'What time is it?'

'I'm sitting here making small talk with someone whose natural expectation is that the next person who rolls through the door is there to give him a blow job. I'm trading off a five-year friendship, give me a break.'

He hung up on me. My manager. I was off the bus at the next stop somewhere amidst the plastic glories of Oxford Street, trying to make sense of the afternoon, fifteen minutes behind schedule. He met me at the plate-glass doors of the record company office, manhandling me through them in reverse.

'Dickon Brand,' he barked to a quailing receptionist, beside himself, literally dancing with rage. For once I could see it his way. He paced me down the corridor into a small studio set up for a solo performance. The sound-proof doors closed behind me with a muffled thud. It might as well have been an execution chamber. A brassily coiffed, low-cut secretary appeared, batted her false eyelashes at me and steered me into position. No drinks were offered. She pressed a button on the intercom and spoke to a shadowy someone the other side of the smoked glass.

'Should he start Karl? Or would you like to talk to him first?'

A throat cleared. I screwed up my eyes to see better beyond the murk, but my adversary was well masked. After a short pause and some creaking of what sounded like a heavyweight leather jacket, he declined. 'Nah, let's hear it Katia.'

It. I decided not to retire without a fight. If this was a swansong, then let it be loud, let it be defiant. Suddenly I didn't want to play anything that anybody could have heard, either live or on the web. I had so many songs inside me, they were going to get a new one.

'Ok, this is *Lovergirl*, thanks.'

It was something I'd cooked up for Cleopatra the night after we'd made love so spectacularly, apparently all that was left of our liaison. It was wild, edgy and masculine, not very characteristic of my current dreamy run of songs, but I thought it might speak to this nameless, faceless executive behind the screens. Who the hell was he to have that much power over anyone that he had my manager practically wetting himself. It wasn't in my nature to give him what he wanted. So I gave everyone what they didn't.

> *Can't see can't breathe can't die can't live*
> *You're onto me*
> *You're onto me*
> *You're sweet hard dark light*
> *Know how to feel right*
> *Into me*
> *You're into me*
> *Lovergirl*
> *Lovergirl*
> *Dance me to your backbeat*
> *Burn me with your black heat*
> *Against the wall for you*
> *I'll take it all for you*
> *Lovergirl*
> *Ah Lovergirl*

I punished that guitar with all the anger I hadn't sent her way, all the passion that was welling up in me again now her absence was sinking in. My addiction was classic. The first days of denial, when aversion says: what you thought you needed all those weeks, all those hours, you didn't need at all. It was doing you bad. It was doing you in. Then withdrawal starts to bite. I might have put it off for a few days, soothed by the honeyed touch of another girl, grief scorched out of me by the desperation of my bid for fame. But I'd woken in the throes of a fever and I didn't know who

I was at that moment. I just knew she was the ghost in the glass and she was dancing for me in a sea of glinting lights on the mixing console behind, as I wanted her, all curve and flirt and sassy sweetness and grace, such grace. Then I looked at her head on and she was Kali moving in with razored fingernails and a ruthless look in her eye.

It wasn't quite burning my boats, my performance was good, but I knew from the pause at the close of the song that they were confused. That Tarzan was explaining why his lyrical songster had abruptly turned into a wannabe rock star.

Someone flicked the intercom on. Then off again. There was obviously some kind of altercation going on back there.

'Shall I play you another song?' I offered, trying not to sound sardonic.

Tarzan's voice could be heard through the soundproof glass in raised dialogue with Karl the Terrible. Then the intercom opened again.

'That's all. Thanks.'

It was over. Tarzan came out looking like nothing I've ever seen but a storm about to break in a frenzy over the Westway. Even now I still remember the sick air preceding that downpour, though I've eclipsed what his actual words were at the moment we walked through the door onto an acrid, fume-drenched street. He conveyed me from the building with the power of his feelings rather than by any physical intervention. If he'd tried I'd have hit him anyway, I was coiled like a cobra with all the venom of those unpaid favours he'd stacked up, and sick to my stomach. It felt like the end of the world. It was the end of the world, though I didn't know it yet.

'There is no fucking label in this town gonna sign you. You were LATE!'

He was right. It was all over before it had begun. But rebellion was building in the pit of my being with alarming violence. I was starting to feel like the Minotaur and I didn't know how soon I would start to roar.

We paced each other down the street.

'I cannot represent you. I cannot manage an individual with the inappropriate sense of time and motion that you seem to possess.'

I stopped mid-track and faced him down.

'No, you cannot represent me because you've signed nothing with me, paid nothing for me, done nothing for me other than a shed-load of virtual garbage which won't make the slightest impact on my music.'

'You're too old for this.'

'Just too old to take it from behind like the other poor hopefuls you rip off.'

'Fine, we'll draw up a list of the nothing I've done for you and take it to my lawyers in the morning. I'll have a share in the publishing of those little dirges you're convinced the *ladies* will be downloading in their thousands. You amaze me, you arrogant little shit.' He dried, his mouth hanging slack, finally speechless at the extent of my ingratitude.

'You can waste your time trying, I'll just kick them out of my set and write new ones and they'll have nothing to do with you or anything you stand for. What you people don't understand Tarzan is that we create without you. You're a parasite not an artist so you're never going to understand…'

His fist was against my jawbone almost before I

saw it coming. It flashed forward and I felt the impact before I realised what he'd just done and was about to do again. The minotaur rage was upon him, as if I'd channelled it all out of myself in that tirade, but his face was frightening and he was going to lay me flat if this went on. He shoulder-barged me off balance like the former rugby player I suddenly knew he was and as I hit the pavement I realised it was all best barrow-boy mockney masquerading as industry nous, when of course he'd been to some public school in the West Country all along. 'What was that you called me?' were the only intelligible words I could make out. They came in spasms through a kind of purple gasp as he landed on me and put his hands to my throat. *Tarzan.*

I hadn't been in a fight since college. I didn't have time to remember how it went, I just knew I had to get my knee up hard from under the bulk of him before he choked me. It was like lifting a mountain then suddenly his grip relaxed and he crumpled away. I'd hit my target evidently. I wouldn't have wished it on him but he gave me no choice. He doubled up breathless on the pavement like a beached fish as I sprang to my feet and grabbed my guitar case. Bystanders were gathering, two kids already arguing about who'd put the boot in first and I walked away without anyone appearing to realise I'd been part of the fracas. *You alright mate…* words floated in the air, could've been for him, could've been for me, it hardly seemed to matter now. My head was spinning, my jaw was swelling and my ribs hurt with the kind of sharpness that made it hard to breathe, but I was free.

I didn't stop walking till I reached her street, sputtering on full throttle like some amateur rocket-enthusiast's attempt at orbital domination, pain streaming off me like a comet's tail. I had no idea if she'd be in. I certainly shouldn't see her if she was. But there were no brakes on this piece of space-bound scrap metal. I was a junkie in the lunatic spasms of cold-turkey, I was crawling on the ceiling, making about as much sense as a psychopath's short story. How short it would be was in her hands.

'Hello?' Her hushed voice breathed down the intercom. My lower body turned to soup. My upper body beat itself up internally. It was hard to breathe at all. Perhaps I would die on her doorstep.

'Cleo.'

There was a pause, then the buzzer sounded and the door latch clicked open. I dragged myself up the two flights to her landing, where I'd been accustomed to looking dolefully at her closed door. This time it was open and she was standing there, her back to the light, everything shining around her like the angel I knew she wasn't. There was no fathoming the depths of denial she could raise in me.

'What's happened to you?' Her soft hands were moving to the places where it didn't look too painful to go. 'D'you need a doctor?'

'I don't know.'

She took me in, propped my guitar carefully in the hallway under her hatstand and closed the door. There was music playing on the big speakers, ultra-cool, bass-heavy. She killed the volume, placed me on her big sofa and looked me over, trying to decode my battered appearance.

'You've been in a fight.'

'So it would seem.'

'But you've just been with Karl Fleet.'

'Busy afternoon.'

She muted the dismay in her face and stopped talking, putting two and two together. Instead she decided to clean me up. She put tea and oranges on the Moroccan coffee table, brought a basin of hot water from the little kitchen and sat down by me.

She reached forward tentatively and I felt her hand trembling. Her eyes were veiled. She looked sad. The white skin of her throat contracted as she swallowed.

The night we met she'd been drenched with the sweat of the dance and the sudden rainstorm that pelted us on the way back to my flat. Her lips parted easily and her tongue darted quick and sweet at mine as if she could communicate those wondrous stories of hers by osmosis, through her cherry-sharp saliva. She slowed into a long draught of me, limp as a murder victim in my arms, the moment at which we took possession of each other and she became my girl.

Her skin was damp, her dress slippery under my fingers. The scent of her permeated my trance and made me rise pore by pore until I thought the top of my head would explode in rainbows, mainlining the essence of her, the sweet animal smell that wafted from the damp hollows I would later explore with my tongue. I held her where I could look at her, eyes bright in the streetlight that flooded the room, hair hanging down salty as a mermaid's. I thought: this is the girl I'm going to marry.

I still have the sensation of that zip peeling apart and how far it ran down the back of her. It was the most erotic thing that had ever happened to me. I slid the silk from her shoulders and let it drop to the floor with a gentle slap. She became softer, unclothed, her curves more absorbing than ever, right down to the five-inch heels she was still wearing. She was a work of art. Escher without the edges, drawing herself into being. I wanted to look at her, every line of her, before I forgot myself, before I forgot the composition of her. She watched me looking, engrossed in her effect, took me by the hand and turned me to face the wardrobe mirror. She wanted the live theatre version. There we stood, a pair of sexual conspirators. She touched the dip at my throat which made me swallow and suddenly I was shaking, out of control. With a ripping of distressed fabric, that shirt was floored in the second it took to seize her in my arms and press her beautiful body against mine. The skin of her breast glowed against me like warm chamois, but we were vibrating together like the reeds of a strange, primitive instrument and this was the way our bodies would make their music for the next three hours.

I put my hand over hers and held it to quell my raging sadness. My eyes closed. Waves of trembling overwhelmed me. A blood-red sea of pain whose tide was endlessly coming in, never receding. She held me so lightly it was hardly holding at all. But her warmth finally seeped into me and slowed the tide, slowed my heart, made it possible for my lungs to inflate a little more in their barbed cage.

Her caller had had the generosity to wait until then. Her phone trilled and she snatched it from the table where our tea was cooling.

'I can't talk now. No. Yes. Around seven is fine. Thanks.' She was off the line. I didn't need to know who it was.

In the duration of the call she'd made her decision. She unbuttoned and gently removed my shirt. A few scrapes and bruises, nothing time wouldn't heal. That was the external narrative. She arranged one of her ample Egyptian cotton towels around my shoulders and dabbed at my bloody jaw with her make-up pads until the skin was clean, the towel stained and the damage clear.

'At least your hands are ok.'

I turned them over, looked at the dirt drying under the nails, looked up at her looking. She lowered her eyes and a small muscle in her cheek flinched. Otherwise her composure was immaculate. I wondered how to let her off the hook.

'Good enough for sweeping streets.'

'Come on, have some tea. I'll get you sugar. No, I'll do better than that…'

Nimble as a cat she jumped up, disappeared into the kitchen and returned with a jar labelled in faintly medicinal script and containing large brown sugar crystals suspended in a thick liquid that took their murky, mysterious colour.

'What d'you call this?'

'*Rumkandis*.'

I liked the sound of the word on her tongue. With the passing of the initial shock, my withdrawal symptoms were moving into a more imperious phase.

'Again?'

'It's rum and sugar. A German girlfriend swears by it.'

I realised in a kind of swoon that I would try and get her to sleep with me again. I pushed my cup forward and she spooned in some of the elixir. I held it there until she'd upended half the contents of the jar, then stirred it slowly, watching her watching me.

'Aren't you having any?'

She hesitated, the ghost of a smile playing at the corner of her mouth. I knew perfectly well she didn't drink alcohol. But this wasn't, really. It would have been like saying chocolate liqueurs were out of bounds. Or that you couldn't cook with red wine. She took the merest spoonful and stirred it into her tea.

'Smells beautiful.'

'It does.'

So does cyanide. But I took a deep draught and let the warmth infuse my bones. It felt like that moment when you've been in bed with a raging cold for two days then suddenly your body decides it's well and in defiance of death all of a sudden wants to connect with the nearest female. Any female. The cleaner. Your little sister. And here I was unexpectedly reunited with the woman of my dreams. I was horny as hell for her. The angst of the previous weeks evaporated. She'd made a decision without me, it still felt like the wrong one, but that was my take and I had no right to trespass on her freedom.

'What were you listening to? When I came in?'

'It's a drum and bass mix of a song I'm working on.'

The towel slid a little further off my shoulders. I felt like Marilyn Monroe. She bleated a giggle and threw me a striped running tee-shirt she'd pulled out of the cupboard to preserve my decency.

'Sorry, it's got paint on it somewhere from when I was making papier-mâché with my nephew.'

My skin thrilled to know that she had a gentle

side, a playful side, a side that invented games for children. She was human then, no siren. I pulled the cotton top over my head, soft as a kid-glove with all the washing and wearing. Strange and comforting to think of it next to her warm body.

'Can I hear some more?'

'Sure.'

She grabbed the remote control and while she twisted round to select the track, I tipped what I could of the remains of the *rumkandis* into her tea.

The sound flooded my senses in a way I didn't associate with her at all, but she'd been working up her programming skills and the fruit of her labour was this dreamy, trance-like pattern looped but off-synched against a darker, equally hypnotic pattern, and then – how could I have missed it the first time? – her voice, ethereal, haunting, and by the end almost operatic. One simple line, like a mantra, building different harmonies as she swept the world away.

> *Root in me*
> *Grow through me*
> *Breathe through me*
> *Sequoia*

It was hard to find words that didn't fall short. 'It's beautiful. Brave, I think.'

She wriggled her toes in her dance tights and glowed. 'It's therapy.'

'If all therapy felt like that, what a world it would be.'

'That's a sweet thing to say.'

She rested her head on my shoulder. 'How d'you feel now?'

'Right now? I'm dandy.'

'You shameless flirt, I'd give you some punishment if you hadn't taken too much already today.' She stroked my hand. 'D'you want to talk about it?'

I crooked my head round to look at her up close but it hurt too much. 'I'm sure your manager will give you the low-down when you see him.'

At this she moved away to get a better handle on things. 'You split already?'

'It was short but intense. Bit like us.'

She coloured. Her hands fluttered. She took a sip of the rum-laced tea in an attempt to light her through the forest, and as usual it wasn't the way I'd predicted, we were down a narrow pathway heading for the thicket without a torch before the end of the first sentence.

'D'you think we'll make it?' There was a look I'd rarely caught in her, trouble in mind. 'I've got six months, maybe a year to get my career up and running. Then they'll pull the plug on me.'

'They?'

'My family. They're my main investors, I owe them all this. I can't let it stay that way, it's too much, it's my ball and chain.'

'You're doing great, Cleo. You'll be massive.'

'No one knows that. It's just putting yourself in the best place and the rest is down to luck and timing.'

She came back to nestle. Fledgling with a razorblade concealed beneath her downy feathers. 'Promise me something?'

'Scary?'

'Try.'

'I'll try then.'

'In a year, if things work out and I can make a go of it, buy my freedom… if you can make it too… can we try again?'

The words were out. They were as monumental, as immutable as a curse, terrible in everything they entailed. It was an impossible promise – impossible to make, impossible to fulfil.

'Does that mean it's over?'

She was crying now, the tears streaming down her ivory cheeks, a deliquescent Madonna. 'I need it to be real. You can't live on dreams.'

'Half the world tries.'

'Half the world starves.'

'Come on, you're not going to starve whatever happens.'

'I mean starve emotionally. Creatively. If I can't do this, I don't know what I'll do. It's all I love.'

It was the nearest to truth she ever spoke. There was no place for me in that love. Not even for a song.

She was laughing now, bittersweet, on the edge. It was me who was crying, I realised. She reached forward to touch the tracks of my tears with her finger, then her tongue, stem the flow with kisses before the salt could reach the wound and hurt me. But I couldn't stop. My mouth twisted and I realised that the animal sounds in the room were the braying of a man whose lover had quit the game. The salt hit the wound despite everything she could do.

I must have frightened her, balled up on her sofa like an assault case. She sprang into action with the serious stuff, a bottle of Armagnac she'd been keeping for medicinal purposes. She pressed one of her delicate painted teaglasses into my hands and held her slender fingers over mine, pushing it to my lips. I fought her off, sending the little piece of glittering fragility shattering onto the parquet.

Later, I wondered about karma. There was a girl I'd loved when we were seventeen, a lovely girl with long black hair and a red mouth, whose virginity I'd taken in the meadow behind my house that summer, and when I told her some weeks later it was over she'd almost fainted in my arms. She couldn't take it. She'd lain on my front lawn for two days and nights with a bottle of rum and coke for company, weeping and sleeping by turns. I couldn't look outside the window although my mother had told me to go out and comfort her. I'd hidden in my room with my vinyl and my guitar and I played all the songs I'd ever written for other girls, until her friend came and took her away. I didn't see her for two years, then we bumped into each other accidentally at someone's party and she was with a tall, well-muscled guy who certainly didn't know who I was. She gave no sign that anything had ever passed between us, except one little quail of the mouth when she said hi. Bravery. And I'd shown none. Not even enough interest to write a song about it. There were too many others.

So now, this Cleopatra, tyrant queen of my heart, had told me I was incompatible with her career plans and left me as desolate as that poor raven-haired beauty. It was over before it had even begun and all I could see was the wasteland of my life without her stretching on into the future. I knew, then, that I would do something radical. It would start the minute she kicked me out of the door, but she'd have to make that move first.

For a long time she sat very still, kneeling at my

feet. She was the Sphinx, but I would never get anywhere near solving her riddle. All that content I would never access. All that richness of beauty I'd banked on, and lost. All that mutual discovery, all that conversation I'd imagined would accompany our gradually unfolding relationship. All the joys I could have brought her. But I was nothing. She'd told me I was nothing. The day's events had told me I was nothing. What would it be like? Being nothing?

After a while, I recovered enough to watch her watching me, feeling like a specimen dredged up from the darkest depths of the ocean. My face creaked with spent grief, swollen as a sponge. My eyes sank into my head like a crab's, while hers regarded me dispassionately, pink-rimmed, her face very pale, but otherwise with no outward sign of trauma. Hell, she even cried beautifully.

I hadn't consciously noticed she'd taken a few hits of brandy since trying to administer it to me. Now I understood her unearthly stillness. Her lips curled around the pearls of her teeth and suddenly she threw back her head and laughed. It tinkled across the room, like the glass shards that were dangerously near her bare feet, a most musical and seductive sound, but she was in the wrong movie. We both were, that was the problem all along. It sent a chill down my spine, even though the shaking had subsided. The laugh evaporated as quickly as it had come, and she eyed me again, remorseful but with a playful twitch at the edge of her mouth as she pulled herself up onto the sofa next to me. It took a while. When she spoke, her words were uncertain, like badly shaped felt cut-outs.

'This is supposed to be for you.'

She took a mouthful and leant into me, with a fire

in her eyes that said *you know you want this*. She kissed me, pulling my lips apart with her gentle fingers as she emptied the liquid into my mouth. It burned like heaven on my tongue, and my heart pumped wildly at the audacity of her first aid. There was nothing I could do against her. I was in her hands, where I wanted. At that moment I felt I'd have been happiest if she'd killed me then. Give up the ghost.

'There's a reason...' she began, her lips moving against mine as she spoke, everything her body said in utter contradiction to the crucifixion her mind was imposing on us – there are times when chemistry talks louder than logic, and she was in the throes of an Orphic dilemma, each limb stretched to breaking point by the ecstasies of her Thracian phantoms – '...why I stopped drinking.' Her body was suddenly limp against mine and my arms closed around her. But it was fear I felt, not desire. I wanted to protect her. Her lashes brushed the dried blood on my face and made me wince. 'Why is it you smell so divine, lover?' She breathed against my neck, inhaling my scent, blood, testosterone, the sweat of a day fuelled by aggression and madness.

'Why was it, Cleopatra?'

'Why?'

'That you stopped drinking?'

'Ah...'

She struggled to put her thoughts together, heaved herself suddenly out of the black lagoon, the seaweed streaming violently from her limbs. 'I miss her so badly sometimes I think she'll pull me under with her. I drank a glass of wine at the memorial... like a kind of last communion, and I thought: you know, if you drink another you will never stop, there is something in you, like there was in her, something wrong, something that can't stop…' she was gripping my arms, the fear rising, '…like this. You know why I can't be with you my lover. Because if I fall for you any further I will sink to the bottom of the lake and never come up. It's too much. You will drown me.'

She was crying again. I kissed her then, her marble brow, for the promise she'd asked of me, and for what I'd failed to comprehend. Stroked her back until the tears subsided. Eventually, I heard her breathing softly against me and knew she was asleep. She hadn't slept in my arms since that first night. If I just stayed still, here on her sofa, maybe she would just sleep sweetly against me, and maybe in the morning, we would be healed. Maybe.

At five minutes to seven, I remember looking up and seeing the hour on her hand-sculpted Salvador Dali clock above the door, the entrance intercom buzzed, committing violence on the serenity that enveloped us both.

She jumped out of her skin, wide awake and on her feet in a split second, her face stricken as if she'd been slapped.

'Whoah, it's ok!' I'd surfaced into her nightmare, was on my way to answer the door, but she was back in that different movie again. She pushed me away with a dangerous look in her eye.

'It's not.' She stabbed the intercom answer button but her voice was soft as a kitten. 'I'm just getting ready.'

'Aren't you going to invite me up?' said the visitor below. The day turned its evil eye on me just as surely as if she'd rewound the tape and substituted a different edit for the past two hours: it was the voice of Karl Fleet.

I yanked open the door and walked out into the dark without looking back, shouldering my guitar as I went.

3.

The waitress arrived with a large plate of bacon and eggs and a mug of tea, which she deposited between them.

His look was baleful, but his hunger was greater than his pride. He chewed vigorously. The mask of his face was prominent around the mouth, a strong jaw beneath the beard. Determined. Stubborn perhaps. She let him eat quietly, without firing questions. She was used to interviewing documentary subjects. Used to giving people space. They usually talked when they were ready.

He watched her throughout the meal. She took small bites of an almond croissant so he wouldn't feel awkward. And how was he going to feel awkward, she chided herself inwardly. It's the first decent meal he's had in days, weeks maybe. Without staring, she tried to work out how thin he really was. It was his forearm that gave it away. Somewhere she could look without seeming to pry. It was emaciated, the wristbone showing beneath the frayed cuffs of his wrecked and stained jersey as he put down his cutlery. Politely. He'd been well brought up. It pained her. She swallowed, a sudden burst of adrenaline making her heart pound in her chest, her ears.

'D'you want a bed for the night?' The words were out of her mouth before she could stop them. 'I don't think this is very sensible for you. Perhaps I can help. Put you up for a few days.'

He seized her hand between his own cracked palms and looked into her eyes. It was a simple gesture but it floored her. She'd never seen anyone drop their guard quite that guilelessly. She felt suddenly like crying, her skin tingling with the danger of an apparently selfless act. The next moment she was cursing herself.

Her phone rang. Never had she been so grateful to be interrupted. She was in an absurd situation, committing herself to foolishness, and why? Some futile revenge act upon the homoerotic banner her daughter seemed determined to hang from the rooftop? But she knew that was not it. This was something all her own. She wanted the danger she felt sure she was inviting. She wanted absolution. She wanted… what? She knew exactly what Stephen would say the moment she told him. It was inappropriate. Impulsive acts of charity were not something they could afford, they'd had to fight just to keep the business afloat, to rear their own child to the point at which she could achieve some kind of independence, why take on another burden, however temporary? Did she not want that space they'd finally earned in which to be a couple? All of which was entirely rational and correct.

'Hi.' She was already on her feet and waving her cash at the waitress. 'I know, I'm on my way, tell Pam I'd like to see her before… yes. Of course she must. See you shortly.'

She realised he was still watching her as she hung up, and she was suddenly floored with shame. She had no right to set up an expectation she couldn't fulfil. She put money on the table between them. Too much money.

'I'm sorry, I have to go.'

He nodded. He knew, of course. It was apparent in every pore of her body, she was burning with self-recrimination. She left the café empty-handed, leaving him stranded but fed.

There was a to-do list, scribbled sticky notes from Ally, phone messages and numbers, a collage of leads trailing to meet her at the office door. Just as things were heating up, she felt something hollow at the heart of her commitment. At about one-thirty, when Ally had gone for lunch, when there should have been a lull in the stream of phone calls and texts but wasn't because of the award, Mia realised that she was giving out the same approved information on autopilot. It was the first time in her producer's life that she hadn't felt completely absorbed in the company's mission, in Stephen's directing, in their creative force as a duo. Their new film project was still embryonic, existing more in Stephen's head than in her own. She realised she hadn't yet got a handle on it. She didn't yet feel the passion that would be necessary in her fight to get it made. *Lovergirls* was still the project in her bloodstream. Projects completed were like newborn infants, they needed all her attention to get out there. And there was something unfamiliar clawing at the edge of her consciousness. The lovergirls blossoming all at once in her life, the new development of which she was taking cognizance. She was unsettled but she was dealing with it, she thought.

Strands of music drifted in from the bright early spring street. She put down the phone, relieved at the temporary respite from her own voice. As she did so she realised with a stab of longing that she wanted to make a music film. It was like suddenly being inside the body of Caliban, all her inchoate yearning breaking out in an unholy rash on her captive skin, a howl to the unadmitted teen spirits that lurked in her heart, little understood. A second later a surge of adrenaline prompted recognition.

> *Can't see can't breathe can't die can't live*
> *You're onto me*
> *You're onto me*
> *You're sweet hard dark light*
> *Know how to feel right*
> *Into me*
> *You're into me*
> *Lovergirl*
> *Lovergirl*

If she'd been made of more impressionable stuff she would have found the connection uncanny. As it was, in the space of twenty-four hours he had given her the germ of a new idea which hung in the balance between masochism and inspiration. She didn't understand his suffering, she just knew that it was real. She didn't know what drove him to play on the streets, she just knew that he couldn't help himself. He was in the grip of his muse and she was drawn by this strange energy, fascinated by it.

At two-ten Mia received a message from Stephen. *With Stuart at Halcyon, join us for lunch. Beeb local 3pm. Love.*

She couldn't leave the office unmanned with all that was going on. She knew that Stephen would forgo the pleasure of her company if it meant she was pushing things forward. Company business came first, it had been an unspoken pact between them over the years. Still she was touched that he'd asked her out to lunch, treating her as in the old days when she'd been his young protégée and lover, when it had all felt so urgent and raw, when she'd been carving out a sense of who she really was and trying to live up to his belief in her.

She sent him a text. *Hands full.* Love back at him. Started peeling off the sticky notes one by one, each of the calls in turn, another press opportunity fulfilled, another task completed, between the incoming traffic that left the list growing at the tail end even as its maw was satisfied. During the afternoon she was aware of the strange counterpoint of her own voice, husky from all the chat, with the glass edge of Ally's jocularity and the distant thrum of a guitar somewhere down the street. Probably he thought she had the wherewithal to make him famous. If she'd been less busy she might have been irritated by his insistent noise outside her window. Instead, the clamour of her professional life kept her buoyant, afloat on his sea of dreams. She was busy, her channels were open and he entered her bloodstream.

Stephen called her at three forty-five after the BBC interview, all had gone swimmingly, he was on the evening regional programme at six. Mia told him she'd record it and to take a cab over to Notting Hill Gate for a feature interview one of the Sundays had requested. She'd spoken to all the arts editors, the urgent deadlines were done, she'd put the others off till tomorrow. She'd see him at home. For the rest of the afternoon she drew up a revised version of the budget and finance plan for the new film. At five forty-five she flicked on the news and checked her social media accounts while Ally programmed the recording.

'In his element look at him!' Ally wriggled into her fake leather jacket, freshening up her bright fuschia lipstick with a glance at her compact mirror. She was tall, curvy and presumptious. She adored Stephen's interview persona, it made her giggle for some reason Mia couldn't fathom. She shut down her laptop and with a flick of her honey-coloured hair she was heading for the door. 'Seeya tomorrow, doll.'

Mia nodded, lulled by long familiarity. 'Go paint the town red, hussy. And give that busker a kick for me on the way out.'

Ally's laughter echoed down the stairway in concert with the clacking of her heels.

Onscreen, Mia watched the body language of the man she had lived with and loved for twenty years. She knew all his mannerisms so well, the spark in his eye, the upward curve of his mouth, the demonstrative spread of his hand. She listened to the interview with admiration and a trace of awe at his articulacy. He was still the smartest man she had ever met. Too clever for TV. She enjoyed the way he ran circles round the interviewer's sluggish brief. For her it was only about getting the message out. For Stephen, it had to be a conquest, there had to be proper answers to the mediocre questions: why did he choose to make a film about female sexual perversity? How did he go about finding out the girls' secrets? Were they really as naughty as the film made out? Did he ever think they might have behaved differently if he'd been a female director? What about Dalila, his new discovery? etc etc. She knew it all ad nauseam, but he always made it seem new.

There was a break in the music. Perhaps Ally had taken her at her word. She flicked off the TV as Stephen's piece finished and took a break. She couldn't fathom her need to hurry downstairs, but she reached the street breathless. He was packing up, ready to move on as heavy, dark clouds gathered overhead. There wasn't much time.

'Can I ask you something?'

He looked up with that twist of a smile that made her heart wrench. 'Got a request?'

'No, I wondered if you should see a doctor.'

'I'm feeling fine.'

'Your feet.'

He looked at the ground. Contemplated her with a half-nod. And so it was settled between them after a fashion. Mia knew the local drop-in clinic, having worked in the area for several years. He had, till his recent misfortune, lived further east and was still an interloper in the West End. She took him up to the office so she could fetch her stuff. He waited, taking it all in. He offered to carry her bag.

'That's sweet of you, I can manage. I'll book a

cab, then you won't have to walk too far, how's that?'

The inadvertent gleam in his eye told her it was the nearest thing to bliss he could imagine at that moment. Mia dialled and spoke to the controller of the local taxi firm, still not quite sure what they were doing in the same space together. He looked down at the street, craning forward, his knee jerking as if to an invisible rhythm, his body in perpetual motion, restless. Was he looking out for his dealer? She thought again of Stephen's words as the unwashed smell of young male reached her nostrils. Stale sweat and a faint aura of ammonia. A wave of revulsion hit her along with bewilderment as to how she'd got herself into this position. What was it about him that had got under her skin this way? It wasn't compassion it was craziness, the same craziness that had swept her out of one established life and into a new adventure all that time ago, but why this?

He turned to face her, his back against the melodrama of the sky, blinding silver overtaken by rolling banks of darkness, his face in shadow, but she could see he was staring at her, a distant thought forming.

'Were you ever an actress?'

It was the naïve question a teenager would ask. 'Why?'

He nodded, considering. 'Just the way you looked. In your green dress.'

'I always preferred it behind the camera.'

'I don't think I believe that.'

She gave him a beady look. He didn't know her. Who was he to judge?

The intercom buzzed and she answered to the taxi driver waiting below.

'Let's go.'

She let him precede her out of the office while she set the security alarm, then followed him out into the street, the world roaring in her ears, wondering what she'd done.

The drop-in clinic was busy. They waited for an hour in a reception area peopled by the down-and-outs, the tragic cases of inner-city rough living. Cut and bleeding faces, bruised and battered limbs, a sad host of limping, hobbling, shivering, grumbling individuals. A pulling of hair and a gnashing of teeth. Her companion watched, drinking in the stock of human woe. It didn't seem his destiny and they both caught each other sharing the thought.

'Sure you want to be here?' he murmured.

'No. But I want to know you're ok.'

The young Indian registrar called them in at last. Mia realised she didn't know her companion's name. She was standing in for his mother, but she wasn't and she had no precise relationship to call on. She explained the situation as far as she understood it, which was very little, and asked him to remove his shoes.

She flinched at the state of his feet. Where before they had been bloody, now they were an angry red, an infected wound clearly visible on the side of one of the toes. The registrar sighed, not quite inaudibly, then got on with the business of taking a history – by which means she learnt her musician's name was Tom Pavelin, last known address a hostel around Tottenham Court Road – then of cleaning, sterilising, dressing the affected area and administering an antibiotic shot. Five steps to salvation. It was over in twenty minutes. Tom Pavelin was allotted precisely the time given to any other homeless person.

'You will have to keep this clean to avoid the infection spreading,' said the registrar, his brow furrowing, forseeing the pointlessness of his own work. 'Also you should wear socks to prevent chafing.'

Mia covered her mouth to prevent the smile that overtook her from showing. It wasn't funny. Many horrors beckoned, from septacaemia to gangrene. But then she caught the look in Tom's eye and suddenly none of these were real, just phantoms conjured from the serious young doctor's years of learning at the sharp end of the NHS. All he could do was patch them up and send them out again, to return a week later with worse. The dregs of the city who couldn't look after themselves. Waifs and strays with less common sense than a dog.

'You should irrigate this with iodine and change the dressing twice a day,' said the registrar morosely.

'I can do that.' The words were out of her mouth like the unit first aider before she'd considered, and with them her fate was sealed. The script feathered in her hand and she was on her way to the pharmacy before it started to sink in.

It was a curious ride home, locked into the back of a cab together, a metal box thrumming with the sudden, torrential rain that broke upon the city, filled with the odour of him which threatened to overcome her. In the heated interior he basked and threw off the boots. The white gauze dressing grinned at her like something out of a comic book.

'What will your husband say?'

She looked at him coldly. Presumption was not something she cared to add to his repertoire. She felt ill, constrained in a space whose atmosphere of street stench and wounded soul intensified with every breath she took. A space in which the discreet atoms of her being were slowly, inexorably overwhelmed and extinguished by the rude new compound forming in their place. She was the weak element and she would be transformed, resolved, her crystal structure forever changed by this chemical reaction. Faintness made her open the window. She felt the chill night air and the rain hitting her face and closed her eyes to the assault.

'It's just for a day or two, until you're on the mend.' *Don't expect a free billet you little taker. Don't think my husband will say anything at all, you are nothing to us.*

'Of course.' He scrutinised her, catching her mood, iron in the sky, in his soul, what would it bring if she were unkind. What was he doing in a cab with a woman almost old enough to be his mother, held together by her generosity, but something else, something he was too raw to fathom. What were they to each other at all?

As so often, the house was dark when they arrived, Stephen doubtless being treated to a second bottle of chianti up the road. She was relieved not to have to explain immediately, but she still felt like a fugitive as she led him limping down the steps and unlocked the basement front door.

'Always liked garden flats,' he nodded, making conversation. It was increasingly awkward. She glanced at him as she led the way in and de-activated the security alarm.

'It's our house, our daughter lives with us.'

She could sense him re-evaluating the situation and it irritated her to see his mind working with what felt akin to the calculation of the burglar, though she knew it was simply gaucheness. It embarrassed her the way he suddenly hesitated in the cloakroom. She realised he'd caught sight of himself in the mirror.

'Look, don't have second thoughts on me now, I've had a long day and I've got to check my email.' She slung her jacket onto its usual hook and led the way in. She flicked the dimmer on the kitchen spotlights and their high-tech haven was revealed like a wonderful stage set glinting with copper and glass. She saw it in a flash through his eyes and felt momentarily ashamed. Then she saw what she'd brought in from the street standing on her clean floor and panic overtook her.

'Let me show you the bathroom.'

She took his guitar and placed it carefully beneath the coathooks, then led the way upstairs. She'd never been conscious of what she'd possessed until that moment. It had all been accrued gradually over years of a long and industrious relationship, acquired with the natural growth of layers of skin, a veneer over her life's achievements, and by now she had no perspective on her social level except through the filter of the films they made.

The house was a tall terrace, two rooms on each floor. She and Stephen had a large bedroom on the first floor, facing front, where the windows took in the evening sun. Lottie's current room was at the back of the house, one floor up. The upper ground floor had been traditionally where guests, au pairs or lodgers had been housed, a rear-facing room tucked behind the hallway with enough space for a small bathroom, presently used for production storage. At the front was the home office. They climbed slowly up three flights to the attic. This had been variously Lottie's den, the home cinema, an edit suite and a writing room. Remnants of all these functions remained. It was the only space unspoken for and she showed him in.

A double bed slung with Turkish bedspreads nestled below the eaves. Bookshelves lined the wall, crammed with old production materials, research volumes, novels long read and archived, boxed up equipment. The TV was several years old but it had been a good one, slung together with DVD player and satellite receiver and the hi-fi system which Lottie had used whilst dancing round the punchbag which still hung from the ceiling. Photos and memorabilia festooned the surfaces in a kind of timeline, a historic tableau of a relationship, a family and all it contained. Mia led him past all this into the ensuite bathroom where she turned the taps on full blast. Steam hit the mirrors in the bright light. She lifted towels out of one of the cupboards. Worn but clean. Bright but not tasteless. A world of colour and pictures, a carousel of order and purpose unfolded around him and he stood at the centre of it, letting it wash over him.

'I'll leave you to it. Put your dirty things outside the door and I'll see if we can rescue them.' She was kind, distant, an authority figure. She was in control. He wriggled out of his sweater and draped it over the towel-rail. There was too much fatigue for shame. The change was so great he was stunned into silence, withdrawn into himself. She felt a stab of pity, seeing the foul teeshirt clinging to the concavities of his emaciated torso. She left him, closing the door quietly and trying to conjure enough defiance to account for herself when Stephen and Lottie got back. *It's a couple of days. An act of kindness. Nothing more.*

4.

My mother once got a friend of hers to read my palm. I was fifteen, giving her the runaround and she was looking for answers. In reality she didn't have to look further than a kid growing up in a small town without a father, but that's hard to take when you've poured all your love and care into someone and they come back at you with angry words, bad deeds and sad results. Instead of giving me a clip round the ear and locking me in my room – she couldn't do that, I was six inches taller than her and strong for my age, besides it went against her liberal principles – she would feign indifference in the hope that I'd get bored and stop my rebel-without-a-cause pose. The problem was, it wasn't a pose. It was where my chaotic hormones and untutored instincts were driving me. I wanted conflict so I knew how far was too far. But conflict wasn't in her nature. I'd say: *I'm going out to get drunk.* She'd say: *ok, but you'll have to make your own way home can you crawl that far?* Or, I'd say: *I'm going to beat the bastard that took my girl.* She'd say: *ok, but make sure she doesn't give him your mobile number.* She was a terrible mother for a wayward boy. The kinder she was, the harder I plunged the knife in.

She was drinking moonshine with her hippy friend Jenufa when I came in one day from school and announced I was going to London. I remember it was hot weather and I was sweating from the walk home across the fields. She giggled and told me if I was off to make my fortune perhaps I could use some guidance. I told her she'd go blind if she drank any more, but still I was curious and I sat next to Jen, whose bangles clashed gently as she took my hand and turned it over in hers. She had soft, cool skin and long, delicate fingers. They weren't like my mother's hands at all. As she folded, probed and stroked the lines of my burgeoning musician's palm, I imagined them clasped around the root of me, as if I were a plant, a fleshy amaryllis shooting skyward to the sun in its unfolding riot of red. My penis stiffened against the harsh grey fabric of my school trousers, my face hotter with every phrase. It was probably the most exciting encounter of my limited life to date, but she seemed unaware of my physical response. In soft, murmured phrases she told me a story of my life. Most of it I've forgotten, but she traced my heartline with her finger and told me I had a great capacity to love and to hurt. She showed me a break in the line that meant loss. I told her I'd like to have my hands on any girl at all at that moment, that's why I was leaving town, London was full of chicks falling over themselves to get laid.

Thirteen years later and no wiser, albeit in the city of my choosing, I stooped over the spotlit basin in that sudden, immaculate box she'd put me in, dazzled, dazed and confused, the extractor fan roaring in the back of my mind. I didn't recognise the person in the steam-shrouded mirror, a scrawny man of indeterminate age whose features were obscured by dirt and matted facial hair, a crazy glint in the eye that spoke not of creation but of the blank wasteland of pain.

Part of me wanted to run, but the sound of water thundering into the bath dissolved my will, little by little. I watched the white tub bubbling audaciously. I was bone-weary with resistance. It was time to change tune. I peeled off the greased, once blue-striped layer that had lain next to my skin for the months since my girl had betrayed me, and let the dull fabric finally drop to the floor. I could barely conjure the strength to strip off my jeans, but the rest practically fell away from my body, like rags from a carcass. I eyed the noxious pile in the middle of the gleaming tiles and wanted them gone, it didn't matter how, just out of the world, obliterated.

Shaking with the effort of my personal de-rig, I took a deep breath of the faintly perfumed steam that permeated my unconscious and climbed into the bath, the first time my body had touched water since that lie had propelled me from one life into another. I was shocked at my body, bony and blue-white as an axolotl as it slid into burning clarity. I breathed. I submerged. I became still. I held my breath until the pulse beat in my temple and the red sunset behind my eyes began to turn to black starry night. Should I go now? Slip away into the dark like the fugitive I had become? Who would know?

She would be left with it all. A miserable corpse and a heap of woes. She didn't deserve it. My body crashed upright, showering beads of water over the floor. Better live.

A lightness flowered in my head. The decision not to die was a kindness to her that flooded me with ease, like a gift. I would return her goodness to me. I knew this with the certainty of a baptism. I was confirmed. All would be well.

I grabbed the bottle of shampoo and set to work with the back-scourer that till then had resided innocently on the bath side. I scrubbed away at my suffering until my skin throbbed. Mortification of the flesh. When I'd finished, the brush lay battered and denuded where I'd found it, but I was clean, stripped of all that had held me down. I pulled the plug and let the filth drain away, lost somewhere under the streets of London, dried myself with towels as clean and rough as cats' tongues. I removed the sodden dressing that couldn't do me any good now. The wound was still inflamed, but then my whole body was inflamed, where was the difference? I dabbed it dry, let it ooze as I inspected the rest of me. My nails were an affront. I foraged in the wall cupboard, found a pair of clippers and set to work. Grey parings sprang into the wash-basin. I was amazed and repelled by their length. They wouldn't wash away. I gathered them as best I could in my fingers and placed them in the bin. I sat on the perspex toilet-seat and turned my attention to my toes, working round the blisters and calluses as well as the pain would let me.

Hobbled by too much rough living, I craned to inspect my reflection. More caveman than hobo let alone boho. The beard had to go. She'd have trouble persuading her family and I didn't want to cause offence. I fished out nail scissors and razor and attacked the growth that shrouded my face. I missed my trimmer but it was ancient history, left behind in a house I dared not revisit. Stiff from the heat of the bath, I peered crookedly at my leprous reflection. The beard came off in patches, filling the sink with black curls like a nest for vipers. I looked like a moulting hen. In happier times I might have snapped it on my phone and sent it to a mate. *Bad facial hair day. Attack of moth.* But I was too beaten down to find it amusing any more. I just wanted to merge quietly with the shadows and not to be an embarrassment.

I cleared up as best I could and emerged in a towel, hit by the cool, dry air of the bedroom, the pores of my skin able to breathe again. I flung myself back on the bed and closed my eyes, not so much a nap as an out of body experience. I knew the moment she was there in the room, I saw her glance at me in a flinched kind of way, I could see her searching, I was watching her every move. She quietly opened the cupboards of her past life and interrogated them for something to protect my modesty, cautiously placing a couple of shirts, a worn pair of jeans, an unopened pack of underwear and a dark sweater on the chair next to the bed. Then she faded into my dream and I was flying over the fields above my mother's house. The sun was shining on the blades of grass and the breeze was blowing up a song.

Up there in the clouds there was a beautiful melody in my ear, the wailala of a nymph whose voice was not of this world but which my heart understood. It was the sunlight singing and it danced in me. I wondered if I'd died after all. But then another kind of counterpoint reached me, the operatic rise and fall of a marital argument. The words were indistinct and happening in another layer of this lasagne house. But they permeated the crust on which I basked and I felt myself sinking inexorably into the meat of the affair. He didn't want me here, that was evident. And she wasn't going to be bossed around so that was stalemate. The duet reached an abrupt conclusion, followed by a rapid-fire percussion solo: high heels against sanded wooden staircase, concluded by a mighty slam of renovated pine door, whether hailing the entrance to sanctuary or exit to the street I couldn't be sure in my mind-fugged state. Then there was a little scuffle outside and the door opened to reveal a smaller, fiercer female incarnation of her in an orange and red layered dress. She had her mother's dark eyes and that have-at-you look, but she was angular, not soft.

She came and stood over me, outrage written across her face, my forked, naked self on her parents' bed like a violation. She was easy to read, nothing held back except the scream. I lay there looking back at her, not in any hurry to cover my manhood. What would have been the point? I felt like an anatomical subject, or worse, a slave. I certainly had no status in those eyes, so there was no protocol to observe. It was a strange moment. She wasn't exactly searching for words, only for meaning. Like her father she couldn't work out why I was in her house. Only her mother knew that and she wasn't telling.

'I think you'd better be out in the morning,' she said. She had a wonderful voice. Hushed and deep. More expressive than the self she showed. It was a voice made for words but she kept those to a minimum.

'What does Mia think?'

She flashed me a look that told me the thief she thought I was, then retreated, closing the door firmly. She'd have locked it behind her if she'd had the key.

A hush fell upon the house. Everything I did was amplified by that hush, like I was stranded on a silent beach by a dried up lake somewhere on the dark side of the moon. I could hear my eyes swivelling in their dry sockets as I scanned the ceiling and walls for any clue to tell me why I'd washed up here. She'd *rescued* me. That was all.

A repetitive sound like a low-flying helicopter drummed in my head and I realised it was the sound of my body shivering. The cool of the room was no longer pleasant. I heaved my body into a sitting position and felt the weariness kick in. My body ached with the pain of those long months living rough with only the spirit of Kali for company, eviscerated, beaten and finally, stunned into silence. I knew I could not go back there and live. Living meant something new. I had no idea what the morning would bring but for now I was committed to finding a way of staying under that roof for a few hours longer.

Though she'd seen me naked, sleeping, she'd expect me dressed outside my padded cell. I looked at the neat pile on the chair and my eyes pricked with tears. I wasn't sure why. Then suddenly it felt like online mathematics for a three-year-old: select one shirt out of two, one pair of underpants out of five, and the rest of the elements drop magically into position with a fanfare.

I tore open the plastic bag containing white boxer shorts and slipped on a pair. They were loose on me, but then I guessed her husband was better fleshed than I was, and she'd discarded these as being the wrong size. Was he a big guy? I couldn't remember who I'd seen her with. I remembered the suit. He was important enough to be wearing that suit in public. And here I was putting on his rejected underwear. It was soft, good quality cotton that hugged the skin. Did she touch him through that cotton? Did those graceful fingers stroke him hard and make him beg to slip inside?

I tugged the shirt over my head, did my best with the jeans and opened the door of my prison. Adrenaline assailed me. Invader landing new territory. Ready for the kill. Fight or flight. Strange that my body wanted to behave like a Viking, balled up and ready to commit murder, while my mind decided it had more to do with the lunatic taking over the asylum. I hesitated in the shadows, the echo of a song in my ear, listening for opposition, but it was eerily quiet except for the pounding of my heart.

A portrait of Shelley's ghost loomed towards me in the gilt frame of a Baroque mirror, the angularity of the jaw all the more startling for the absence of beard, the eyes and mouth suddenly too large. But who would take me for a poet now?

The dimly lit corridors of the house wound tightly around each other like embracing odalisques bejewelled with wall art: abstract canvas, childish scrawl, wood carving, screen award... with every step I slipped a little deeper into wonderland. What I could learn from these promiscuous walls was hampered by the thought of that sharp-eyed pixie who'd appointed herself guardian of her parents' affluence. I longed to stay and look, but I wouldn't be held a thief. No loitering on this first adventure down the three flights to the basement where I guessed her mother would be.

Through a door opening off the main hallway I glimpsed a flickering screen, caught the classical roar of a film soundtrack. Was this the lair of the alpha male? I hurried past, feeling like a fugitive, bare feet punished by the fashionably rough stair covering, floorboards groaning with the weight of this fragile frame dragged by leaden limbs down, down, down, head burning in anticipation of what I'd find at the bottom.

She was sat brooding over her laptop like Circe. She glanced up as she heard me. I had startled her and she coloured. She didn't look me up and down. She didn't need to. She could take in the totality of me at a glance and know that I wasn't a street urchin. Transformed from pig to man in the space of a couple of hours. She was nervous. The phone purred at her side, winking blue like a genie wanting to come out and play. She left it in the bottle, for now. 'Are you hungry? I can make a quick pasta.'

'I'll help you.'

It wasn't quite a smile, but her face softened. She moved fast, flitting like a moth, touching the surfaces lightly. We skirted each other in this blazing, opulent space, she pulling out pans and knives, I following, snooping, trying to learn the geography but it was like a chinese puzzle and I was slow, picking up on her impatience and lamed by it somehow. We didn't look at each other.

Like the sorceress's apprentice my hands set

shakily to work at a wooden board chopping garlic and mushrooms, half relieved at the mindless focus, half maddened by appetite, while her dance around the stove continued, tossing and agitating what I passed her into the warm olive oil while the sea-salted water boiled up a storm. I could almost pretend I had a legitimate function here. It reminded me of winter evenings with my mother, the two of us cosy and closeted against the collage of daylight hours we'd left behind. Except there was this mighty subtext: *are your husband and daughter at home?*

The phone rang again. She ignored the genie crooning in her ear. *What's happening Mia? I'd like you to call me back.* The answerphone beeped, went back to sleep.

'I've really pissed Stephen off actually,' she murmured into the *alio e olio*. The first of the sort of intravenous confessionals we were to adopt.

'Is he a jealous guy?' I couldn't help it, I longed to ask her questions.

'Maybe.' Who wouldn't be with a woman like that? There was class in every move she made, not blue blood or any of that crap but real class. Intelligence. Grace. Not all of this was apparent to me at once, but at that moment I was as curious as an alleycat, I wanted to hear every word that dropped from her lips.

'He trusts you doesn't he?'

'Of course.' This time a flash of danger in those dark eyes.

'Is he joining us?'

'He's out.'

'And your daughter?'

She exhaled. A half-smile. 'She's in. But she won't

be joining us.'

She shredded herbs from a window-sill pot into the giant bowl in which the barely cooked spaghetti was tossed and we sat together at the scrubbed table. She served me and watched. She pushed her portion around the white plate but ate little. We were quiet but the space between us was heavy with questions. Once the edge of my hunger was blunted, they started to spill over. 'Should I go?'

'I don't like going back on my word.' She clenched her jaw with a stubborn little movement. 'I don't see that it's such a big issue.'

'It might be for them. Some nobody you've dragged in off the street.'

She sighed at me, impatient, though she knew it was pretty close to the truth. 'I don't see it that way.'

'Might not be safe.'

She almost laughed. When she did that it was quite beautiful. She had to look away then, I was onto her.

'Life is about controlled risk. I took a gamble.'

'Will it pay off?'

'I have no idea what you mean.'

Hostile now. I'd probed her too far, too much like an equal and she closed me down. She started to clear the table. There'd be no evidence of a cosy supper when he got back. She poured herself a sly glass of white from the hi-tech fridge and stacked the dishwasher, while I hobbled over to the cloakroom and retrieved my guitar. I didn't need to drink, I was still intoxicated with the novelty of being indoors. I lifted my instrument out of its case and began to tune. It was battered and cracked after all those weeks on the street, and my fingers were calloused, but when I touched the strings, I knew I was home.

I played six songs at one sitting, without looking up, without pause. Some time during the third one she came and sat on a footstool near to the sofa where I'd perched. She wrapped her slender arms around her legs and listened like a child. She was so deep in thought she didn't move when I strummed my way to a close. She put her head on one side, exhaled softly, looked at me and said: 'This has to be a film.'

We were quiet again then, somehow easier with each other now she'd understood the connection. There was nothing difficult, just the complex gentle flux of two bodies sharing the same space. I wondered what she meant exactly. Did she want to make a documentary about me? *Streets of undiscovered gold?* Or was it some drama she had in mind? 'Has everyone got a film in them d'you think?' I ventured.

'No.'

She wasn't giving herself away that lightly. All at once she was on her feet with that instinct she had for breaking the moment, always. I was new to it then but I came to recognise her defences. In this case, I could see I'd provoked it. Pushed too hard and she shied away. Her mother's instinct springing to protect her.

'I'd better do your foot.'

It was wonderfully mundane, wonderfully kind in the same breath. She reached for the pharmacy bag from the hospital. She'd had it on the kitchen worktop all that time.

She knelt by me. I let her bathe my feet in steaming water from the elegant scrubbed steel faucet. She had a little ceramic bowl whose colours seemed to leap out of it into the room, blue and white, birds and flowers, a foreign land in miniature. That's what she was to me, a new horizon.

'Where's that from?'

'Siena. D.H. Lawrence's paradigm of the ideal city. Never mind the Guelphs and the Ghibellines stabbing each other in those dark alleys…' she smiled, a flicker of mischief. 'The little shops are full of this stuff but I liked it.'

She opened a door in my mind, her references easy, natural. She'd travelled and she offered me all those worlds in the palm of her hand, trickling the water over my foot again and again, her hair falling across her face, concentrated. Madonna or Magdalen, I couldn't tell. No woman had ever washed my feet before. If her husband had entered the room at that moment the game would have been up.

But he would have been mistaken. I was being nursed for my own good, what could I do but sit mortified by the contrast between her fine, capable hands and the abused state of my feet. I wasn't Christ, only the Leper. The water was hot and my skin was raw. She was hurting me. Pus oozed into the bowl and all I wanted was to cry 'stop', but she was nothing if not thorough. When she did finally stand to pour the soiled water down the sink, she was sweating and so was I. She let the air dry the foot and began to clear our traces. I watched her back, watched her business. She was balled up, somehow, but I didn't know if it was me, or him, or the imagined conflict in the space between. She came to me again, dark-eyed and frowning with that concentrated look I came to know. Always senior. Always in control. Always on the edge. She could have knifed me then, but I knew she had other weapons at her command. On this occasion, iodine. Christ's name crossed my lips this time. The pain seared through my nervous system and blinded me.

'Sorry.'

I couldn't tell her it was all right. She'd taken my breath away.

'I have to do it otherwise the infection might spread.'

I nodded, steeling myself.

'That's why you're here.'

So that was why. I struggled with a stab of pain of a different kind. She hurt me all right. But she healed me too.

5.

Mia unfurled the gauze bandage from its spotless clinical wrapper and did her best to cover the wound. Her scalp prickled in empathy as she imagined the hurt she had dispensed, would have to again. What nagged at her, gave her pause, was the look of him. He was feverish, she could feel the heat, saw the glaze in his expression. She remembered from some research she'd once done for a classical music documentary that the composer Scriabin had died from blood poisoning, and the absurdity of it crazed her, made her order him upstairs.

'Please go to bed now.' It came out wrong, but it had the desired effect.

'Had enough?' He thought it was because of Stephen of course, but hell, she thought, he wouldn't go just because I tell him he's looking a bit under the weather. He's not my son. She pressed a foil of analgesics into his hand. 'You need to rest. And I need to talk to my family.'

He hauled himself to his feet, limped to the stair. 'You win.'

'It's all right. We'll look after you.'

She was a pop-up hospital drama, how ghastly. The script wasn't hers. She didn't know what she was doing. She couldn't wait for him to leave the room and give her some head space. 'Get some sleep.'

With a last hangdog look he was gone, dragging his stooped young frame upstairs. She hoped he and Stephen wouldn't meet in the hallway, she knew who would have the better of it right now. Her husband knew his own value and it gave him power to vanquish any opposition. She knew his confidence of old. She had always admired it, had loved his strength, but it was too much for this situation. He had nothing to fear and yet he would make this young man suffer for the two things he clearly possessed that Stephen no longer could: youth and beauty.

Mia opened the fridge and poured herself another glass of the chilled white wine. It was a good one, organic, Stephen ordered it direct from California, a friend of theirs with a vineyard. The warmth of the alcohol flowed through her lower abdomen and thighs and made her feel more generous, if less in control. She remained aghast, turning the situation over and over in her mind. Did it make it more or less acceptable that he was a fine musician? It made her action more comprehensible – to herself at least. It tore her notion of charity to ribbons.

She was musing in a half-doze, feet up on the sofa where he'd sat when her daughter's velvet tones nudged her into alertness again.

'Has he gone?' Lottie stood in front of her with a critical glint in her eye, bristling warning like a cat.

'He's sleeping in the attic.' Mia offered her a space next to her.

'Why?'

'Because he needs help. He's got himself into a mess.'

'I wish you could hear yourself, Mia.' Her daughter had called her by her name since she could speak, but at that moment Mia wished with all her heart she'd just call her 'mum.' She'd longed for years to hear the word drop from Lottie's lips even by accident but it was too late now. The girl was precocious beyond her years and had never had a normal childhood anyway. Now she was going to lecture her like a frosty old headmistress.

'You're out at college all day, you won't even see him.'

'I can smell him.'

Mia eyed her uneasily. Her daughter's predilections were so deeply buried she didn't even know what they were. Still waters run deep. They were alike in that sense.

She put her arm around her and they held each other quietly. She felt the sinews of her daughter's frame stretched so taut she wondered how all that tension could be in such a young body. The cost of being clever, of being the only child? The price of being separated from her half-siblings over those long stretches of time? The never-satisfied longing for absent parents? Did the fibres of her body reach out for a union she could never attain?

'I'm sorry I couldn't give you a brother,' she said softly, felled by the inadequacy of the words, regretting them the moment they were out of her mouth.

Lottie gave her a sidelong glance. 'That's so not it, mum.'

Mum. She'd said it. Mia decided not to tell her what she should have, years ago. There are some kinds of sadness that go too deep, that you can't admit, even to yourself. Those you carry to your grave. Instead, she stroked her girl's hair and felt the delicacy of her cranium under the roots, that mysterious shape she'd known since the breast, known even in her dreams long before she was born.

'Sometimes the reasons we do things aren't clear to begin with.'

'You really don't know what you're doing, do you?'

Mia sighed. There were plenty of answers she could give. Few that would leave Lottie's control of the universe intact. Mia longed to ask her about her feelings for the dark girl Dalila but she didn't want to wound that monstrous, fragile ego by asking. Oddly, their relationship was halting at that most ancient of barriers: sexual attraction. Why was it so hard to be frank, open and honest with the people you loved the most? Hardest of all when they were your offspring and most in need of the honesty? Lottie was beautiful, with a luminous, sensitive face that radiated intelligence – presently marred by a frown she recognised all too well as her own – the grace of a dancer, the quick hands of an artist. She was the mirror of her relationship with the man who was her great love and all the more precious for it. How was it right to delve into the dark corners of the girl's psyche and expose her to the grey dawn, when she was still groping her own way toward maturity? It would have been cruel, because it would have been in her own self-defence. There was nothing she could say to justify it to herself so she took the chastisement she felt at that moment she richly deserved.

'He was sleeping naked *on the spare bed*,' Lottie growled. Mia's mouth twitched. She wanted to share her hilarity but again there was the brick wall. Of course she knew, she'd seen him for herself.

'He wouldn't have wanted to put those street clothes back on.'

'What's he wearing, dad's cast-offs?'

Mia nodded, almost happy to be caught out. Lottie eyed her suspiciously.

'Be careful, you don't want to join them.'

There was a moment's deadly hush before the anger flashed up in Mia. She wanted to slap her own daughter. It had never happened before. The air caught in her lungs. 'Don't. You. *Dare*.'

'Why so angry? You wouldn't have brought him home unless you'd fancied him! But how could you, Mia, he's nothing. You're married! To a brilliant, lovely man!'

The moral bluntness of the young. Mia stared at the brittle little judge she'd created and felt a wave of fury. She wanted to drown her presumption, her easy condemnation. It would take a lifetime to learn the complexity of the human heart and she herself was only half-way there. Lottie was barely off the starting-blocks.

'This is ridiculous, I won't hear you talking that way.'

'Tell him to go.'

'I will not. The boy needs a few days to get

himself sorted out and you are going to have the charity to put up with the inconvenience.'

Lottie shook her head and sprang for the door. 'I'm going to stay at Dalila's.'

'I'm sure she'll make you feel better.'

Lottie's cheek flared, angry tears springing. 'I'll see you, mum.'

She grabbed her bag and jacket from the hall and left, slamming the sidedoor and clattering up the basement steps. Mia listened to her feet hurrying away down the street, breathless. What had she done letting her daughter leave that way? One thing to have a dead hand on each other, not to want to share the same space, quite another that she'd *gone*. In anger. She snatched up her mobile and texted. *Sorry. There is nothing here to stop you coming home later. Dalila is welcome you know that. Love you.*

At midnight, she was drifting uneasily on a clear gold wave the colour of Californian grape, dozing in a bed too big for one, in sheets that smelled of the love she still, inexorably, bore her husband. When he came in, she heard the front door close. She heard him enter the study beneath her and close the door. She heard his feet moving around, steadily, quietly, purposefully. She heard the feet of the big leather sofa scrape gently across the polished boards. She heard a cupboard open, then close. She heard him lie down on the sofa. Then nothing. So he would sleep alone tonight, he was that angry. This had never happened in the twenty years she had known him.

There was a buzzing fever in her cranium but she was tired suddenly, knowing the worst. She would not go to him now, it was too late, and too early for reason. There were three of them in the house but the geometry was all wrong. A cuckoo in the nest and a panther on the prowl, the smell of bloodshed yet to come. She pressed her eyelids shut and weariness overcame her in a tearless spasm.

At dawn, she realised with a sickening swoop of the stomach that she was alone in bed when she should not have been. She knew at that moment she had caused a rift in her marriage that had not been there before. She couldn't fathom what, in this tumultuous week, had caused this to happen. A sweat broke out at her hairline when she thought of the young man asleep in the attic, the cause of it all. But how could he be the cause of anything? He was only a symptom. Some sign of an infidelity that went too deep for words. Some need for freedom yet to be fathomed. It had to do with... she wasn't sure what. She knew she had fallen headlong into a kind of borrowed adulthood when she took Stephen to her heart. And before she had stopped falling she was already a mother. And now she was falling again. This time towards adolescence. What was wrong with her?

Anxiety and a need to confront her worst fears propelled her out of the bedroom and down to Stephen's study. *His* study. She rarely spent time there of late, all her thinking took place in public, down in the kitchen where family, friends, cleaners, all were free to come and go around her as she worked. She had no study. Maybe that was it. There was no sanctuary. No place to call her own. She belonged to everyone and not to herself. And yet, she'd chosen to express this lack through the acquisition of another dependent. Is that what he was? Her rebellion. Her kick-back. Her unsuitable thing.

Stephen was asleep in his shirt, hunched uncomfortably under the spare duvet, a cushion for a pillow. The room smelt of stale alcohol. Mia stared at him for a while, startled that he was suddenly a stranger to her. She reached out to touch his arm. This had to stop.

'Stephen…'

He shrugged her off and turned to the wall.

'Come to bed? I'll make some tea, we can talk.'

'I'll come to your bed when he's gone.'

Like a bad romance. She couldn't believe that those lines could come from the mouth of the man she'd loved and partnered for so long. She felt cut off at the knees. It really was that simple. That chemical.

'Please. Don't do this.'

Seeing that nothing more was forthcoming, that sense would be withheld until she acted, she left the room and sealed her husband into it.

She had a crisis on her hands. She had to tell the boy to go, he was nothing to her. And yet she was furious at this enfringement of her authority. Deep down, she wanted to hurt someone and the rage terrified her. Fighting panic at the irrational turn of events, she mounted the stairs two by two until she reached the attic door, heart pounding. She didn't knock, she went in but he was at the door shaking like a leaf, his eyes unseeing. 'Mia.'

The world turned a full revolution in the moment she took to realise that he was dying. Bright spots tingled before her eyes, angels dancing on the head of a pin, the vision of a fluorescent lit ward filled with the raving and the destitute where she would have to deliver him to breathe his last. A moment later he collapsed at her feet.

The time for reflection came later, as she sat in the waiting room those endless hours of the bleak morning, with a peculiar, debilitating sense of trespass that lamed her, sent the thoughts drifting from her mind, weighed her eyelids down, her phone, finally, silenced.

Somehow she had persuaded Stephen to help her lift him down the three flights of stairs to their car, when the ambulance failed to arrive. A collaboration of an unfamiliar kind, an unbidden emergency, guilt-laden, like shifting a corpse into the boot by dead of night. But this was in broad daylight under full view of well-heeled neighbours setting off to work, embarking on the school run, their good-mornings ringing hollow in the clear air while they sweated in their gross manoeuvres like assassins.

'Fantastic PR,' muttered Stephen, but Mia could see the fear in the line of his jaw set against the stench of the grave, while he grappled like Jacob with the Angel, manhandling the dead weight of the youth into position against the car. He had done this before, in much worse circumstances: earthquake, riot, revolution. Death could not daunt him. Mia felt a pang of admiration for her husband. While he opened the door she clamped the boy between her own body and the metalwork. She never knew a human being could weigh so heavy. It was all she could do not to let him slip to the gutter. Her muscles trembled with the effort, then her husband was pushing him inside like an inconvenient courier package and they were off into the waking traffic. The morning news accompanied them through the grid of a city so familiar yet somehow losing its precision as fear of this impending death thundered in her brain, pressuring her into silence while Stephen gave the plan of action.

He always had. That's why he was the director. He had, she sensed, directed the whole of their life together with such consummate ease, that she had never been conscious of it till now. As she listened she felt a sudden awakening, a terrifying clarity. She was someone else. She was outside her previous life, looking on. All she could feel was the burning in her bones to reclaim for the living this soul crumpled in the back of their car.

The hospital took one look at him and the fast-track kicked in, oxygen, plasma bag, heart monitor, the lot. He was up to the intensive care unit within half an hour of their arrival and all at once they had become the guardians of a hapless, fragile youth the colour of parchment with lips like a butterfly ascending. Stephen was furious, bile-driven. He must have family. Why was it, in this world of global communication that no one could find him a parent of his own? he whispered furiously at Mia. Society was drifting apart under the force of its own indolence, its own complacency. The whole thing was self-inflicted. The boy wasn't abused, he was self-abusing, a wanderer on the face of the earth, another useless dreamer severing connections at his own convenience... and now? Just another problem to be solved.

Mia couldn't fault her husband's logic. She even agreed with him. She knew perfectly where the anger came from. She just couldn't connect the words to the person prone in the bed before them.

She also couldn't find the words to tell him that

their own daughter was also adrift in the city. That she had no idea where Lottie had spent the night. She palely suggested that Stephen pick up the pieces of the day and man the office while she finished up at the hospital. Another debate about the parameters of duty. She needn't stay, she'd done everything she could. Leave her contact details with the nurses and come with him. Mia refused. She needed to know the situation was safe. She'd do it for any member of her production crew, she couldn't just walk out. Livid-lipped, Stephen left the ward. She watched him, a stranger to herself.

Nor could she say why the day stretched into evening and why, still, she was cut adrift on the tide, a raft without a sail, directionless, numb, waiting for the IV antibiotics to kick in, waiting for the triumph of the human will over micro-organism, waiting for him to pull back from the brink.

It took three days. Finally he opened his eyes and stared at her, with the insolence of the newborn. His mouth twitched.

'What the fuck happened.'

'You nearly died.'

'Christ, my head feels like a punch-up in a bar.'

She stared at him. He looked like a badly drawn puppet and yet her heart was beating so hard she could hear it in the room. Life was an absurdity.

'Been here long?'

'Yes.'

'Still married?'

It was beneath contempt. Ungrateful little idiot. As he tried to sit up she found her hand shooting out to stop him, anger galvanising her. 'You are not going back on the street. Tell me the truth.'

His eyes closed, evasive. 'Truth is banal.'

'Maybe. But you have a mother and it isn't me. You have a life and it isn't here.'

He struggled to the surface like a drowning man gasping for air.

'Make one call.' She pushed her phone into his hand. He flinched from the contact, sending it clattering to the floor.

'I can't.'

She shook her head in exasperation. 'D'you think there's anything you've lived through that I couldn't understand?'

'No.' The veil lifted for a moment, there was a brief connection before weariness swept over him.

Mia pressed the nurse call button, re-pocketing her phone. She remained standing, as if that were any kind of defence against the hours she'd sat at his bedside.

'I'm leaving now. You're in good hands.' She looked down at him with a kind of vertigo, life rushing back to shore as the nurse appeared.

'I'll write it for you in a song.' He exhaled the words rather than spoke them.

Fighting frustration, she buttoned her jacket, watched the curtain rise on the dumb-show of medical ritual.

'I'll come back tomorrow. There are things we need to discuss.'

His eyes flickered, came to rest on her once more with perplexity. Unable to bear it, she turned and walked out, not looking back.

Stephen's mood when she returned was strange rather

than estranged, his irritation transmuted into a creative spurt on a script he'd been putting off for at least a year. She was glad to see him at work in his front-room study, the angle-poise burning, his face concentrated in the bluish glare of the computer screen. It was a familiar sight from their years together and the routine of it reassured her, made her feel she was returning from a day at the office. The turn of her key in the panelled front door sounded just as it always had. The hallway aroma of polished floors and Earl Grey tea was overlaid this evening with a smell of baking that greeted her like a blessing, for she knew that her daughter had come home.

It was almost as if nothing had happened, three days swept away by the strength of a family unit that refused serious breach. Or perhaps it was only swept under the carpet. She put her head round Stephen's door, his squirrel's tangle of old scripts, DVDs and correspondence, walls lined with shelf upon shelf of master tapes, volumes on film theory and practice, theatre plays, novels. The room that spoke his character so clearly, that she had always loved. She was careful with her tone.

'Have you eaten, darling?'

A Mozart piano concerto was playing softly in the background. He finished his sentence, as he always did, turned with his sudden smile as usual, and it was almost as though she'd been transported back to the early years. Almost.

'Lottie's downstairs,' was all he said, but she knew what it meant. A truce. Peace and reconciliation might have to wait longer. She kissed him on the cheek and found herself tremulous with relief as she descended to the kitchen. Her daughter was removing a batch of brownies from the tin and putting them to cool on a table that was laden with her efforts of the past few hours, Mad Hatter's tea party meets junior school cake sale. She was flushed, her sloe-dark eyes glowing like animated coals, hair flying out Medusa-style, sleeves rolled up.

'Hi?'

'Hi.' She came forward immediately to hug Mia, her skin smelling of warm chocolate. Mia's heart contracted, she fought the welling of tears. 'Expecting someone?'

Lottie eyed her sharply: of course it was her home-conjuring spell for her mother and Mia knew it. Offerings to the gods to bring back the person she loved most in the world, and with whom she had exchanged angry words. It was a comfort spread for her father and herself in case they were called upon to hold their own vigil through the night.

'You should try the lemon drizzle,' said Lottie. She looked almost frail as she crossed to the stairway and bellowed for her father. As she returned, Mia could see in the childish jut of her chin the little fist of tension that drove her. 'Is he ok?'

A short-circuit back to the source of unease. Lottie had always had this ability to cut to the chase. Too much the only child, always trying to see inside the adult minds that puzzled her.

'He'll be fine.'

Her daughter nodded, relieved to be absolved. 'You were nice to try and help him.'

Nice. She didn't like the elephants in the room crowding her in this way. Why was it that a simple act of kindness brought a mudslide of consequence fouling up her path? Remorse, desire, arrogance, what was it all about? She so much wanted the slate wiped clean, to be rid of the complications, to have everything simple again.

'And Dalila?'

'Yep.'

What did that mean? That the girl was fine too? That they were tight as mice, sharing their secrets beneath the moon? Was this the beginning of tales never to be told? It was hard to face up to the individuation of a child, the more so when you'd shared a peculiar intimacy, a life less ordinary, for so long.

Stephen's feet creaked in his office above their heads. But there was someone else in the house, she'd missed it in her hurry to salve her bad conscience.

'She's here? You should've said!'

She'd caught the faint scent of cigarette smoke through the crack in the conservatory door and went now to fling it open.

It was her absentee step-daughter Hattie, eyeing her with that sardonic curve to the corner of her mouth that was the mirror of her own mother's. 'Alright, Mimi?'

Lottie's laughter sent a chill down her spine. Mia felt set up, trapped by her own absence into a place of vulnerability, suddenly the guest in her own house. Hattie, who had been promising to come round for weeks and failed to show, was now suddenly all too present, along with the end of her cigarette which she ground into the sink Lottie had just cleaned. 'Let's have some of that chocolate cake, Cissi!'

Mia bridled at the horrible diminutive, more at the apparent conspiracy between the two sisters. 'She's coming to stay at mine for a while, Mia. Sound ok to you?' Hattie homed in on the table with a predatory air and the slightly dismissive quality that let everyone know who was boss.

Actually she was the boss, at twenty-seven, of a coffee shipping and roasting outfit that served several of the main high-street franchises, already a high-flyer. Unlike anyone else in the household, she had a natural business mind, an eye for the main chance. She wouldn't stay in coffee, it was just a suitable peg to hang her money-making talents on until she could dream up her next scheme to take over the world. She was tall and rangy, long chestnut hair tucked into her fashionable winter jacket which she now took off and slung onto the chair, letting her hair fall over her face as she leant greedily over the prized morsels. She was casual to the point of rudeness and didn't expect an answer, but that was her St. Paul's style: she had a first in Classics from Oxford, an MBA from the Judge, she'd studied for a year at Yale. She was, by any standards, a wonderful success story in child-rearing. Stephen's ex-wife Kate had poured her creative talents into her daughter, especially after Jaco had gone. She'd had too much loss in her life, something Mia carried like an undercurrent but could never heal for her, still felt she'd set the domino-run in motion even though the pieces really had nothing to do with her. Poor Kate. Poor both of them: these two women, one so ruthlessly alive, the other so traumatised she would never see the extent to which she was projecting onto her successor, living with the symbiotic closeness of underwater creatures, dumb to all but their mutual need.

Lottie had been ten when her idolised older brother had left for university in the States, and a subsequent career at the UN that covered her pin board map with more spots than her diminutive body during a late dose of chicken-pox. All her pre-adolescent years she puzzled over how this rugby-playing, outdoor-loving, sketch-writing, mischievous kindred spirit could be snatched from her, melt away from their everyday like snow on water. That he rarely wrote she experienced as something so inexplicable, it had to be closed down and put somewhere safe, safer than a secure prison, a strong-box in her soul. That was when she started writing poems, all of them from his point of view at first, willing herself into inhabiting a fictional version of him. By the time Skype reached them, he was a stranger living with his boyfriend in Cologne whom she got to know again as a friend, but the umbilical identification had been lost. Who knows how or if it had affected her sexuality, Mia wondered. Life threw so many challenges at one's offspring, only ambition, creation, acquisition – running full tilt for the finishing tape – could get them through the rest of their lives. And here they were suddenly, gathered together as if nothing had happened in the intervening years, eating French chocolate cake and muffins and chattering like children, the past softened by as if by a sudden fall of petals.

So this was how it felt when your child left home. Mia felt oddly bereft, cheated by the casualness of it. Did anyone think she should be consulted? Apparently not. Apparently Stephen knew all about it. Apparently marriage made them one and the same and the decision had been made. End of story.

As Mia watched her two daughters teasing her husband, something crystallised in her mind. Fate had delivered her a story. It said: you have to prove you are more than the child bride. You have to find your own voice and make something of it. At the heart of the story was a mystery. Like any good story, it was submerged and needed excavating. It would take time and research, like any new documentary project. For that, she needed a base where she could meet her subject and work on finding that story. She knew in her guts that she was on to something that marked her transition into a new creative identity. She was starting to understand the eros of the relationship between subject and documentarist, the same compulsion her husband had woven in and out of the fabric of their marriage apparently with impunity, had moved on from each time the project was completed, before it became a threat. How was this any different?

She rented an apartment in her name, a dingy lower-ground floor one bedroom flat in Shepherd's Bush. She gave a plausible cover to the estate agent, in case the paperwork ever made its way into the wrong hands. She had never done anything like this before, knowingly breaking the rules. There was a decision she had made, long ago, but that was something different. This was just an extension of her everyday logic, the only way she could see at the precise moment she passed the agent's window of making things right. There was a scribbled cover note in her head that said it was a future bolt-hole for Lottie, but she knew that was a lie. She was going to keep him.

The relief on Stephen's face was palpable when she told him he wasn't coming back. He didn't ask her any questions, he let her move around her own space without comment. He made coffee, left it on the desk for her where she tried to piece the intervening days back together and catch up with her email. She handled the other company business, knowing all the while that she had a secret, that she felt truly excited for the first time in years, that at least part of that excitement was the knowledge of a transgression that shouldn't have been one, if she had loved her husband less.

When Stephen went to write in his study, she ran a search on Tom Pavelin and discovered a handful of aliases, minister, academic, dentist… and musician. She flicked through the Google listings: gig dates, interviews, reviews. The music press knew about him, if not the nationals. That was better for her: something still to be discovered. A few more keystrokes and she was looking at a nicely composed picture of him on a bridge, and a website that had clearly been designed rather than thrown up by accident. There were photos of a recent studio session. A shot past the profile of a dissolute guy at a big mixing desk, Tom Pavelin a small out-of-focus blur behind the soundproof screen: the power picture, encapsulating the imbalance of the music industry. Another of him clamped under headphones singing at an old-fashioned analogue mic with an enigmatic, dark-haired girl – was this the one who had led him so far down the road to self-destruction?

Blazing a trail through the venues at which he promoted artists, she wrote up a documentary proposal about the new East London music scene, the flowering of the small-scale event in a post-download world. There were crossover happenings, music, dance, theatre, in a proliferation scarcely seen since the sixties. It felt fresh and dynamic, the obverse of the manufactured and branded world reaching the ears and eyes of the youthful majority.

He was discharged a week after admission, with a polythene bag of medication and a batch of paperwork of which Mia took temporary charge. She hadn't told him the plan, just that she would be collecting him.

He'd lost the gauntness that had so disconcerted her, the bruises where he'd been manhandled to safety now fading. He'd regained the half-beard which made a man of the street of him. She had brought him new clothes to go home in, jeans and tee-shirt, underwear, socks, trainers. She waited for him to change behind the curtain with the suspicious eye of the nurse on her, aware of the sidelong glances of the other male patients. She had on a moss green business suit and court shoes, formal, his social worker perhaps. But she wasn't fooling anyone. He emerged looking oddly ordinary, not quite himself. More like a son than ever.

'Let's go,' she said, leading him out past the eyes of the watching world. He stopped to recover his balance once or twice, weak and light-headed, but compliant. It was only in the car that she told him.

'What does your husband say?' he said. It was meant honourably. It sounded quaintly old-fashioned and she smiled despite herself, his presumption too naïve to be taken seriously.

'It's a stop-gap, I'm just trying to help you.'

He nodded, struggling to decode what she was saying. He hardly spoke during the drive, she heard her voice retailing the details, a jet-stream of logistics, in full producer mode. She'd set up a production space where he could stay while he got himself back together, she'd give him a key and keep the spare, she needed access for the project. That was all.

She drew in outside a white stucco villa, parked the car in a space too tight and walked him to his front door. She held out the key and he looked at her, almost punch-drunk with the enormity of the gesture.

'I've never had my own place.'

Brushing aside awkwardness, she gestured him forward. 'Make me a cup of tea and we'll discuss the house rules.'

He opened the door and let her in. It smelled faintly of new paint and damp plaster. The agent had told her it had just been done up by a builder who was selling on. She'd been lucky to get the last one because of some problem with the lease. The carpets were cheap but new. It was clean and whitewashed throughout. She'd had a bed and some basic furniture brought in from a local house clearance place. The sheets were fresh from the packet. The duvet was one she'd unearthed from the linen cupboard at home, one of Lottie's old ones.

'What d'you think? Will you be ok?'

It was the first time she'd seen him lost for words. He picked his way across to the galley kitchen like a cat on a hot tin roof and filled the kettle.

She sat down on the sofa, on a loose cover the colour of autumn and let him serve her, enjoying his discovery of the unfamiliar space. His belongings – a couple of carrier bags and his guitar, propped in the middle of the floor – were meagre enough. He eyed them ruefully, then her.

'I take it I'm not expected back then?'

He sat down on the floor cushions opposite her and they eyed each other across the battered coffee table.

'I haven't discussed it.'

He nodded, the body language vaguely uneasy between them. They sat in silence and drank their tea. She heard him swallow in the quiet of the room. He opened the guitar case, lifted it out and stroked the strings very lightly, tenderly. It spoke to him with the uncertain voice of an estranged friend. But that was his home, she realised. Nothing she would give him. Thus it would ever be. He took time to tune, bent over the body of the instrument which he clasped to him like a child, his hands moving softly, fluidly. He closed his eyes and the song came out of a lull, a kind of trance.

> *The sweetness of a razor*
> *In my fair one's hand*
> *The hair that tumbled down her back*
> *Bloodied in the sand*
> *She knew she was my all-in-all*
> *My life, my promised land*
> *She sold me to another man*
> *Marked me with her brand*
>
> *There's music sweet enough to kill*
> *There's damage in the street*
> *A voice to strangle all your hopes*
> *And wind you in its sheet*
> *There's tales that no one else should tell*
> *And blues so dark they're black*
> *A woman in a brazen chair*
> *A body in a sack*

She threw me from the highest point
The lights went whirling by
A deathly dance of high-rise towers
Across the midnight sky
She sharpened up her scarlet nails
She knelt upon his knee
And when the body hit the ground
She knew the man was me
Ah ahh
Ah ahh

He was doing exactly what he had said, giving it to her in a song. She felt she was listening with her whole body and still it was only half understanding, a fable too oblique to be truth. She would never really know who he was. The last notes faded into the blissful smile that swept across his face.

'Missed this poor cracked old box.' As he turned to her, she was startled to see he was laughing, maybe crying at the same time. 'Too long lying on my back.' Suddenly mischievous: 'For all the wrong reasons.' He was transformed in the time it took to improvise a three-minute piece of nonsense.

'You just need to fall in love again,' she said. She knew it was all that would save him in the end. He was born to be a lover, any fool could see it now, it streamed from him like a meteor's fiery tail. His look flashed at her, quicksilver across a wind-ruffled river.

'Anyone ever told you you're a dangerous woman?'

'Yes.'

'Has anyone ever called your bluff?'

'Not often enough, probably.'

He was playing again, looking at her, wondering if he was reading her right. She decided to start interviewing her subject. He could comply or not, she could decide what to use, or not.

'Would you go back?'

He eyed her equivocally. 'Depends how big the mess is.' A new riff started up, spiked and a little jazzy.

'You were doing some interesting stuff.'

He shrugged. 'You step off the train, it leaves without you.'

Mia smiled. 'That never really applied to the indie music scene. You just took time out. Made yourself a bit of an enigma.'

He was listening, even as the ripple of his pick continued. 'I left plenty of people in the shit, I'm not sure they'll want me now.'

'I don't want to be the excuse for your not trying.'

He smiled like every musical rogue in history.

'*M-ia... oh Mia... doncha forget me down he-re... Got a fist-ful of sorrows got-ta buy me some be-er...*'

She eyed him. 'My side of the bargain looks like this: I don't charge you rent or bills, you're working for me on a documentary project. I'm going to need to recce some venues and artists to get a broadcaster pitch ready and we're starting work tomorrow.'

As she rose, she knew he was looking at her legs. Incorrigible. 'I'll let you settle in. There's food in the fridge and the hot water's on.'

He kept right on playing. She would have found it insolent in anyone else. '*Gonna drink me some courage and burn up that old fe-ar...*'

'What time does the Charlatan open?'

A moment's pause. 'My, you have done your

research.'

'I'll pick you up at six tomorrow. You can show me around.' And she was gone. It was a trust game, but she couldn't tell yet if he knew the rules.

Evening broke in a melt of orange and they followed the meander of Brick Lane with its studenty coffee shops and loud little boutiques thrusting for attention, small ephemeral businesses like excitable butterflies overblown with their own gaudiness. Alongside them bloomed groceries of all nationalities, Bangladeshi, Lebanese, Chinese, hosting equally unnatural colour combinations of the edible kind, citrus, legume, herb and spice, all of it bursting to life from the drab houses that ten years earlier had been the old East End and could still, she felt, revert to its impoverished decay if the money, youth and excitement were sucked out overnight.

The sound of the streets was different here, more closed in, more present somehow. Maybe it was her unfamiliarity. The roar of passing mopeds, the pumping sounds of a nearby vinyl store, the percussive shouts of shop owners and the violent scrape of closing shutters percolated her senses and she drank it in, heart working to the beat.

Another roar, a low, continuous hubbub punctuated by falling-glass laughter shattering the diesel-stoked air, and he was leading her into the sudden, banner-shrouded courtyard of the venue. She saw his jaw clench slightly as he crossed the threshhold and made space for her to enter.

The scent of sexual potential hit her like a pressure wave. Without turning her head on her way to the bar, she took in a myriad glimpses of scarlet smiles, petulant pouts, butterfly lashes, sly glances, glitter and gloss, silken tresses, sculpted stubble, piercings and tattoos, velvet and vinyl, the whole world in motion, shifting and shiftless.

She hadn't told him she was bringing her camera. She didn't know if she'd use it, yet it gave her feeling of power, of unfolding potential as she fingered the lens where she'd strapped it under her jacket. The touch of a button and these fragments would be part of social history, part of her own document. Then again, if she took out her phone she would simply be one of countless others freezing moments in their friendships, kiss-and-tells for preservation online, for sharing, daring, tagging, poking, jeering, leering… the only way in which anyone seemed to commit themselves in this peculiar ocean of collective desire.

But desire for what? Flirt? Boast? Tease? Torment? Adulation? Relief from the tedium? Lasting love? A quick one in the toilets? Exchange numbers and fail to show? Lifelong friendship but never touch? Platonic, diatonic, febrile, nubile… Mia felt she was absorbing the underlying mood through her very skin, despite her filmmaker's armour, leather jacket over teeshirt and well-worn jeans, footwear for moving not posing. She drew the eye. They drew the eye. An unlikely couple with shared intent but different body language. Handsome, vulpine male and carelessly attractive female. Was it so clear she was eighteen years older than him? She started, catching herself approaching the bar mirror in his wake: it was the fact that they looked a couple at all that threw her off balance momentarily.

'What d'you want to drink?'

He was a different person tonight, wired, overemphatic. 'I'll get them.' His hand was on hers even as she reached for her cash. And a look which she well understood. *This is my patch and I buy the first one.*

'A bottled beer is fine, love.' *Love.* How did that slip out? His mood trashed her *sangfroid*, he was profoundly ill-at-ease, trying not to show it, courting disaster with every sidelong glance. She learnt why in the moment that followed.

'You fucker.'

A punch landed on his arm from the opposite side, a shade too hard to be entirely friendly. Tom turned as if a bolt of electricity had shifted him, revealing a shorter, blonde man with disconcertingly pale eyes whose pupils bored into his interlocutor. The lips were narrow, the expression sardonic. 'Still playing then?'

'Let's move,' Tom said, pushing the bottle of Indian lager into her hand and steering her away from the incipient abuse that was threatening at the lips of his adversary. His hand went up as if to brush away the moment, eyes flicking uneasily across the room in scansion of likely resistance. Then swept her suddenly into the midst of a group, all of whom seemed younger than her daughter.

A tall girl, half-Chinese, with raven hair and black eyes and fur-trimmed wristlets despite the heat, stepped into his space and curled herself into him by way of greeting. Like the Cheshire Cat, her smile remained long after he had cleared the embrace.

'What time's your set?' he called to her. The club sound system made them all shout to each other as if across the deck of a ship.

''Bout ten, you here for a while?' she replied in a rich Pacific cockney alto ever on the verge of cracking, seagull wheeling over a choppy sea. His hand lightly brushed Mia's back as he introduced them but his eyes were on the girl.

'Tigerlily fronts an experimental electro-folk band. Jade de Sade.' The girl blinked at her quizzically. 'This is Mia, a film producer friend of mine.' It was that easy. Instant caché. The black eyes widened imperceptibly, fixed on her with a predatory quickening of interest, and a dark-nailed, slender hand extended to hers in a lacklustre but artful embrace.

'How d'you know Tom?'

It's complicated, thought Mia. *But then again, all too simple.* 'We're developing a project together.'

The girl lit up in smiles to Tom. 'At least you dumped us for a good reason.' She laughed. 'We got some new songs tonight, you might take us on again.'

Tom didn't smile. The suggestion of a shrug, while around the girl coalesced the amorphous body of less open-hearted band members: a bespectacled, etiolated, would-be intellectual who probably wrote the songs; a burly red-head, no messing, protective; a quiet girl who played keyboards and percussion; a slim, besuited Cuban trumpeter who shouldn't be there at all but he'd just married Tigerlily the previous week apparently. 'Wait till you hear him, omg!' said the girl. 'Horny as fuck.'

Mia took a draught of her beer and looked for translation, cohesion, but why look. This was a world whose language was simple, oblique on the surface, controlled by subtext, most of it subterranean, squatting beneath the surface like the body of an iceberg. On the surface only the chaotic undulation of small waves. The room tilted gently, moods shifting imperceptibly beneath the raucous overlay. She waited for her mind to adjust to the wash of intent, the empty words and fast draining glasses. Decibels both assisted and impeded her as the first warm-up act took to the floor. A female singer-guitarist with a shy olive face and a frizz of warm brown hair, perched on a stool plucking her opening riff, long enough to calm her treacherous heart before leaning to caress the mic with her sweet-lipped monotone. The room accordingly adjusted its volume upward; the girl, unmoved by its indifference, pushed out her sound across the phalanx of crushed, intent bodies.

'Is it always like this?' Mia wanted to say soul-destroying, but she knew she didn't understand. Why play to indifferent strangers? There was neither guts nor glory in it.

'When they know you, when you're a bit higher up the ranking, they'll pay more attention. Rouge only started on the circuit half a year back, she's doing well to get this venue. At least she's got an audience.'

Mia glanced at him. He was wise to the scene, she needed his knowledge not to feel hurt for the girl. But she was still irritated with his easy use of her function. 'Don't you think we'll get something more interesting if they don't know who I am?'

He pulled deep at his own bottle, flicked her a sidelong glance, wrong-footed.

'I don't want it to be a talent show.'

'Of course not.' A fleeting, mischievous dart of a smile. 'It's not that much of a risk, is it?'

She was laughing, despite herself.

'Just get your bloody camera out and video her, we'll see if it's any good later.'

Mia flushed, but it was impossible to tell in the bar lighting. He knew her moves already. She felt

90

jaded. An intruder. She flicked the camera out of her jacket and raised it with her free hand. 'It won't be great quality…'

His guitarist's hand reached out to a nearby stool and swept it into play. He straddled it in the same move, pulled her hand and camera to rest over his shoulder.

'Instant tripod, let's see how we do.' And suddenly she was clamped up against him from behind, the heat of his body stabilising her picture and destabilising her mind in one gesture. He, on fire with his own intention, was oblivious to his trespass on her body space. They had a project together, of course this was the obvious way to get the footage, but it compromised her, lamed her authority, made them equals in the quest to create. The camera whirred in his ear, her arm snaked across him, she had to lean against him like a lover not to lose her balance. He'd tipped her into a space from which she could not reasonably retreat until it was over.

6.

I shouldn't have done it but we were making up the
rules as we went along and suddenly she'd breathed
immortality into me. She was a goddess, she'd given
me a second chance at life. It was the first time in
months I wasn't hurting. My body slammed into
reverse gear, I had to have someone that night. I just
knew it couldn't be her. She was beautiful. She was
classy. She was my senior, my saviour. She was
married, I didn't want to mess with her life, it was
probably too complicated already.

It took an effort: even dressed like that in her
beat-up jeans and jacket with her hair all mussed she
was obviously made of finer stuff than anyone in that
room. Obvious to me, but not to them. She'd
disguised herself well and I felt like the keeper of
some secret religion. At moments we were close
enough to feel each other's heat, but keeping it

professional. At least, that's what I thought. I'm not sure it was what she thought, but the body of a twenty-eight-year-old male doesn't play the same games as the mind of a sophisticated older woman.

In the name of research she'd taken me back to one of my happy hunting grounds from the time before I'd cut loose, a cool indie warehouse with cheap cocktails, good music and late opening hours. A lot of people I knew were there and with her next to me it was like looking at them from the other side of the glass. Same old crowd, give or take. Some bands I'd already promoted there before. They couldn't remember why we were connected. Too many legal highs for most of them even to remember the week before. But she was cool, she leant on my arm and it was like a passport to something interesting happening, talking to all the girls, Tigerlily, Rouge, a chanteuse called Alicia, like they were the most interesting people she'd ever met. She'd get them on her side and in a minute or two they'd be unfurling themselves like flowers in her hand. She seduced them. If I'd gone at it the way she did, I'd have been in for a fine old party. As it turned out, thanks to her, I got two for the price of one. For no price at all in fact.

Nursing my drink, I decided it was like surgery. You cut out the diseased part, stem the bleeding, stitch up the wound and the body learns how to live without what was there before. I'd excised the tumour of Cleo's poisonous love and my body was figuring out how to take its first steps forward into a new world, tentative at first, and a little shaky. One thing I was sure of: I wasn't looking for anything meaningful. I'd been through the desert forty days and nights, felt the freeze and burn, the parched throat, the dimming of vitality, the onward struggle with unseeing eyes, the divorce of mind and body from any reality but looming mortality. I'd gone to doomsday for that woman and I couldn't go back there. But as I listened to Mia pulling stories from the girls' lips like a conjuror, euphoria warmed my body and I needed to hold some sweet flesh against mine.

I didn't quite know how. I felt like a dancer in a minefield. There were plenty of people who wanted to talk to me. One who should be avoided at all costs. I kept Mia close, masking myself from the unwelcome attention of anyone who might come through those glass doors. Tarzan was in one of the gig spaces keeping watch on his latest protégé. I wouldn't be going there. I hoped he'd disappear as soon as the drinks tab grew too long. And there was Emmeline, that cellist in my ex's band, eyeing me across the bar. Though she was sultry and bejewelled, I would not be persuading her to open her legs other than to play her instrument.

Though it would have been preferable not to sleep with a musician at all – I might want to work with them in the future – Mia's pornographic murmur was proving too much of an aphrodisiac for me to fuss over details. I felt the evening drifting my way as she started a discussion with Alicia and her younger sister about the relationship between sung speech in the French ballad, *singspiel* and Dietrich, and the mumblecore of the new folk vocal line. My older woman was good. Quick on the uptake and almost too clever. If she'd been less voluptuous I might have found it pretentious but it wowed the girls. All at once they were giving it back as good as they got, plus more of their life-history in ten minutes than I could have extracted in an entire evening. Alicia had been in London for five years, had studied modern languages at UCL, was researching a PhD in some dark corner of linguistics and taught three days a week in her faculty. She wore her French accent proudly. And here we were, suddenly singing at the bar, lines from Piaf's *Je ne regrette rien*, Brel's *Ne me quitte pas*, Schoenberg's Pierrot Lunaire…

> *Den Wein, den man mit Augen trinkt,*
> *Gießt Nachts der Mond in Wogen nieder,*
> *Und eine Springflut überschwemmt*
> *Den stillen Horizont.*

The words flowed like a sweet narcotic, Mia filming the whole interview on her phone: which turned us on the most she wanted to know? Alicia opted for Brel's tragic pull, but to me there was nothing more sublime than this moondrunk text.

> *In nightly waves the moon pours down*
> *The wine one drinks with eyes alone*
> *And springtide floods*
> *The still horizon...*

I got Alicia to do it for me again slowly in German and felt my flesh stir. She was willowy, with a long curtain of blonde hair and liquid eyes that held you as she spoke. Her right nostril was pierced with a delicate gold stud. She wore her nails long, and a ring that held an eye to ward off evil spirits. Her little sister was visiting her for a long weekend. Darker, more curvy, with an ample, soft bosom. Arched eyebrows like her sister's and a birthmark on her cheek that made her shy. On the other hand, that might just have been landing in London for the first time. She was only seventeen. Her name was Florence.

During the evening we dipped in and out of each other's consciousness. From time to time I'd glimpse them chatting across the room, or smooching ironically with each other, as I instructed Mia in the vagaries of the music industry. It was, in her words, a useful session.

At around midnight, Mia declined to come dancing with us and took a cab home. She offered me a lift but a sharp glance accompanied by a twitch at the corner of her mouth told me she knew I was better left to take my own time.

'You do remember your address, don't you?' she quipped, as she wrapped her silk scarf around her neck and gave me a peck on the cheek. 'I shouldn't like to think of you lost on the streets again.'

More maternal than my own mother. I tapped my phone at her – it was all stored in my little magic rolodex the size of a contact lens. With the slightest of nods, she left me and swept out through the clammy crowd.

We did dance in fact, after another mojito for the girls and a sneaky joint out back where the boys stored the barrels. A chilly wind rolled us into a nearby blues bar awash with laughter and smoke and driving, heavy rhythms. We were sucked into the warmth, the movement, the twist of limbs, the movement of hands, hips, the glitter of sidelong glances, the swish of hair against cheek, the undulation of flesh beneath damp clothing, like

Matisse's dancers, an unending circle linked by desire and the will to live.

It was three-thirty when we tumbled out of the cab, paid for by Florence's pocket-money, down the steps into the apartment. My apartment. A mellow warmth suffused my loins as I anticipated the rest of the night stretched out before us. All done and paid for, all care left outside for someone else to stumble over.

Alicia was no introvert. Perfectly uninhibited, she eased me onto the sofa where she could reach my mouth with hers and gain better access to my skin. She tossed my jacket insouciantly onto the nearby dining chair and opened my shirt buttons, her long nails brushing lightly against the hairs of my chest. Florence watched her sister in a wistful way, taking off her own clothes almost absent-mindedly.

'Attention aux pieds, mon amour,' murmured big sister, 'tu sais, c'est la zone du corps la plus sensible…' all the time caressing my neck just below the ear with her tongue. Occasionally I'd feel the sharpness of her teeth against the skin of my earlobe or my throat, but never too much, just enough to sharpen anticipation. As she did so, the hands of Florence slid discreetly beneath the hem of my jeans and unzipped my boots. There was something at once tender and fierce about the way she applied her mouth and tongue to my toes, an unfamiliar sensation that clicked almost immediately into arousal. Alicia must have felt me stirring against her thigh, for she hurriedly removed my shirt and took her tongue and gentle teeth to my nipples. I lay back with the sensation of being done to that I imagine a woman might feel, and no compulsion to change roles. It was the best therapy going, Smokey Robinson playing through my mind like a distant soundtrack, the girls converging from opposite ends of my body. Sexual healing *à trois*.

I had Alicia's tongue in my navel like an overactive sea anemone and suddenly I was hard as a rock. Florence was pulling my jeans down over my hips with a glint below her sweeping eyelashes that said she'd be up for whatever I could give her. In this pincer movement it was anyone's guess which of them would try first. It seemed Alicia wanted to run the show, so little sister got to look and stroke while she kissed me deep. Then she turned and swooped down on me like some beautiful predator, took me into her throat so fast it had me gasping, gazing at those shapely hips thrust into the air, skirt up around her waist. I slipped a finger inside and felt her body twitching with the tease, her throat vibrating like a tiger. It was all so close and hot there was a moment it could have been over before it had begun, but she withdrew to undress and let me cool down a little. She had a good body, athletic and well-scented, with breasts that tasted salty from the dance. She was graceful and responsive. When I put my tongue to her she shuddered, uttering French expletives under her breath. When she seemed ready I took her in my mouth. I knew she'd come if I carried on but she was saying *Non, non* and pushing at me like she wanted a ride so I took her on board reverse cowboy style and she went off like a firework in about ten seconds. I was counting hard because I didn't want to come myself, she'd taken me unprotected. She cried out loud and long, then her head flopped forward in a cascade of blonde silk and she slipped off me, kissing her sister full on the mouth. I could see Florence surrender. Then I could see she was using her tongue. I rolled over to watch them for a while. I wasn't sure whether they'd done this before or whether the double act was just something to which I'd been the catalyst. Still breathless, Alicia pushed her sister back towards me with a *'prend-le'* and a sly smile at me. Tentatively, Florence straddled me and we kissed, sweet and slow. She'd taken off her pretty top and her breasts pushed against my chest, her nipples grazing me softly. I felt her moving moistly against my lower abdomen, easing lower, reaching for me, I knew I had to do something, I knew I hadn't a single thing in the house. It wasn't mine. I'd barely lived there. I just knew it couldn't be like the last time, catastrophic. I turned my head to Alicia with what sounded to me like a distant groan, *we should be protecting your sis, right?* She was quick to the rescue. That condom was stretched over my manhood in less time than she'd taken to orgasm, then she was kissing me, her sister was kissing me, climbing onto me, tighter, hotter, stiller. She hovered in mid-air, her cheeks ever more flushed, her eyes rolled back, hardly seeming to move at all, then she was slipping down harder, punishing herself until she came in a huge, shuddering gasp, riding me like a queen as I surfed her wave and finally grounded with what felt like a throat full of gravel, in one of the most intense experiences of my life.

We slept together like kittens in a basket, curled around and over each other and dead to the world for some hours before dawn started to poke its steel fingers through the dull red curtaining. As I woke, the first person I thought of was my married woman.

These graceful sisters were like a gift she'd bestowed on me without even knowing the extent of her own bounty. I was lying in the big bed she'd provided, the most comfortable bed by far I had ever inhabited – and there had been a few – with absolute absence of anxiety. That was what she'd given me: loss of fear. I felt a surge of love for this mysterious saviour of mine. Lady Mia. Perhaps I'd wear a miniature of her concealed around my neck and pen sad ballads to her. At the same time I felt as mischievous as one of those kittens. I happened to be lying on my left side, and I kissed and touched the soft and musky neck of the girl lying closest to my reach. It happened to be Alicia, another little skirmish began while Florence slept into the breaking day. Big sister was secure in her sexuality. She knew how to turn herself on, greedy but light of heart, without struggle.

Our mouths being tacky from the night's adventures, we made tea and drank it among the bedclothes. I basked in my satiety like a rock star. My needs were simpler and less destructive than most rock stars, but by mutual understanding I would be allowed to kiss and say goodbye and dismiss them from my door an hour later, knowing that it was a completed episode, and there was no call for repetition. Florence's eyelids fluttered and there was a moistness about them as she gave me a parting look. Little girl. She might have liked it to continue for a while, but her sister would put her straight, I was sure of that. Plenty more like me in London town.

As their footsteps disappeared down the street into the hazy morning rush, I lay down in the untidy nest we'd made, breathing their mingled scents. The room coalesced around me like a noiseless hive. My body turned slowly to honey. It was not a sudden epiphany, more a sense of filling with golden light, expanding from a glowing point in my heart and loins to fill my limbs, my head, the whole of me. I loved the world, was the world.

I must have drifted off, as the next thing I was aware of was the front door buzzer drilling through my unconscious, letting all the light escape. Like a punctured balloon spiralling across the room, I surfaced giddily. Had one of them forgotten something? The key sounded in the lock sending me scrabbling for whatever it was I wore the night before, like a faithless gigolo. She was in the doorway in some elegant cashmere coat and her hair curled. *Curled.* She'd never done that before. I was used to her bedhead look, had occasionally wondered what it would be like to ruffle that blonde-dark mop, to knot it between my agile fingers.

'Sleep well?' she intoned, with the merest hint of irony.

I slithered into my tee-shirt and boxers, mustering some kind of response. 'Like a baby.'

'Glad to hear it. Found the thermostat and everything?'

She was enjoying this too much. She opened the tall cupboard in the hall and tweaked the switch I'd slammed to max in the early hours.

'Leave it like that then perhaps the planet will survive.'

I retrieved my jeans and joined her in the kitchen, where she already had the coffee on. Two mugs, Alicia's and mine, nestled side by side on the breakfast bar. While the coffee-maker burbled, she whisked them into the sink and rinsed them, without so much as a flicker. What a woman. My mother would have sent me a laser-beam look along with the appropriate sarcasm that might trigger the minutest degree of payback for a lifetime of self-sacrifice.

Nor did she react to the other clues, the brightly-coloured thong I discovered scrunched up on the cistern when I went for a belated shower some time after she'd been to powder that straight nose of hers and spray some of her expensive perfume. It must have been Florence's but it looked like a piece of kiddie underwear and I stuffed it into the bin, disconcerted. When I poured Mia the coffee she'd kindly presumed to make, there was a little scrap of paper lying on the worktop, torn from a miniature diary and containing the words ♥ *you so much sexy*. Young Florence was going to take a few days to recover from our night of bliss.

I have never been one for secrecy. Tongue always hanging out and heart plastered on my sleeve. I'd left notes on my scandals everywhere I went through life. Until Cleo. The tsunami that swept my history away. I stood on the mud flats staring into the rising sun and the broken disaster of my life. Or rather on the kitchen tiles, the brief glory in the comfort of strangers fading with along with the morning mist and the curl of steam from my coffee cup.

Mia had hung her coat in the hallway, such as it was, and was leant against the kitchen bar in her dark two-piece. Poised, unhurried, something of the film star about her. Waiting for me to wake up. I realised that I was behaving as if I was the guest in somebody else's flat. So used to dossing on friends' floors, I hadn't actually got around to taking possession of my own place. Perhaps I still didn't believe it was my own.

'Won't you sit down?' My voice sounded too husky for the circumstances, and way too formal. Clark Gable and Joan Crawford in one of my mum's afternoon black and white films. What we did together on wet Sundays when I was small. What a disastrous childhood.

'I'll stand if it's ok. I thought I'd take you shopping.'

The laugh burst out of me before I'd had a chance to think. 'I'm old enough to find my way to the corner shop, don't worry.'

She eyed me with a flash of impatience, motioned me next to her on the sofa. 'Let's put it this way…' She called up a memo board on her tablet and started constructing some kind of chart. 'You've been on the streets. You're recovering from some health issues. Whatever work you were doing is currently unavailable to you until you piece your network back together. Until that time you're working on a music documentary with me, so your CV won't completely fall apart in the interim. You have no other identifiable source of income unless you'd like me to drop you at the job centre. I would consider it a courtesy if you'd let me dress you in such a way as not to embarrass me professionally. We have a meeting with a major broadcaster at three.'

Put like that it was difficult to argue with her. She knew if she handed over the cash I'd probably blow it all on a leather trenchcoat or something equally ill-judged.

In fact it wasn't awkward at all. She knew what she was looking for, and she knew where to get it. In three hours she'd acquired me a trousseau fit to marry me off. Or at least to fill that wardrobe in the corner of my bedroom.

No one had bought me clothes since I was about ten. My mum would have to whinge at my dad for weeks over the phone to pay the maintenance so she could send me to school in something that didn't have holes in the knees, elbows or toes. But this woman had money. She drove me the few blocks to Shepherd's Bush Roundabout, where we rounded the corner to that vast cathedral of consumption that was Westfield. If you couldn't spend, you could always look. All day if you liked. It's just that nothing was different to anything you'd find on a high street anywhere else in the land. Everything was a franchise. Nothing was unique. She apologised for this most profusely but we agreed it was the most practical way for me not to look like a piece of street refuse.

In the centre of the mall, a capoeira demonstration was taking place to thunderous Brazilian music. We strode from door to door like fellow conspirators, dipping frequently into the shops to get away from one kind of noise only to hit another. Soft rock. Smooth jazz. Dubstep. Vivaldi. It was amazing the diversity of aural stimulation retailers thought would persuade bemused shoppers to buy. Occasionally she'd ask me a question. *Do you prefer the elasticated waist or the soft cotton seam? Are you a thirty-two or a thirty-four?* We rummaged in bins of special offer socks, riffled through railings of jackets, sweats, tees. She explained as we continued our whirlwind tour of the menswear stores that when she'd started out in television she'd often had to help out the costume designers on film shoots. Actors got through more socks than you could ever believe possible. Inside-leg measurements and collar-sizes held no terror for her. She negotiated the place like a well-honed search engine, handing me one carrier bag after another, oblivious to the occasionally curious looks of assistants or till staff. She did everything with grace, suggesting, never dictating, but ruthlessly conveying to me what she preferred in the raising of an eyebrow, the pursing of her glossed lips.

By the time we perched on barstools with our tuna ciabattas and freshly pressed orange juice, I felt like one of those dowdy women on a TV makeover show. I could see myself next to her in the mirror behind the baristas, sporting a new jacket and tee-shirt over a pair of well cut jeans with some designer label I couldn't have afforded in a million years. She'd got a keen eye for prices but she'd still spent a few hundred kitting me out. Of course, she was much too cool to be looking back at me in the mirror. She was texting someone on her phone. Her husband, probably. Or her daughter. I was too cool to ask. I just knew we looked good together.

'I like your hair that way,' I ventured.

'Thank you,' she growled, still texting. I put up my hand to touch the curl nearest her cheek. It sprang back against her skin as I let it go. Was she blushing?

'Are you?'

Still looking at her touch screen. 'What.'

'Blushing?'

She put the phone down. Met my eye and quailed somewhere behind her optic nerve. I knew I'd got through but her armour was up in a flash.

'Don't push it lover boy.'

I smiled, took a large bite of the crisp bread and chewed with relish, enjoying the sight of her polite nibbling. 'You've got a crumb, just there.' I licked the tip of my finger and stroked it away, without disturbing the glossy lipstick she was wearing.

She half-smiled, sighed, batted me off impatiently. 'Look, you're old enough to understand about professional distance. None of this will work if people think you're my toy boy. I'm sure you wouldn't want to be anyway,' she added, in case I was getting ideas above my station.

I nodded wisely. Though at that moment I couldn't see anything wrong at all.

Of course penniless musicians have always revelled in their penury. In the eighteenth century it would have been a smart way of getting inside the petticoats of a patroness: *here am I, young, gifted and poor, all I have to offer is my music.* And my body. Gorgeous gentry in their tall powdered wigs and whale-boned waists panting over their golden boys. An unbroken line of patronage stretching across hundreds of years, ever since music gave the church a kick in the arse. Probably it was all much more unbuttoned then. Expected even. Wealthy couples married to each other's fortunes and held together by the mutual acceptance of each other's dalliances on the side.

So here we were sitting in a smart, glass-bound office in Victoria and she was pitching to this commissioning editor like a real power woman. I was high on her thrust. Her trust. She had her Mac on the conference table and here was a pretty decent-looking promo she'd cut together of the musicians we'd filmed last night at the club. I didn't know she could edit. And she'd manipulated the picture quality to give it a crazy, spontaneous feel, a little grainy, but more colourful and so exciting. Nice, trashy little captions in overblown courier typeface like a late-night sixties journo filing from a smoky jazz club. I'd have hired her to make me a music video there and then although I'm sure I couldn't have afforded her rates. She'd cleverly used snippets of my voice feeding in and out of the performances, occasionally cutting to me looking *not bad* as a kind of host, a narrative presence running through the sequence. She'd taken sound bites and laughter from people I knew were just ordinary wannabes, like all of us, and made them look amazing. It was the poetry and rhythm in the way she'd cut them together that made it all lift off. It just worked. You were going to watch this thing. I could see the TV guys – and she'd got three of them in the room by banking on her own reputation – lapping it up. I could see they wanted it.

When had she done all this? While I'd been letting myself be serviced by two willing and very able young ladies last night? When else would there have been time? I felt gloriously undeserving, more than a little shamefaced, and completely in awe: this was the way to run life. Take it by the scruff of the neck and shake it into the shape you required it to be. Don't take no for an answer and build everything you do on what's just happened. Then you're on a roll, your career is moving forward, you're as good as your last piece of work, you're constantly active and alive, people who matter are noticing you, you've got the media onside because of your talent, not because of how much noise you can make on Twitter. It took age and experience married with superior intuition and willingness to connect beyond generation, beyond tribe, beyond status.

I must have had a kind of ecstatic look on my

face. The look of the cat who got the cream, who knows how hard to lick and where to get more. I realised suddenly that there were several pairs of eyes on me, *weighing me up*: the mascara-swept gimlets of the commissioning editor; her sidekick's deep-set scowl; the development kid's shy, kohl-painted gaze; and Mia's warm glance pretending bare-faced scrutiny like the others, playing the game while the corner of her mouth twitched. She looked away a fraction before the others. All this took place in seconds, the time they took to decide I had The Look. The boss eyed my battered guitar-case. Would I play as well as present and interview? she wanted to know. I was open to suggestion, but of course I was a musician first and foremost so happy to oblige if it fitted the brief.

This seemed to be what they wanted to hear. A musical guide was more interesting than a talking head. There was the possibility of a spin-off album, at least a download from the station website. There was talk about slot lengths and times, VOD rights and audience interaction. Something about two-way promotion and shares in ticket royalties. A lot of legalese about the waiving of artists' rights. It was getting pretty heavy from what I could glean. They clearly sniffed a format they could make loads of money from and of course the artist would be the dung beetle trodden under foot in the scramble to coin it before the interest ran dry. Mia told them her lawyer would correspond with their business affairs department and draft contracts would be exchanged before the end of the month. There was more talk about delivery dates and timing between recording and broadcast. This was where I lost the thread, but the fish was still on the line and we left the office after an hour feeling that we'd done a pretty good job.

It was then it happened. One of those spur-of-the-moment things you think nothing of at the time but which etches your soul like acid on gold. We were on our way through the high-tech nineties hangar of the reception area, and she was thanking me for helping her convince them, it looked as if we had ourselves a pilot at least, when I dipped my head to hers and kissed her softly, very quickly on the mouth. It could have been a friendly, high-spirited thing if it had been her cheek of course, the sort of thing media folk do all the time and think nothing of. But her mouth. She was not the sort of woman you kissed on the mouth with impunity.

Neither of us reacted on the surface, we were still laughing and talking and had barely broken step. The screens continued to play out their images of daytime programming, the commissionaires had their backs turned variously, the receptionists continued to cuddle their laptops and answer their phonecalls, wired to their earpieces and staring ahead at the thronging street outside. But as I made way for her through the revolving glass doors, there was a tiny fluster in the way she left the building. A sea change.

7.

She took Stephen out to dinner that evening at the little Italian restaurant in Blenheim Crescent they'd been to for years, particularly when they had something to sort out. As so often in the past, it happened spontaneously, a feeling of something drawing to a head, a need to be in company, not just each other's, neutral terrain perhaps.

Stephen had no idea where his wife was up to in her head. It had been a peculiar couple of weeks, but there were few outward signs. Her charity-drive was over, the boy discharged and declared fit to face the world, presumably now dossing on the floor of one of his musical friends. She was vague about the details but she thought he'd be able to look after himself. She looked lovely, hair falling softly about her shoulders, her clear skin animated by the trace of a flush, an intensity in those darkest of eyes that he couldn't quite fathom. She seemed a shade graver, yet somehow more herself, more present. It was subtle, the change, perhaps no change at all.

She'd come in from her meeting slightly later than expected and he knew it had gone well from the way she'd swung into his arms, laughing. Her heartbeat was strong against his breast. She was going to tell him something, she was nervous, he could always tell.

'So? They liked it?'

She nodded, turning from him and throwing her coat over the back of a kitchen chair.

'Yes. Ball rolling, anyway.'

'Are they going to commission it?'

'That's the idea.'

She was half-beaming, half-frowning in the way she did when things were going well. Never quite trusted the moment of elation.

'Fantastic, darling! I can see I'm going to have to watch my back. Unless you were thinking of hiring me as director?'

His hands were slouched in his jacket pockets, playful in that arch way he had, and not quite daring to believe, she pulled him close again.

'I'm buying you dinner.'

He smiled into her hair. 'What kind of answer is that?'

'No answer at all. Let me leap in the shower then I'll tell you everything.'

It was dark and warm at Luigi's. They sat at their usual table, tucked away in the interior gloom, away from the street door and from prying eyes. All the edges were somehow growing softer, the caramel cashmere sweeping from her shoulder to the worn leather seat, the glow on her skin, the drift of hair around her face, haloed by the undulating yellow flame between them, the island of candlelight that cocooned them and softened the edges of the debate. Even the jazz was soft, late-fifties mood stuff, Chet Baker or something, he couldn't quite place it. The wine was excellent and mellow. The room spoke in hushed tones of seduction or surrender. There was no need to fight. Why should he even have thought of it? He was blessed with the most stunning woman in London as his wife. Full of life, spirit, generosity, and this new creative energy which had so startled and impressed him. He wanted to set her free so she could soar now, really have the career and recognition she deserved.

'It was a joke of course. About directing. They'll need the young guns to make it work, I'm far too long in the tooth.'

'You're not *available*. You don't think I haven't talked to your agent?'

She was laughing in that open-throated helter-skelter kind of way she did when they'd first met, like pebbles on chamois, rolling and all soft-hard edges and curves. If you'd had to write it down phonetically it would have been impossible.

'You should direct it yourself.'

The way her pupils dilated, it was clear he'd hit the mark without even aiming for it. So that was the game. He broke into a smile which brought her up short and almost snatched her breath away, though she rolled on through it like a kid in a playground. 'I probably will. If it's a bunch of music promo newbies it'll be down to me to be puppetmaster.'

'You *are* a producer, aren't you darling?' He leaned

in to top up her glass, challenge flickering in his eyes. 'Clever. Good for the company. Something new and ballsy.' He sipped, turned the warm liquid in his mouth, put his head on one side. 'No yearning for the classical music world then?'

She frowned. 'Long ago and far away.' She was sounding defensive, she knew, but it was one of her painful subjects. One of only two they never spoke about. She didn't know why. Maybe it was time to push the boundaries and find out. 'Pop is for everyone, on all platforms, by any means. More alive than it's ever been, shambolic, unpredictable. It's seething with idiots, savants, clowns and suicides, but at least it's not stiff with monstrous egos.'

Stephen was laughing at her by now. 'Put like that why would anyone want to give them screen time?'

'It would be like dredging up all that stuff from my childhood,' she smiled appeasingly. 'This'll be fun. Noisy and raw.'

He was thoughtful, as they dug their way into the antipasto. 'As long as you think it's creative enough. I'd still love to direct a movie for you.'

She didn't think he'd make a play for her. And now he was moving in on her creative space again. Master of the pincer movement, how did he do that?

'You should get back to that screenplay of yours.'

'I'd love that, of course.'

He was watching her eating. The sun-dried tomato was sharp on her tongue, making her salivate self-consciously. The gaps in the preceding week opened up like cracks in the pavement. She felt suddenly nervous.

'I hope these people are worth so much of your time and energy.'

'I'm only filming the ones who are worth my time.'

'Just don't want to see you throw away your talent.'

She wanted to find him patronising, elitist, out of touch, but deep down she knew he was right, that he meant it in her interest. It made her resentful. She felt uneasy, her appetite draining away.

'He must have triggered something fairly momentous, darling. Are you ok?'

A cold start flooded from the crown of her skull down her forehead. Illogically, she felt giddy with fear, though what, really, was so very menacing about the scrutiny of her husband, eyes crinkled in half-amusement at her passion for a lost cause?

'Of course.' She levelled with him, met his eye solemnly. *I'm not a cheat, whatever else I am.* 'Don't tease, it was well meant, however it turned out.' Her words sounded quaint and old-fashioned to her. Too many excuses, it was bound to sound suspicious. 'I'm sorry I upset Lottie though. How d'you think she is?'

Stephen put out his fingers to touch hers. 'Honestly?'

She nodded. Their daughter had made no secret of whose side she'd been on during the past week.

'I think she's having a delicious fling. She's just cross with us for being old.'

'Us.' Mia stifled an outburst. She wasn't standing up to be counted. And she resented his assessment, it sounded like an off-the-rails fourteen-year-old, not like her complicated, easily-wounded daughter. Stephen chuckled provocatively.

'Stop projecting onto her, Mia. I know as writers we do it all the time but it's not healthy. Let her get on with screwing the pants off this girl and give her space to grow up a bit.'

Mia stabbed at the blood-red, wrinkled skin of the remaining tomato, pushing it around with the oil-drenched curls of artichoke, feeling his liberalism applied to everyone else except her. Where she was concerned, he was quite capable of turning tyrant. Should she be glad to be loved that much? Involuntarily, her fingers brushed against her lips and she thought of the revolving doors earlier that afternoon.

Stephen leant forward and kissed her gently on the brow, pouring balm on troubled waters.

'So tell me,' she said, 'What is it you've been detained by under your burning anglepoise, night after night? Not Lottie's peccadillos.'

'Hardly.'

'Your biography?'

A smile spread across his face. 'You weren't very interested a few nights ago.'

'I was hatching my own plot.'

'It's a miniseries for the BBC. They called me in for a meeting directly off the back of the award. Anthony's got the draft contract on his desk already. Should keep me off the streets for a few months.'

'A commission?'

He nodded. It was a wonderful piece of one-upmanship, and yet it was protection. It was her husband taking responsibility, stepping up to the mark. She felt suddenly lost, trivial. Her reply sounded querulous. 'That's fantastic, Stephen.'

'I'd rather be directing your script. When are you going to finish one for me?'

She met his eye without flinching, though it took

an immense effort of self-control. Her head was in a foreign state, she realised that anything she wrote then would be a visceral cry from somewhere she hadn't even known was inside her, the blood and guts, the frustration, the sense of being lost. She was spinning off into outer space. She didn't know herself. Where had this anger come from?

'I'm not sure I could write what you'd want to direct.'

'Write me a proposal.'

She shook her head, uncomfortable. 'I can't do it.'

'You never know till you try, Mia. You're too used to being in control. Let it all hang out a bit and see what happens.'

He didn't even see the contradictions. That she'd made her move. He thought he was buying her time. He'd taken a job that was someone else's pitch, was working to a brief in order to take the pressure off her. It was his fight back, his bid to reclaim her. She didn't even know if he'd done it consciously. What she did know was that he sensed nothing of her continued contact with the young man he'd objectified and neutralised, her lost one, her leper.

All at once, the tension flowed from her body and she lit up with the certainty of not having been found out. The freedom of knowing her husband was on her side. Her sense of security spread its glow over the rest of the meal. By the end of the evening they were flirting with each other in a wine-fuelled haze which took her back to the early years.

She kept quiet and took her leper to bed with them. She returned the embraces of her husband with a different appetite. There was enquiry in her fingertips, in the way she used her tongue and lips.

There was adventure in the way she revealed her body, a new expression in the way she moved. As they clutched each other closer and ever more urgently, she kept her eyes closed.

After it was over, she listened long to the breathing of her husband next to her in the bed. A soft rush like the ebb and flow of the ocean on a distant shore. She felt calm, not desolate at all. She breathed with him, breath of life, pranayama. More fish than woman. Each inhalation and exhalation a mantra repeating itself over and over like the flux and flow of the ventilator in the hospital room that long night, moving her away from a self which had crystallised and hardened into something that was no longer her, towards the new self she knew was forming like some strange embryo. She had made her adult self to reflect the husband she had idolised. She had been too young to make that quantum leap. Now, suddenly, she was alive with curiosity, an alternative she. The self in one of many parallel universes she could have lived.

The breaths merged, finally, with her dream in which she moved through a glittering slideshow, an endless series of revolving doors through which she danced, over and over, in the naked ecstasy of movement, losing her mind, losing herself. Like a zoetrope gathering speed, the whirl of glass too fast for dance, she was spiralling upward, shooting through the open roof and into the sunlit sky where faceless figures moved free of gravity, bodies arched and graceful as a painting by Chagall. She was drawn towards one naked like herself. It was too bright to see. She closed her eyes against the dazzling light and as their hands clasped in the dance, she felt only the warmth of skin against her breast, the twining of limbs, the soft brush of lips on hers.

She awoke to the smell of coffee and a warm space in the bed next to her. The first birds were singing in the deepest of dawn blue skies. A light was on in the hallway. He had Radio 4 on in the kitchen, she could hear it drifting up from the conservatory. She stretched her toes and sighed. It had been the way their non-production mornings had started all the years she could remember. The routine of a long and happy marriage, the serene and luxurious knowledge of shared habit. What right had she to inhabit this blissful state of security and know that in an hour or two she would be off on her latest adventure, albeit in the name of work, with a young man who had no idea of or respect for professional boundaries, who the previous day had been acting as if she was fair game?

Coffee came, and the loving embrace of a husband who had been writing at his PC for an hour and a half. She shook the dreams from her head and drank herself eagerly into a state of wakefulness and gratitude. She would have to put some distance between herself and the boy if it was going to work at all.

It was with some irritation that she stood on his doorstep some time later, having rung the doorbell for the fifth time with no response. She didn't want to use the key, it was against the rules she'd set for herself, the protocol she'd drawn up in her mind about renting a space on behalf of a third party. Nevertheless, it was a shared workspace as well as his home and they had made an appointment to meet at eleven. It was eleven-thirty.

A text trilled its arrival. She flicked on her phone with a start of relieved annoyance that changed at once to compunction. It was Lottie, inviting her to a live poetry and art event she was holding that evening. One of these endless pop-up happenings that incorporated 'secret' into its title in order to make itself sound sexy. She texted back. *What time?* The evening was supposed to be set aside for more ad hoc recording, she'd be working with Lars, one of her regular cameramen, to pick up better quality test footage. Presently, it showed every symptom of being a disaster in the making. She inserted the key in the lock and entered the apartment. Signs of his recent habitation. The clothes she'd bought him unbagged and piled on the sofa. He'd taken most of the labels off, they were all over the side table. The debris of a hastily consumed sandwich on the kitchen counter. An empty takeaway coffee cup. The laptop on the workstation was on, a new screensaver collage of downloaded album covers. He'd found something profitable to do with his time at least.

Her text messages, however, went unanswered. His phone was currently unavailable and requesting that she try again later. He couldn't even set that up reliably. She sat down at the computer to look for clues. His Facebook chat page was still open. He had made no attempt at concealment. Someone implausibly named Cleopatra had tried to catch his interest. He'd left her dangling in the void, had engaged idly with one or two females making propositions of varying degrees of lewdness, had embarked on a long and playful exchange with one Jewel, the precise nature of their relationship unclear. He had answered indifferently to a couple of musicians asking to be considered for slots. Face aflame she sent him a message. *Aren't we supposed to be meeting at yours?*

Knowing she was in the wrong, she opened up his email programme and brought in his mail. While she was waiting for the queasy mixture of spam and bona fide messages to load, a new message from Tom Pavelin flashed up at the bottom of her phone screen. Her heart leapt with painful anticipation.

Sorry Mia am running late could we meet down here later?

A stab of anger and disappointment. She fired him back a reply. *Where are you?*

It took several minutes for his response to come. Whether from bad connectivity, bad conscience or distraction at his end, she had no idea. She scanned his inbox and saw that he had made one or two vague arrangements in anticipation of the day's work. Nothing that she couldn't have done herself tenfold and more. Nothing that was written in passable English either. She felt punished and put soundly in her place.

She boiled the kettle, washed out the cafetière and noted he had made time to stock the fridge with semi-skimmed milk, a couple of smoothies and some yoghurt. Anticipating invalidity? She imagined the bender he'd embarked on after they'd parted. He probably thought she was going to make a film star out of him. Her lips burned with humiliation. She poured her stiff black brew into one of the brightly coloured cups she'd chosen when kitting out the place, tried to regroup her thoughts. She realised she was *waiting* for his reply. She had never done this for a man in her life. The technology hadn't existed before and it was not, she decided, a step forward.

Old Street how about 4?

She stabbed the keys as if she'd been levelling a slap to his face. *Suggest you let me know when you are next available I have other plans.*

He was tail-between-legs now: *Sorry my bad*

She logged off without bothering to reply.

Lottie's event was underway at the Shoreditch gallery when she arrived in the early afternoon, contrite and sweaty from the tube and feeling every inch somebody's mother. A lithe, attractive youth she recognised as one of her daughter's fine art coterie, was suspended from a harness near the ceiling, where he was fixing wire sculptures to a continuous monorail criss-crossing the room overhead. Each piece was mounted on runners enabling them to glide almost noiselessly in perpetuity. The gallery owner, an elegant woman in a rich, crimson *kurta* and waist-length black hair, glanced up nervously at the unfamiliar air traffic, sensing health and safety issues, while art students and occasional members of the public admired, sipping their green tea and jasmine. A divided screen on the rear wall flashed up a flow of graphics, snatches of poetic text, against which Mia observed her daughter giving the okay to the projectionist before turning.

'Mum!' Lottie stepped across the room into her arms.

Something political just for a change, she chuckled as she held her mother tight, smelling her hair. They'd decided to look at global displacement.

'Can you stay for a bit? I'm about to do one of my slots. We go on all day till midnight. Couldn't get a licence beyond that, but hey. What d'you think of

Roland's aerial hardware?'

Grounded, Roland was unfastening his safety straps, flushed, animated. The two of them kissed, intimate, complicit. As Lottie turned away to set up her microphone, he took Mia's hand warmly. 'Great you could come Mrs. Chancery, Charlotte wasn't sure if you'd make it. She's amazing isn't she?'

Mia looked into the sparkling black eyes of the young man and her throat contracted, momentarily overwhelmed by the image of a potential son-in-law. Finally, she remembered to smile. 'Endlessly inventive.'

'We worked on the installation together. It was her idea to engineer the sculptures into movement. We've had them all suspended from the ceiling in our flat while we made them.'

Our flat. Mia watched him, reeling. Of course she had watched her daughter with pliers and wire cutters from her early teens and knew how nimble, how artful those fingers could be, bending the spun metal to her vision, just as she would later subjugate language to her poetic will. The remarkable self-possession and dignity of her daughter turned her world on its head, not for the first time.

In the five minutes it took Lottie to arrange her performance space, Roland dropped into position several pieces of the sky in the jigsaw puzzle that had been her version of her daughter's recent life. She was the driving force behind the artist's co-operative they'd set up with a scholarship she'd been awarded, raising local grants and private sponsorship to run a series of events to promote their work. A radical spirit like her father. A hard worker, a fixer like her mother.

'I haven't even offered you a drink!'

Mia took the iced elixir Roland handed to her. 'She just drives all other thoughts out of your mind, doesn't she?'

Mia smiled with a secret glow, thrumming with the secret satisfaction of one who knows the value of her offspring. She was thrilled, no longer overwhelmed, absorbing the sound of her daughter's deep, melodious voice as she spoke into the microphone. The hubbub settled, all eyes were on the spell-binding mermaid of a girl, seductress and oracle, Calypso and Cassandra. She spoke her poetry and the world slowed.

> *Identify cataclysm*
> *the catch in the throat*
> *the catch*
> *shoal of the lost*
> *splintered*
> *flowing over the dustbowl land*
> *fish rolled in sand*
> *mother and child hand in hand.*
> *Wings. Wings beat.*
> *Beat of rain on corrugated roof.*
> *Coruscated woof and weft of all we leave*
> *heave and grieve*
> *sieve and strain*
> *skein of geese stitching their arms across a silken sky*
> *V for victory*
> *coded in feather and sinew.*
> *Downthrust and no trust and tanks rust and*
> *always sky*
> *pearl grey as a deathshead*
> *steel grey as the metal fighter*
> *dull boom and clatter of the all nighter*

tearing the air
wide
a rent in the fabric that covered life
here
take cover
here
move under
here
thrown asunder
here here here here
becomes there.
A little letter thrown like an anchor
the 't' where terror begins

Mia couldn't judge whether the poetry was good or bad. She could only feel the power of the performance. The roll and murmur of her daughter's delivery. The hypnosis of her conviction. The seduction of a scene drawn like a Japanese pen and ink sketch against the backdrop of colour, always colour, the graphics sliding and shifting across a rainbow screen.

There had been several actors on Stephen's side of the family. Mia's own parents had both come from that protestant-coloured stable where 'showing off' wasn't quite the thing. Study hard and acquire a skill, yes. Compete for prizes, of course. Justify your right to perform in a public space. So different to now, when any sixteen-year-old had the front to get up and yell into a mic. Mia saw with gratitude that her daughter had not only the courage to perform, but the intelligence and intuition to captivate an audience. It was a gift. Something that made her magnetic and watchable. Something that made her completely different from her mother.

There were other poems, a touching flow of ideas on statelessness, migrancy, urban poverty and isolation, about what impels the human race to wander. At the end of the recitation, the applause was warm and prolonged. The room had filled without her noticing, the air humid with concentration and human idealism. And love, she couldn't put it any other way.

She watched her daughter step out of the charmed circle into dialogue with admirers clustering round to quiz her about meaning, message, method. Mia homed in on certain phrases as she observed the group, surprised to learn that the poetry was all extempore. Lottie worked from pictorial sources, studying long and late online and in archives and galleries, the imagery burning itself into her mind, leaving the play on words behind. A natural flow of subconscious reaction. Not so ingenious, perhaps, but certainly effective.

'Too modest!' intoned a female voice next to Roland: Dalila. Mia greeted the girl with what felt to her like a Judas kiss. She hoped it didn't seem as reluctant to the recipient. Roland laughed with what Mia suspected was a touch of complicity.

'How are you Dalila?'

'All good, Mia, how's you?'

Mia nodded, brushing aside the over-familiarity with a smile.

'What did you think?' This was Lottie, joining them pre-emptively.

'So great, darling! Well done you.' For the moment Mia held her close, she felt the lightness of her under the disguise of the dispossessed she had adopted for the day. A long and detailed analysis followed. Dalila had caught some of the performance on her phone. Roland slipped his arm around Lottie's waist and made her watch despite protest. 'Moments recalled in tranquillity and all that, you need to internalise it not just spout it!'

Mia agreed wholeheartedly with him, struggling to read the body language. In her predisposed eye, Roland behaved like a lover, but then so apparently did Dalila. So did the two co-operative mates who joined them to look at the footage. Intimacy and androgyny fuelled the hothouse.

'I'm going to upload it on YouTube now, it's too important to waste. Don't argue, you look great.'

'It's not about me, it's about ideals. Situationism throws the message to the four winds, it's the antithesis of memorialisation!'

Sighs of mock-annoyance from the group. 'Times change! You have to get the message out there!'

And so it went on. Feeling herself on the margins of the debate, or at least, too equivocal in her opinion to support Lottie's argument, she gave her daughter another kiss and left amidst waves and smiles. When she reached the door, they were already collectively pinned to the screen again.

She had not managed to reach Lars, though she trusted him to be at the rendezvous they'd arranged at five. He was working on a commercial shoot somewhere high above the city, the Gherkin again probably, putting his mastery of time-lapse panoramas to good use. She didn't want to send him a text and look as flaky as her host, she'd never get him to take the thing seriously. She decided to head over to the Charlatan and show him the venue regardless. They needed to play around with sound and the external mic she'd inevitably be holding as part of the minimal crew. If Tom could be bothered to turn up they could try some screen tests of the presentation style. If not, they'd film the bands and at least she would partially have saved face. But she was not happy. She had sold herself short. She had made herself dependent on someone whom she knew in her bones was bound to disappoint. She turned her face to the blustery afternoon, with its heatless dazzle of sun dipping between sweeps of charcoal cloud and the dark angles of tall buildings.

8.

She'd offered me something amazing on a plate and I had no idea why. Suddenly I'd become the Pied Piper of Shoreditch, a broadcaster's USP. I needed a room full of allies not people I'd shafted or let down. There weren't many I trusted.

I did trust Jewel though. Whether she still trusted me remained to be seen. We had a history, one of those ambiguous, open-ended stories in which I seemed to specialise.

I'd been watching her in a piano bar one of those nights I'd been hanging around for Cleo not to show up, watching the long titian hair, the undulation of her velvet-encased body, the graceful, sinewy movement of her arms, the surprising speed, strength and delicacy with which she traversed the keyboard. She was playing jazz standards, Ella Fitzgerald, Billie

Holiday, with a precision that blew her cover: a classical pianist on a moonlight job. She wasn't beautiful, but she had sad grey eyes and a sweet, quizzical mouth painted russet to match her velvet. She was like an autumn bird and she soothed me with her lack of guile. I asked her where she'd learned to play. It sounded like a chat-up line and it was.

We started a game. I requested a song, she tried to play it. If she succeeded, I'd put a drink on the tab for her. If not, she'd do the same for me. The alcoholic version of strip poker, but she was a cool hand and her memory led us down all kinds of liquor-soaked alleys, ploughing through the refrains of a dozen tear-jerkers in a kind of medley, me calling the next song during the chorus and her smiling into the key change. She was so good, I started to sing along and in the end we were just laughing in each other's arms.

I delivered on that first whisky, we'd earned it.

'What's your name?' I asked her.

'Bathsheba. I know, it's such a mouthful no-one can say it.' Her Irish accent lilted in my ear, nestling there like a small, soft bird. 'At home everybody calls me Jewel.'

'Suits you well. You'd have to be a topaz, or a smoky quartz. Maybe a black opal.'

I was getting in too deep, I could see it in her eyes, pushing where I had no right to go. Something happens and before I can stop it the damage is done. On the other hand, I wanted to say those things. She was worth it, and besides, a notion was taking shape in my mind.

'Would you think of jamming with me some time? I'm looking to put together a band and I'd like to see if we could… work something out.'

'What kind of music d'you play?'

'Experimental folk.'

'What does that mean? Scarborough Fair with death metal?' She was laughing at me now.

'Oh, I love Scarborough Fair. But tonally more unpredictable, more jazzy, less traditional.'

'Sing me a line, then?'

I played the chords in my head and gave her an opening verse of a song I'd written for Cleo those weeks ago when I thought we were going somewhere. The Irish girl caught the first phrase and stroked some chords against my melody. A new vista of clear sound opened around me, stripped of the unrelenting fingerpick of my guitar.

Washed up on that urban beach below the South Bank Centre, watching the kids jumping wall and flipping their skinny bodies onto the stones, ripping the rubber from their trainer soles and punishing their ankles, I decided to call her. It was hard to tell what mood she was in, with all the street sounds at my end and the classical cacophony at hers. She was rehearsing, said she'd call me back. Feeling a little fishy I walked along the strand below the aquarium and mounted the steps onto Hungerford Bridge.

I'd never set foot inside the Royal College of Music. Now I was striding out with the Albert Hall in my sights, past its Patron enthroned in blinding Hyde Park sunshine and deeper encased in gold than King Midas. Jewel was doing alright if she was part of this establishment. My phone screen pointed me down Queen's Gate and Prince Consort Road and suddenly there it squatted, unfolding its vampire wings in the wintery sun, a neo-Gothic monstrosity with bigger pretensions than St. Pancras.

I didn't really look the part, still masquerading as hip TV presenter, but they could probably do with a laugh at my expense. I strode through the main doors and asked for Bathsheba Connor. The doorman told me to wait in the lobby, they'd be out by five-thirty. She was part of the elite squad, playing with a piano quintet in some upcoming chamber concert, but I needed to grab her as soon as she finished, the timeline had hold of my lapels and it wouldn't take no for an answer.

'I'm her brother. I've come to collect her to visit our sick uncle,' I lied. The doorman gave me a *how dumb do you take me for* look, but he let me through to wait outside the rehearsal room.

I wove my way past students ten years my junior carrying precarious, precious instruments, following the seductive sound of a piano trilling and rippling its way around the sharp sweetness of the string section. Even though it wasn't my kind of music, it was buoyant, life-affirming. No one could be wrong who could write music like that, no matter how long past its sell-by date. It brought a smile to my face as I looked through the glass of the door and saw her, fingers flying up and down that keyboard. It was the exhilaration, the precision timing, that really got the hairs at the back of my neck. The group accelerated to the end of the movement like a sailing crew catching the wind past the finish line, and suddenly all that rippling was gathered up in the final chords that nailed the piece into place in my mind.

They all sat listening to the director of music's notes. Nobody else spoke. There was no whooping and hugging. No questions. They packed up their instruments. Jewel lowered the piano lid, put away her music with deft hands and was the first to leave. I could hear her soft lilt approaching the other side of the door. 'See you tomorrow!' Then she was practically in my arms.

'Tom.' She looked as if she was about to faint.

'Hi, Jewel.'

She took a step back, flinching away from me. 'Long time no see.'

'It is.'

She looked me up and down. 'You doing alright, then?'

'Pretty good.'

She wanted to turn away. There was nowhere to go however. The corridor was narrow and dimly lit by stained glass, and she couldn't push past me without making a considerable effort of will, a scene. I could see her heart wasn't in it. The next moment her grey eyes were filling with tears and her lower lip trembled. I held her softly against my new jacket, hoping she wouldn't stain it.

'Where did you *get* to?' Her voice shrilled into my shoulder like a querulous kid. I absorbed the hurt as best I could. 'You never showed up!'

'I...' Thinking fast, it was hard to find anything that didn't sound callous. 'I had to go away.'

'I didn't know if you were dead or alive, you just – *disappeared*.'

'Yeah.' Radio silence. The longest of my career. 'It was nothing personal.'

She pulled away, the nearest to a flounce she could muster. 'Of course not.'

'I was ill for a while. Try not to be angry.'

The beady look didn't suit her and she knew it, she was trying very hard to stay livid but her soft heart wouldn't let her. She tossed her red hair and looked at me. A long, complicated look.

'Are you over her now?' Because she knew all along what it had been about. I tried to muster a tender thought for Cleo but I could scarcely recall her face. Perhaps it had worked. Perhaps I really was over her. The thoughts must have been written across my face like cloud shadows racing over a sunny field, as I realised she was biting her lip in an effort not to cry. She nodded, resigned. 'Well, you and I were never going to be lovers, were we?' It sounded so sad, I felt like crying myself. I decided to lighten things up.

'Come and play with me?'

'I can't, I have to practise.'

'Don't they ever give you any time off for good behaviour?'

She shook her head wryly. 'Not if I want to hit the grade. Eight hours a day is what it costs.'

'A little jam session can't do any harm?'

'Jam today,' she was laughing despite herself. Not a sulker, she wanted the sunshine really. We grabbed a coffee out of the machine and headed for her practice room.

She jazzed around, warming up her fingers while she waited for me to get out my instrument. She eyed it in my arms with a certain pity. 'Looks like a battered baby.' There was a shift in her mood as she took in the visual contradictions. Clothes straight off the peg. Guitar on its last legs. 'Perhaps you need someone to buy you a new one?' A mischievous little smirk that goaded me into song. I played her the three I'd been working on. She listened hard. 'You've changed your style a bit.'

'Changed my life a bit.'

We started over with the first one. It was a waltz, country-flavoured, indigo-washed, clean and sweet. A story about a man who tries to impress but whose efforts fall short. The story of my life. All of them are. Pieces of myself, like transparent shavings of flesh, pictures extracted from my cells, revealing something and nothing of who I really am because, in truth, I still have no idea.

I knew she'd pick it up and run with it. She wasn't straitjacketed by structure, she could let it go and fly. Her musician's instinct leapt in and did the job without her thinking too much about it. All that time spent at her fiddler daddy's knee must have rubbed off something tribal, no escape from those Celtic genes. The way she stitched chord colours into a song made me think of a mediaeval maid bent over her embroidery, a Lady of Shallot lost in her mirror of sound. She brought out the poet in me, as I knew she would before I got lost out there on the streets. Perhaps if I'd walked into her life instead of out of my own everything would have been different. But I knew that was just fantasy. There was no going back. We make our choices for a reason. Jewel had value to me in a very particular way, and only in that way. I would have felt like a rapist if I'd ever laid a finger on her, despite her fixing so much of that Celtic yearning onto my graven image. As an affair of the heart, it was a tragic mismatch. It felt like a wanton act, leading her down my garden path but I couldn't help it. I needed what she had more than I needed not to hurt her. And maybe, as a creative partnership, she'd get something back in the end. Maybe.

We must have played a couple of hours together without stopping. When we finally took a break, I felt this was a kind of music that might have a future. It wasn't a glasshouse constructed on quicksand. It was more mature: the foundation was secure. The second thing I felt, though I wasn't sure how it related to the fact that I'd kissed her earlier that day, was a need to share it with Mia, to show her faith in me was justified. I don't know precisely how I thought this would work, I just knew that Jewel reflected a facet of my better nature, made me a better musician, perhaps a better person. The third thing I sensed was that the building was completely empty and that the doormen had probably locked us in for the night. Jewel snorted with laughter. 'What, like the public library? Wait while I fall asleep under a newspaper like my friends.' She threw a copy of the Metro over her face and slumped over the keys like a dosser.

'You hungry?'

She peered out expectantly. 'Of course. I've got to learn *Alborada del Gracioso* this evening. We work till midnight here.'

'Somewhere round the corner?'

That presented some expensive options, but luckily Jewel had her regular Italian café where the pasta was homemade, cheap and tasty. We had seconds on the house, licked our fingers, thick as thieves. I was stealing her away from her practice time but she didn't seem to mind. She was in everyone's good books.

'They gave me the performance prize last term.'

'Kidding me!'

'For the Rachmaninov, and ya missed it. Scamp, yous.' She was camping it up like her ma. But at least she was still speaking to me. I paid the bill and asked her if she'd like to come dancing. She looked at me with her head on one side, considering. In the end it wasn't temptation enough. 'I've got a date with Maurice.' I nodded sagely. She saw right through me. 'Ravel.' I'd come a poor second in that company, I realised. 'It was nice seeing you though,' she added. She was slipping through my fingers, I had to ask her then. 'Jewel.'

'Tom?' She had a mischievous glint in her eye.

'Would you play with me again?'

'I might if you practise.'

'I mean on a regular basis. Maybe write some songs together?'

'Like a duo, you mean?' Her eyes were merry at this, but the corners of her mouth she kept pulled tight to frighten me off. She was already receding into the shadow of the Albert Hall.

'Yes. Think of a name.'

'*You* do that. And get your new girl to buy you a guitar or I'll build you one out of orange crates and string. Go on with you.'

She turned on her heel and left me, slightly giddy at the speed of the day's developments. I wondered if Mia would include an instrument as part of my terms of employment and started musing on the best way to ask as I turned towards the tube.

I don't know what happened then. Something about the way the light turned in the sky, blinding silver shot with dark, dark grey like the sweep of a bat's wing, like the flourish of a matador cape, like the swing of *her* hair against the stage lights, and I was on my knees, crumpled over my own wash of grief, tears pouring down my face and the howl I'd suppressed finally bursting from my lips. *Nevermore*, quoth the Raven.

A young guy with a big black beard and kufi stopped to put his hand on my shoulder and ask if I was all right. And I knew I would never be all right. No amount of kindness, no amount of generosity, no amount of success would ever make up for what I'd lost in Cleo. I couldn't tell him. I couldn't speak at all. I was weeping like a five-year-old in the middle of the dying day. I knew from his face that he understood. He had a kind, sad gaze that told me he knew about love, knew what it meant never, ever being able to give that love to the person you'd fixed on for all eternity. What a miserable condition it was to be human. I thanked him for his offer of prayer, told him I'd be fine as a couple of Japanese tourists hurried past us looking nervous. He asked where I was going, escorted me gently in the direction of the station like a grandson looking after some wizened ancient. I felt as old as time.

He turned me abruptly into the door of the pub we were passing. 'I wouldn't normally say this, but you need a drink my friend.' He took out his wallet and bought me a double whisky and himself a bitter lemon. We stood together at the bar under the eye of the suspicious-looking publican who clearly thought we were in the middle of a lover's tiff.

The fire hit my belly and melted through my bones and I started to feel the wave of despair drift quietly to the door and leave. I'd drunk so little over the past three months, a shot went a long way.

'That's better, right?'

My face somehow managed to shape a smile. I nodded back.

'I don't know your sorrow my friend, but Allah is great. Remember that.'

He wasn't a pushy type. He gave me a pat on the arm and left. In the space that opened around me, soft rock pummelled my ear like a rabbit in boxing-gloves, anodyne music from a planet I rarely visited. The barman collected the empty bitter lemon glass and threw me a baleful glance. I realised there was a little card on the bar towel containing the address of a local mosque. I took the hint and shouldered my guitar, slipping the card into my jacket pocket as I left. Salvation could wait, I was heading for another drinking establishment.

When I'd left Cleo's apartment that night I'd run past the dark car waiting outside for her, under the black sky like some crazed mannequin in perpetual motion, helium balloon with the string cut, soaring into the icy upper reaches of the atmosphere, nothing to pin me to earth except the bottle. Alcohol-fuelled oblivion, followed by the worst night of my life, lying in the gutter staring at the cold, cold stars. The inebriation was a meagre flame. What came after was the bone-cold chill of death, but I couldn't stop circling the way she'd left me for ambition. A whore in the name of her art. She'd have found a way of explaining it with her beautiful words and twisting my mind so I'd believe what I wanted which was that we could have a future together basking in our own success like walruses on ice, but instead I beat myself black and blue against the walls and pavements of this city, my not-so-padded cell, willing the physical pain to blank out the emotional for so many weeks I forgot who I was. I kicked over the traces so thoroughly I lost myself and became some madman with a beat-up guitar the cops avoided arresting, till…

… I woke on my back on a scrubby patch of grass staring at the lurid night sky, no idea where I was, a leaden chill beneath me and the pre-dawn air creeping its way down inside my jacket and clawing me awake. My hand hit the empty bottle at my side with a clatter.

Retching, I staggered to my feet with a blinding realisation: I owed better than this to the person who'd saved me from the streets. Mia was my saviour. Cleo was a vain, self-seeking starfucker who had sacrificed me on the altar of her ambition. Why pour libations to a flawed goddess? Was I going to drink myself to death over her? The least I could do was to go home, sleep off the night's godawful binge and try to shape up. Cobble myself into the potential TV presenter my older woman needed me to be.

I started to recognise the skyline, the sixties tower blocks winking their acid lights beyond the trees, the pincer movement of the traffic beyond. I found myself staring at a place I knew, the twice derelict club and former public toilet with its strung lights sadly extinguished. I'd have been down there last night had it been open. I must have staggered a good way along Kensington High Street and the back streets of Olympia in the early hours before collapsing on Shepherd's Bush Green, ironically a stone's throw from the warm basement flat to which I still – thanks to this mysterious woman whose motives I didn't remotely understand – had the keys, and which I entered fifteen minutes later armed with a flat white and some emergency food from the twenty-four hour shop, another of my nine lives gone.

The central heating kicked in and warmed my veins and the coffee calmed the spinning edge of the world so that I could see my laptop screen at least. What a lame apology for a human being, so buffeted by each and every moment, unable to face up to the opportunity she was offering: dragging me into something resembling a career.

A brief trawl through my inbox told me all the reasons I was afraid. All those ghosts of months past were starting to squeeze through my wall of silence with their banshee wailings and their boo-woo-hoos. As I feared, I'd been seen two nights ago. Walking. Alive. A couple of trolls were busy at my social media sites and there were some who would like to give me a beating and worse in real life. All my debts still owing, all those let-downs still smarting. I had to make myself believe those I'd surrounded myself with would forgive and forget, move on, accept the uneven hand the street side of the music biz had dealt them.

I deleted a torrent of obscenities and tidied up my pages, sent a few emails. A clean sweep and a blank page on which to write my future. Fame was my best chance of protection against these sad-brains. I knew that they'd fade away the minute something more than a vlog filmed by a friend on their phone was on their TV screens. Nothing attracts success like success. A hint of some of that gold dust rubbing off on their tarnished wings and they'd be creeping around offering to carry my cables and mic stands.

There was a nasty long email from Tarzan that gave me a bad feeling in the pit of my stomach. Enough education and time on his hands for vitriol to mature and fester. He'd seen Mia, scented money, old school network on overdrive, attached a claim for breach of promise and lost income.

Mentally I was already closing the box on all the songs he'd fingered. I had to stay ahead of that downward drag. New songs, new identity. I reached for my guitar and started to play around with some idle thoughts riding in on this gathering wave of fatigue, a book of goddesses. This heaven was ruled by a woman in a sea-green dress, neon colours dancing in her hair, holding out her thread of pearls to a ragged dreamer. Jazz chords inflamed and made strangers of my fingers while my folk sound rested quietly the shadows. I thought: my Irish girl is going to have fun with this.

As if she'd read my mind, a *New Message from Jewel Connor* flashed onto the screen. *The   Scarlet   and   the Black*. Her suggested band name. It was 5.33 in the morning, had she been up all night wrestling with that one? It was a novel by Stendhal she told me, avoiding the question. Was that too literary? I kind of liked it with its blend of socialist, anarchist colours. *Chess-board. Dark and dangerous. Elegant and violent. The harlot and the jack*. She sent me a big LOL and we bantered our way through the next ten minutes. I thought: this might just work. Then the interruptions started as people got home from the clubs, or started waking to the new day, depending on their end of the social spectrum. I told Jewel I was heading for bed, which was the truth at the moment I wrote it. We'd be meeting anyway at the Charlatan that evening. I'd introduce her to Mia.

A new box opened *hi* from little sister Florence. I bit my lip and ignored it. It felt mean, but that was trouble brewing if I let it. She'd get used to my silence in time. Someone else wanted to call me *manwhore* just for the hell of it. I seemed very good at making enemies, it's a shame I couldn't earn money that way. My erstwhile flatmate informed me his short film had been accepted to some underground film festival in Minnesota. Kind enough not to mention the rent I owed him.

And then Cleo had the audacity to message me as if we'd never left off the conversation begun all those months ago. It was 6.40. *You were wrong about Karl that's just a business arrangement* as if I'd done nothing but mull this over and over in the interim. It's true I'd given it some time. But not enough to warrant replying. I stared at her words for a while, heart pounding, granted, but the overwhelming emotion was anger. And a healthy seasoning of scepticism: what did the woman take me for? Did she think the string by which she held me still intact? Exasperation propelled me finally from the screen and towards the bathroom.

I'd been asleep for a blissful ninety minutes when I became aware of the front door bell ringing. Insistently enough for me to grab fresh jeans and tee-shirt before approaching the spyhole with the illogic of the half-dream: if Tarzan's man had discovered enough to doorstep me then I'd be ready for him.

It was a girl. Slight, fair-haired. Was she the upstairs neighbour after her missing post? A burglar's paramour come to case the joint? Shivering, a bright-coloured mess of wool clutched around her against the morning chill, she didn't look dangerous so I unlatched the door.

She was in before I asked, slipping past me like an apparition. 'Cold this morning,' she murmured, dark velvet voice sending goosebumps up my arm, a *what the hell* kind of alarm prickling at my scalp. Trying to catch up was like surfacing very slowly through a pond thick with protozoa. 'I wanted to apologise,' she span round lightly so that we almost collided, 'I wasn't very polite last time we met.' If this had happened in a bar I'd just have smiled vaguely and perhaps waited to be reminded where I'd seen her before. But when someone drops in at 8.20 in the morning, you're supposed to know. I'd already put out my arms out to steady her, it didn't even feel that awkward. This was going way too fast and she was the one leading the dance. She looked at me with her mother's eyes and for one giddy moment I thought I was losing it.

'I hope you're better?' Her smile was irresistible, pure Audrey Hepburn, guileless, open. 'Charlotte Chancery.' She extended a delicate hand. 'Mia's daughter.'

'You look kind of different.'

'Do I?'

'You were all spiky last time.'

'You were stark naked.' Laughter rippled out of her, infectious. It was difficult to mistrust her. 'Please don't think I'm being nosy or anything. It's just… I've seen you in the street. I'm staying with a friend round the corner.'

I must have looked doubtful, her eyes went kitten-wide.

'Surprised you recognised me?'

'I'm an artist. Naturally observant.'

'Not stalking at all?'

Meanwhile she was making herself comfy on the sofa, drawing her legs up under her and stretching out her stocking-clad toes. 'Why should I wish to do that?'

And why. It felt like a ridiculous question even as it came out of my mouth.

'Bit early for a social?'

She fingered her bedhead tendrils innocently. Politely covered a yawn. 'I know, sorry. Any chance of a cuppa? I've been working all night.'

I wondered if I should tie a thread to the doorframe to lead me back through the maze. Instead I filled the kettle and flicked the switch. 'Has your flatmate run out of teabags?'

'He's asleep. We've been at it with pliers and wirecutters for twelve hours.' She held out her little paws to me so I could see the wear and tear.

'You sound a fine pair of burglars.' A flash of a catsuit and mask, shinning up drainpipes in the dark. 'Or is it S&M?'

'It's dynamic sculpture.'

'Sounds intellectual.'

'It's an installation with moving parts. We've got to set it up in the exhibition space today. I hope it works.'

Little Miss Fixit. How much did she know? 'How is your mum? She's been very kind to me.'

Only a fraction's hesitation, she was good at the game. I just wasn't sure if we were playing cat's cradle or kiss and tell. 'She's fine. She's got a new project.'

'Aha?'

'The indie music scene?' She was eyeing the corner where my guitar was propped against the sofa. 'You're a musician aren't you?' Those doe eyes darted back to me, quizzically.

'On my good days.'

'What kind of music?'

It was like being interrogated by a flower. So open and lovely it was impossible to resist.

'Acoustic. Folk with a jazzy feel. Or jazz with a folky feel. It depends.'

She smiled, hands cupped around her mug of tea, bundled up like the house elf. 'Go on, play something!'

The neighbours were moving about on the floor above so I took my guitar and tuned the strings, started fingering a riff which drifted into my head on a sunlit mote of dust, casting my line to hook a new goddess for the roster and it didn't go quite the way I'd expected. This one turned out to be Terpsichore, unravelled by the music from her gaudy woollen outer layer, leaving it like a shed skin on the floor as she began to dance.

I was used to jamming with musicians. It was different each time, but the parameters were always driven by the sound. I'd made people move on the dance floor plenty of times and it was a great kick. But I'd never conjured this kind of movement from any human being and it kind of flicked a switch in me. It was as if I'd been given 3D glasses when before the world had been flat like a postcard. She flowed like honey. Those limbs that had been swathed, veiled from me, were suddenly unleashed, loosed, curving, splitting apart to show me everything she was, undulating softly around my one vibrating string, wheeling from wall to wall to my abstracted chord structures like some demented twelve-year-old in need of exorcism, suddenly flat on her stomach with her legs stretched back, suddenly defiantly on her feet. She arched, flipped, curled, flamed around me as I played and I was completely unstitched by her. She ended in my lap, the guitar was on the floor, she was kissing me, her lips hot on mine and her heart beating like an athlete's against my breast, her breath coming fast. It came faster too as we found ways to get closer, flesh on flesh, liquid gold spilling itself across the floor.

There wasn't much to say afterwards. Entwined around each other we slept as furiously as we'd played and woke blinking at each other like children. It was 10.30. I knew I had to get her out of the flat before Mia arrived, I just didn't put it that way. It was a truce of the kind only lovers of the flesh understand. I told her I had a meeting across town at twelve. If she thought I was lying she didn't show it. She had to be loading metal parts into the back of an estate car by eleven thirty. So we agreed on our separate agendas and it was almost a guilt-free fuck. Except I kind of knew she'd be back in her own good time, when it was time to mess with my head again.

We dressed and took the bus to breakfast past the dizzying sunlit plane trees of Shepherd's Bush Green, down Holland Park Avenue and into Notting Hill Gate. A bit too close to my recent transgressions for comfort. She wasn't bothered. Her mother always took the tube. Her dad was in the middle of a new screenplay and wasn't going out. How that guaranteed our invisibility I wasn't sure, but she laughed it off.

We drank latte together in a tiny café in the hinterland of Portobello Road. Like her mother, she was had that same forward push that made things happen. She'd made us happen, just like that. A seducer. Like me. I was still in that weird post-coital cloud which she seemed already to have leapt from, no parachute required, like Athena armed and ready to fight. Half spooked by her I watched as she set up her day's agenda, which seemed as complicated as mine was becoming. My phone vibrated in my pocket. A slightly vexed exchange of texts with Mia began: why was I not at the flat, we'd arranged to meet and set up the evening's test recording... I measured out my words, punctuated by the close observation of her daughter's clear skin, tousled hair, the delicate shadow above her full upper lip, *that mouth*, no idea where this was all leading. Sculptress's fingers tapped away at the smartphone, accompanied by the same determined frown which I recognised as Mia's. But this little live wire was something different from her progenitor. A bit too much mischief going down for my liking.

'Do you dance in public? Or was that just for me.'

She flashed me a glance. 'I'm not sure.'

'Why not?'

She sat back with a sigh. 'I did ballet when I was three. It was the only way they could get me to stop charging around. Settle, centre, prepare, position three, all that. I didn't really like it. I just never stopped. It was a kind of framework, everything else was so fluid. Mum and dad took me on the road a lot when they were in production so I was always part-time at new schools. It was pretty chaotic.'

This was the most she'd said to me since we'd met. Was she going to open the window for me, just a little? Just enough to let me jump out?

'You do your own thing then? Freestyle?'

'I like art better right now. Messing around with concepts.'

She was waving a fiver at the barista, that was like

her mother. She was about to slip away.

'Would you like my number?' I ventured, unsure of anything except that I was being taken for a ride. Of that there was little doubt in my mind. I'd been hijacked. She paid and put away her phone with an ambiguous smile. 'I know where to find you.'

'Don't you even want to know my name?'

That tickled her. Laughter bubbled out of her like chilled champagne. 'I think I prefer you without one.'

I wasn't sure whether the power chick pose was real or just sparring. 'There are websites you can go to for that.'

'No, no, that's not my thing. I usually prefer girls anyway.'

She'd almost knocked the breath out of me, not quite. 'And how did it compare?'

Her quirky little smile again, completely unscrupulous. 'That might be a long conversation.' She pulled her mess of coloured wool around her, heading for the door. 'I'm up for it if you are.'

She gave me a little wave as she went, leaving me with ashes in my mouth and a guilty afternoon to kill.

9.

Through the viewfinder of the Alexa she watched him enter, loose-limbed, heading across the floor with his club face on and the guitar slung across his shoulder. A bit of a pout, eyes narrowed – short-sighted, she remembered from one of their conversations – shirt and jacket, looking presentable. Only twenty minutes late. Maybe she'd make a professional of him yet.

'He's here, I'll bring him up and we can plan some sequences.' She hoped Lars wouldn't hear the tightness in her throat. *He was here.* She was not to be utterly humiliated then. Whether he could do what she needed was still an open question.

'Have a beer with me?' he invited, as she approached. The kid behind the bar tried not to smirk at them. Eighteen and new to the job that week, still learning to add up in his head. 'Thanks, Ed.' Nothing out of joint with the world, all business as usual.

'And three pints of water, one with ice please,' Mia added.

'Thirsty?'

'For the cameraman. You too, once you start talking.'

He nodded, taking it in his stride, carrying the tray up to the gallery for her like the production assistant. She was grateful he'd decided to play the game, she felt leaden, her palms too clammy for the handrail.

'Hi.' His hand was already out to the man with the hardware.

'Lars, this is Tom.'

Lars shook briskly, keen to get on. 'Let's have a look at you down the lens.'

Like the coloured fragments in a kaleidoscope, everything started to fall into place as they started the familiar process of putting together a shot.

'Over by the red sofa might be nice.'

Lars moved models, musicians, actors around like so many chess-pieces every day, impervious to their charms, other than the pictures he made with them. 'Who's playing tonight, then?' Like the dentist with his gentle patter, keeping the machinery moving, everybody happy.

A moment of utter blankness behind the eyes as though someone had pulled the plugs. Then he drew breath and launched. 'So proud of our lineup this week, kicking off with Virginia and the Wolf, a real heartbreaker, sounds a bit like Laurel... Sam Wright with his big soul voice, he looks pretty great too... Cherry Juice, a bunch of twisted chicks with their cool brand of electronica... new songs from The Scarlet and the Black, and our headliners tonight are the Dumb Waiters, a seven-piece punk-funk outfit from

Brighton, can't wait!'

Turning it on perfectly like a tap. That was his job after all. Eyes pinned to the monitor, she watched how he moved in on the camera with that slightly insolent swagger, the smile that seemed about to break into full sunshine at any moment. The camera loved him. It would probably work if he kept his nerve and stayed sober.

'Nice!' croaked Lars. 'Sounds like a long evening.'

'We keep going till midnight then it's DJs till two. Don't worry mate, we'll let you escape before the place gets too wild.'

Lars wasn't listening, he wanted a plan from the boss. 'Should I take some top shots of the bar, Mia? We can regroup once it starts filling up, but I'm going to have to run around handheld to make it look like anything's going on here.'

'The place is packed by nine, we'll strike some kind of middle ground.' Mia scrolled through her outline. 'I think we should film a couple of songs by the first girl. What time will she be here Tom? Can you do a quick interview with her?'

In the green room a waif with Patti Smith hair and a bit of lace from a charity shop that called itself a dress was tuning down her strings in front of a make-up mirror. The walls were smeary with spilled coffee and the light was harshly fluorescent. A couple of mangy sofas and a table on which last week's beer glass deputised as ashtray were the only notable creature comforts.

'Gin, we're taking you upstairs for a bit of a chat,' said Tom, nodding her out, 'it's for a TV documentary and this room looks like shit.'

Virginia shouldered her guitar mutely and followed them up to the gallery.

'Doesn't anyone complain?'

Tom shrugged at Mia. 'Nobody cares. They have musicians queuing up to play here, why bother?'

'I might get a cleaner in for next time in case we have to take the camera in there.'

'Save your money Mia, they won't thank you. It's down and dirty. That's where the energy comes from.'

Virginia looked enigmatic. At first she was so enigmatic she was hardly there at all.

Lars raised an eyebrow at Mia. 'You look great darling. Forget about us, just fix your attention on the man there.'

'I'm upstairs at The Charlatan with Virginia and the Wolf who's just about to go onstage.' Tom smiled at the girl, encouraging. 'What's the name about? Is there a wolf in your bedsit?'

'It's a pun.'

'Aha?'

'About Virginia Woolf? The novelist? Stream of consciousness kind of rolling around in my head with little red riding hood and bad moon rising and Elizabeth Taylor in the play.'

'Cool. And you're just releasing your first EP next month?'

'Yes, *Girl in a Lighthouse*.'

'Lonely place?'

'Absolutely. No escape except by drowning.'

'And who are your influences?'

'If I say any names you'll just see I'm nothing like them at all. Ask me another question.'

'Where did you get that dress?'

Her lower lip was suddenly trembling. 'It's made

from fragments of my mother's wedding dress. I washed it so you can't see the blood anymore.'

'Shotgun wedding?'

He'd gone for the mischief and now suddenly tears were pouring down the girl's face. Tom took her hand, appalled. Least said soonest mended. Mia circled her finger to Lars – keep rolling. In the edit they'd slam straight into the song.

Mia offered tissues. 'Thank you, that was amazing Virginia. Would you like a drink?'

She blew her nose, looking like a lost schoolgirl. 'Maybe after, thanks.'

With a performer's sixth sense she knew it was time to go. Nothing else existed for her. The camera followed her down to the stage and minutes later she was playing her heart out. Slow, dark chords and a voice that wouldn't have been out of place in a Brecht play, declaiming her strange little tales of woe.

'Sorry, Mia.'

'Forget it and move on.'

She nudged him away, friendly but not taking her eye off the monitor. There were professional lines here that she would not cross. Lars panned slightly as Virginia moved with the music. 'You want the whole set?'

'Just three songs. Let's get a closer frame on her for the next one, see what it's like.'

'She'll do *Girl in a Lighthouse* last if that helps,' said Tom.

'It does, thanks.'

Mia was relieved when the girl had accepted her namesake in a glass, gin well laced with martini and ice, and was chatting earnestly with her small coterie in a quiet corner near the door, poised for a quick getaway. *Girl in a Lighthouse* with its weird passion and poetic side-swipes, was something she could use. From the other side of the bar, Tom gave her a sly wink, his blunder already forgotten, steering a tall, well-muscled guy with an angle-cut afro, towards her. 'Sam, meet Mia who's producing the music doco...'

A warm, dry hand completely enveloped her own. 'Glad to meet you Mia. How d'you want to do this?'

He loved the dressing room. It was minimalist. Quiet. It fitted with his idea of the struggling artist. He was a London boy, a high-school dropout who'd also been on the streets before being picked up by a canny record producer. He sang with a deep, beautiful voice, a throaty tremble on the long notes that made you long for more.

As the evening flowed on, Mia realised the mixtape they were putting together was a gift from someone who perhaps knew what he was doing after all. She watched Tom helping to mic up the girl band with their drums and marimbas and their sixties monochrome dresses, flirting shamelessly in the name of putting on a show, and felt strangely moved at how she'd reclaimed this fragile ego and put it back where it belonged. It was like the tremor of a current beneath the water's surface. The germination of a seed in the darkness of the soil. The inexorable growth of an embryo in the womb. Healing. He'd done it so fast she'd not noticed how hard he'd been working at it. A day or two and he'd put all this together for her. She'd thought to grab a few preparatory sequences, research the potential of the format, plan a shooting schedule for the next few weeks. She'd expected a bunch of student hopefuls, and here was a fully curated programme of artists poised to break big.

'How on earth did you organise all this?' she asked, while Lars was onstage shooting handheld with the Cherry Juice girls.

'Inspiration.' It was a simple answer, but his look was complicated. 'And panic.'

'Stage fright?'

'Fear maybe. That you'd regret what you'd done. I didn't want that.'

'I don't regret it. I like seeing how you work together, all subterranean emotion and instinct. It's so different to my life.'

'Down where the drunkards roll…'

'D'you think you'll grow out of it?'

'I'm not sure. D'you think you'll grow into it?'

He touched her lips with his forefinger. Very softly. For one strange moment Mia's entire life seemed to recede into a parallel space. In the split second that followed, she didn't know whether to kiss him or slap him. She burned in silence, staring back.

'Have you ever performed?'

'Not in the way you have.'

'I'd like to see you onstage.'

'Would you.'

She was beginning to find this ludicrous. He knew nothing of her history, had never heard her play a note.

'You have a beautiful voice. I'd like to hear you sing.'

'I'm not a singer.'

'Maybe we'll have a jam later.'

Feeling somehow belittled, she turned to find herself face to face with an auburn-haired girl. Nothing like the hipsters jostling for space around her. Hot air and loose words would not be her style.

She was from another age, nothing deliberated about her fragility. The clear grey eyes that drew you to her were almost spookily large, the white, almost translucent skin made her look hyper-sensitive, a soft creature more at home in the dark, one that would break if you handled her too roughly.

'Jewel!' Tom hugged her like a sister. Maybe she was his sister. Then again, something about the body language told Mia she wasn't. 'This is Mia. We're shooting that documentary I told you about.'

'Tonight?' She spoke with a soft burr.

'Should be fun.'

'We haven't rehearsed!'

'We rehearsed yesterday!'

'Can we have another run through?'

'Look at the place, there's no time!'

'We don't have to record if you don't feel happy,' Mia offered, more alert to the girl's anxiety, than her tramlining of Tom's big moment.

'Mia!' He wasn't going to let her off the hook that lightly. 'This girl practices at the Royal Academy eight hours a day, she's amazing, don't listen to her!' And with that he conveyed his reluctant partner across the floor into a backroom behind the stage to exercise his persuasion, perhaps to sit down with her at the piano.

'…It's the Royal College anyways…' was her parting shot.

Mia went to watch the Cherry Juice girls, whose trance rhythms now held the room, the night gearing down into that slower pace that comes with increased crowd density and alcohol consumption. Angular, self-aware, they wove a mysterious polyrhythmic web around their audience, while the glitter ball gyrated slowly above the stage, scattering light-confetti over the room. Centre-stage the marimba player softly pummelled her intricate pattern of repeating chords, surging to and fro around the cross-rhythms of the drummer. Into their polyphony wove the rich, dark notes of the double-bassist leaning over her outsize instrument like a suicidal lover and the singer-DJ mouthing her edgy, surrealist vocals. All distinctly artpop, but the floor was happy to groove to it for a while.

Mia reviewed playback while the stagehands reset. The pictures were as good as she'd hoped, fluid moves and cleverly caught moments of faces, hands, bodies, the band from each side of the stage, the crowd seen from the band's perspective. 'Handsome shots, Lars, I don't know how you do it.'

Lars nodded contentedly, fully aware of his own worth, downing water, coffee and bar snacks in equal measure while the room flowed loudly around their workstation. There were one or two curious glances from punters. The Chinese cockney Tigerlily glided past with an ostrich feather pinned in her hair, sporting some locally designed piece of drapery. 'I hope you'll be coming back next week, it's gonna be even more cool. We're playing, don't forget!' And she was off to wrap herself around the next likely looking drinks provider. A willowy girl with long raven curls paused by them momentarily before moving on after her blonde, chiselled escort, wrapped in uneasy exchange. Mia caught snatches of their retreating voices.

'...you should drop it...'

'...taking it too far...'

'...pointless, vindictive...'

'...messing with my people...'

The sense was lost in the crowd. Mia caught sight of Tom's look as he emerged from the back room. He led Jewel the long-way round to the bar, parked her with Mia and went to help move the piano.

The Scarlet and the Black began their inaugural appearance to the sounds of an altercation with the management. Who was licensing these artists to the venue, the troublemaker wanted to know. Why hadn't he been consulted? He got short shrift from the bar owner whose fee had already been paid in cash by Mia, who had the documentation to prove it and signed release forms from all the artists concerned.

'Perhaps you'd like to talk to me about this?'

'And you are?'

Mia extended her hand, conjuring the honeyed tone she reserved for Difficult Artists.

'Mia Cowper. I'm a documentary film producer. We're shooting here this evening and I'd be very disappointed to lose any of the footage... shall we?'

She indicated the back office and smiled sweetly, bathed by the chill of his icy blue stare. He followed, closing the door behind them.

'I don't recall having granted permission for the artists I manage to be filmed tonight.'

'The artists have all agreed with me directly. None of them is signed to any label so as far as I'm concerned they are consenting members of the public.'

'They do not consent without my consent.'

'And what's your name, if I may ask?'

'Dickon Brand.'

'This is a pilot for a major broadcaster. It's a wonderful showcase for them.'

'Not necessarily. It depends.'

'On what exactly?'

'The line-up. They can't appear with anybody who walks in off the street.'

'They're all talented emerging artists, it's not an open mic session.'

'I'm aware of that but I'd like to review the running order.'

He ran a search on his phone, while Mia ran a search on him. He blared loud and clear on Google, mainly sites under his own control. Whether he had any real power she doubted, but she wasn't taking any risks. If necessary, she would keep him talking until The Scarlet and the Black had finished their set.

'Let me be absolutely clear, I don't want my artists appearing alongside the duo who are playing onstage now.'

Mia shot him a sympathetic glance, careful to look as non-committal as possible.

'Can you tell me why not?'

'Let's just say I have an ongoing legal dispute with one of the parties which I don't wish to get in the way of the artists on my development roster.'

'I see.' Mia suppressed a smile. She hadn't realised the pop music business harboured such pomposity in its ranks, but she could read the sharpness in his eye well enough not to wish to excite him further. Her discovery clearly had a talent for getting under people's skins.

'Should we exchange contact details? I don't want to disrupt this evening's recording but I'm happy to talk further. And perhaps you'd be good enough to let me know which artists you do represent, Dickon?'

With a cursory nod he was already on his way out,

not happy, but at least he'd had the chance to sound off. She wasn't convinced the representation thing was mutually agreed, or that there was any contract paperwork that need detain her, though she'd have to do some necessary due diligence and perhaps get the company lawyer to have a glance at it.

'I'll be in touch in the morning.'

'Look forward to it.'

Sweet vocal harmonies drifted to her across the floor, accompanied by ghostly fragments of jazz piano, two voices soaring in tandem over the heads of a densely packed audience who needn't have paid The Scarlet and the Black any heed but for a sense of loyalty – it was his home patch, enemies notwithstanding – yet for a moment the room was hushed, held suspended. What was it that could do this, she wondered, the unsettling melody? The expressive power of the performance? As she listened, the colours in the room seemed to expand around her.

> *When the night turns loud that*
> *Woman in the silken dress*
> *Neon colours dancing in her hair*
> *Seeks the shade of your distress*
> *Turns her back upon the press*
> *And the tumble of success*
> *Pins her money to your ragged coat*
> *And the pearls around her throat*
> *She's the mistress of a dare*
> *Cutting loose and she don't care*
>
> *Angels dancing on the head of a pin*
> *What made you think she'd let you in*

Ah she's moving at the speed of light
Ah she's a comet in full flight
Better break it up before you begin
Better break it up break it up

Mia realised with a jolt that the song was about her. It had never happened before and her cheek flamed with something akin to panic, then pure elation. In all the years she'd been Stephen's creative partner, no matter how many projects she'd collaborated on, even inspired, there was no direct, simple tribute like this. Nothing that said: you are this moment, nobody else made this happen. It was that direct. She found it hard to breathe her heart beat so fast. A split second later of course she knew it had to be about someone else. This man was a lover, he wrote songs for a hundred women and for none. The song was a story, a parable, a tissue of lies, as elusive as the wing of a dead butterfly crumbling to dust in her fingers. She felt anxious, as if the kiss of death were upon her, she was an ageing groupie in a room full of kids barely older than her daughter.

She tried to concentrate on the detail as Lars filmed him over the shoulder of the pianist girl who was really good, sensitive with a lovely voice. Let them have their moment, why crush the life out of it with her own buried needs? Brushing herself down mentally she stepped forward to take a glance at the stage and decide on a possible setup for the next song when he seemed to sense her movement and broke into that smile which had almost been her undoing before. She lit up involuntarily, the high wire artist inside her flipping into the void and for that second there was no one else, just the two of them bound by that invisible spiralling thread, so simple and so visceral she could hardly bear it.

She held that moment inside her through the end of their set and into the next, hardly hearing the applause, though she knew it had been a good first appearance for them and that Tom was surfing his adrenaline rush, now preoccupied with the business of herding together the Brighton group over a bottle of cheap red wine while the PA pounded out their latest EP over the speakers.

The punters knew what they were waiting for and it didn't take long for the Dumb Waiters to have their people where they wanted them: on the dance floor. It was too crowded for Lars to take a camera down among them unless he had floor clearance, and that might just kill the moment. Giving him the thumbs-up, she decided to leave him skirting the wings and grabbing a sense of the eccentric chaos that the Brighton band brought with them, all bright colours, shaven and pierced flesh, high-energy, joyful bedlam. The music was loud: a slapping fretless bass and one of the best drummers Mia had ever heard, led by a punchy trumpet and sax duo who made it impossible to stay still.

'You must have said something very persuasive to him.'

He was suddenly quite close by her, as the crowd jostled them, oblivious.

'I was polite.'

'You're always polite.'

She smiled. 'Not always.'

'The set went ok?'

'It did.' It had far exceeded her expectations and he could read it in her face. 'I like the new songs.'

He took her by the hand, coaxing now. 'Dance? Come on, you should let your hair down.'

She looked up at him, suddenly saw how young he really was and her heart quailed.

He touched one of her stray curls, pushing it back from her face. Oh God, she thought, he's going to kiss me here in the middle of this, and withdrew fractionally. She felt like a nervous teenager, but there he was drawing her into the crowd where nothing mattered except the wild gyrating of two hundred joyous bodies, herself all at once among them in crazy abandon to the accelerating beat. She was dancing with and yet not with him, in a mutual activity of one mass whose individual members separated and converged around her, a continuous shift of randomised pattern, inspiration and perspiration, then he was near her again, face alight with the fun of having got her to step outside the box and move with him in abandon.

They said her great-grandfather had been a show dancer. Bars and musical hall. Unexpected offspring of a Kentish fruit-picking liaison that itself started in abandon and between one year's harvest and the next year's blossom flowered into a love that would last until the worm destroyed the fruit of which they had so heartily partaken. By the time his mother died, the son Gilbert had been apprenticed to a London theatre where his natural talent was honed after the tastes of the age. A graceful man, light of step, masculine, who could lead a woman in the dance and make her feel like a queen, basking in the light of the winking chandeliers, the envy of all the women in the room. And the woman who charmed him to her breast, finally, was Mia's grandmother Elsa.

It was strange, Mia thought, that these things lay in wait to catch us, like cats waiting under the bed to pounce at our bare toes. These codes lying quietly dormant in a billion pulsing strands of DNA, waiting to be sparked into life by... what stimulus exactly? Hormone? Genetic memory? Sound, scent, emotion?

The set ended in a rush of elation that left the punters yelping for more, a bunch of heathens and savages, then when more was not forthcoming, the diehards on the dancefloor were left to the resident DJ and her playlist, while those who had worked up a greater thirst haemhorraged in the direction of the bar. Mia touched his arm lightly. 'Can you do a quick interview with the singer for us?'

'Might need to do it onstage, they've got a train in forty-five minutes.'

How did he even know the time when she had so utterly lost track? That he was programmed to know the start and end of slots she understood, but to care about travel arrangements was something she thought she'd had a monopoly on in life; she was surprised at how much she'd assumed about him, glad at his capacity to surpass her expectations on this evening which had begun with the bar set so low.

In need of a pint and a shower, Lars downloaded the files onto her laptop, keen to get home. 'I'll send you my invoice when I get in, Mia. You should have some nice pictures to play around with for a few days, pending distractions.' He added this with a sly look which Mia allowed, not quite liking the observation.

'I'll do the bank transfer first thing. And thank you,' she leant in to give him a peck on the cheek, an effective distraction technique she was ashamed of, 'for turning a recce into a full-blown shoot at no notice whatsoever.'

'You got lucky. Not for the first time, and I'll bet not for the last.'

What did he mean? He couldn't possibly have seen the only couple of moments that might have given her away. As for the dancing, that was nothing he hadn't seen her do at a wrap-party many times before.

But as Tom crossed the floor with their drinks, shirt clinging to his back, a curl of hair damp on his forehead, it was as if Lars could smell the energy between them. He opened up the first file and set it playing back with a satisfied draught of the ice-cold lager.

'Fucking wonderful.' He eyed Tigerlily, as she slid past them with a sidelong flutter of her absurdly long false eyelashes, and groaned. 'She'd make a grown man cry.'

Mia drank thirstily, eager to separate these two men before they started a conversation she would feel ashamed to overhear and not criticise. She could feel the sweat at the back of her neck, dripping down between her breasts under her clothing. She was thankful that Lars showed no desire to tarry. He downed his pint swiftly and pulled on his Berghaus.

'Let us know how it all looks. I'm off to Glasgow on a short film in the morning. Must've been very wicked in a previous life.'

'Very. I'll call you.'

Tom prised himself away from the footage of the interview with Virginia. Little narcissist, she thought, though not with any conviction.

'Shall we try and find somewhere we can actually hear this?' he said. A different look, now. He was hungry to know how this was all going to play back on the screen, in his head, where was the difference? She had given him a kind of power. Like Pandora, she had opened the box and there was no closing it now.

The club gently but inexorably ran itself down like an ageing car battery over the hours that followed, while they, pinned like butterflies to the laptop screen, reviewed the recorded files one by one, Mia making notes by hand, already putting together a rough edit. The mutual concentration drew them close and created a safe space which neither wished to transgress, they were colleagues after all. Colleagues sitting with their thighs touching under the table. Colleagues who, when they wished to review a particular moment, would stretch past each other to touch the keypad and catch each other's scent. The ambiguous haze which enveloped them was a powerful narcotic which consumed time, energy, yearning. They were both high on the creation of a new screen personality: a young man with good bone structure, intense eyes that dared to dream and a beautiful mouth. A young man whose energy streamed off the screen whatever he was doing. The band footage was exciting, it was what she wanted, a sexy new playlist of what might be hot next month, or what might die in obscurity next week. But it was the interview footage, the way he took the moment in both hands and wrangled into his own form, that made her light up. That was what she was waiting for. The eros of casting was always bound up in the response of the viewing eye, the projection of self-yearning onto the obscure object of desire, the projection of one's own response onto an audience. What was it exactly she saw? Had seen, even when he'd been disguised as a beggar?

She saw it again now as they played through the recording of his set. He was on fire, even with a bunch of new songs, a beat-up guitar and an untried red-head for a co-pilot. He sat forward to watch himself, thigh tensed against Mia's, hands clasped tight against his lips like a fervent worshipper at his own shrine. Bunched to attention, drinking in every second, critical, adoring, impatient, exhilarated.

'I think this might really work,' she said at last. 'You know you're something, don't you?'

He met her eye with a strange, hesitant glance, a fleeting fear perhaps, several contradictory thoughts passing through his mind at once. She'd never seen anyone look at her like that before, so guileless, oddly vulnerable.

'I'll be what you make me.'

'I'm a step on the journey, that's all.'

'It must be great to be grown-up enough to tell the truth.'

Mia watched him, thoughtful. 'You'll be a star if you let yourself. If you don't self-destruct.'

'Or is it just a dare?'

'I've seen you down, Tom. I'd rather see you up.'

The look darkened, told her she was trespassing now. 'You should tell me.'

'What d'you want to know?'

'How you came to be living rough. It shouldn't happen to someone like you.'

'Who should it happen to?'

She shook her head. 'You see, we're dancing round the edges again. You can lay it all down and be free, let your demons go, but you love them too much.'

167

He shrugged her off impatiently. 'Songwriters need their demons.'

'And their muses.'

That was the button. He was scrutinising her sharply, almost willing her to understand. 'Sometimes your muse isn't your inspiration, she's your fix.'

'Can't it be the same thing?'

He shook his head. 'Being on the street was my detox. I thought I wouldn't survive her if I didn't amputate part of myself.'

The pain radiating from him was palpable, like a bleeding child. As a mother she would have done the same for any child.

'Come here,' she murmured, taking him gently in her arms. The breath sighed from him like the departure of a locked-up ghost and there was a gathering stillness, then she felt him tremble against her and with a jolt she realised he was crying.

She pulled back, it seemed too much a trespass. He turned from her, cuffing his face angrily with his sleeve, streaming anguish. 'She killed our child.'

She waited to know how dark this was turning. But the story turned out to be one she already knew.

'Took herself off to a clinic then went into hiding. She didn't want me, any part of me.'

Having pushed him into confessing, Mia was now becoming party to a history that would inevitably exclude her the further he revealed it. She struggled against the fear he would suddenly become banal to her. At the same time, she realised she would tell him what she'd never shared with anybody.

'She probably felt exactly as I did.'

Something about her sudden focus slowed his grief. He turned to listen.

'I was twenty-seven. I had a one-year-old and a career to salvage. It's impossible not to sound callous. I couldn't face being just a mother for the next ten years. I'd have been done for. I'd have created nothing, lived nothing. When I got pregnant with my daughter it was a mistake, the kind of mistake that turns into a blessing, but I couldn't make the same mistake twice and keep my self-respect. Does that sound terrible?'

Her voice had turned very quiet with the sudden overflow of adrenaline, the panic of having tipped over the edge into unwise confession. She didn't know this person. She didn't really trust him. She was kite-flying in the name of empathy. She wanted to make him feel better and at the same time throw her pebble into the pool of female treachery that threatened to drown the male species. Why? To prove to him there was more than one *femme fatale* in the world? He shook his head. It was not the same. She was not the same.

'Stephen thought I had the flu. He had a few days shooting and I left Lottie with a friend and had a termination while he was gone. I've never told anyone.'

'Why?'

'I'm not sure. I wanted to be the one in control.'

'But you were married.'

'Yes.'

'Didn't it make a difference?'

'It made it harder. I put it in a locked box and threw away the key.'

'And now you're telling me.'

'Yes.'

He went over to the piano and sat at the keys,

169

just to have something to do. Under his long guitarist's fingers drifted muffled triads, tonic, subdominant, tonic, relative minor. 'Did you regret it?'

Stunned by the simplicity of the question, or perhaps it was the simplicity of the music, she was surprised to feel the tears pricking. 'Much later. Especially when I couldn't get pregnant again.' He would never know how that felt. 'I always thought it was sad that Lottie was on her own.'

'She wasn't on her own, she had you.' He gave her a sidelong glance which she couldn't quite fathom.

'She had both of us. Probably too much, we took her with us wherever we went.'

'I'd call that lucky. She was bound to turn out special.'

She felt oddly that there might be something more he knew, something he wasn't telling, but the confessional moment drifted into the quietly rippling chords, like cloud forms drifting overhead. It was close to two-thirty in the morning and the place felt unreal. They were alone. She went over to the piano to listen to him figure out his chord sequence, repeating it over and over in an attempt to pluck meaning from the unfamiliar instrument. He was a novice and knew it, suddenly shy of his rudimentary technique.

'D'you play, Mia?'

'I used to.' A lifetime ago. An earlier road.

'Show me how to play this?'

Shaking her head with a smile, she leaned forward between his arms and played the sequence for him with the chord inversions and passing notes that gave it a musical shape. For a few moments, the world slowed on its axis. She hadn't touched a piano for nearly twenty years. No one had ever asked her. And now someone had.

He picked up an approximation of what she'd given him but was soon on his feet again. 'Play it for me, come on.'

He took up his guitar and strummed what he had meant. She started to follow the phrases, concentrating at first, fingers loosening up as she got the transition. It wasn't hard. She could hear the pattern he wanted. The keyboard settled into its long familiar position beneath her curved hands beating wing-like across this newfound terrain, brave new black-and-white world.

'Can you sing a harmony in the bridge section?'
She opened her throat for him, her voice in close thirds with his. In a high, lonely place she glided, along snow-capped mountain peaks that plunged vertiginously into the icy blue lake below.

10.

I had a problem. As usual it took the few days of idleness and self-absorption necessary to blossom into full-blown, slime-drooling, fang-baring paranoia. I was always sluggish after a gig night, and this one had been momentous: my re-launch. Nobody even seemed to know I'd been gone, possibly a measure of my absolute unimportance on the scene. I might as well have popped out for a coffee for three months for all anyone remembered or cared. Show them a fancy camera and they all coalesce around it, gagging for their five seconds of fame.

Perhaps that's a little cynical. Perhaps, like me, they sensed the magic of the digital eye upon them, transformed from slaves into heroes with the sweep of a lens. I loved what the camera did. Its presence in the room adrenalised the evening, gave it flow, a purpose, a buzz. What it saw, I could see again, over and over. I could re-live it, learn from it, fall in love with it. It was a magnet for all our good intentions.

It also gave Tarzan a reason to get back on my case, as dogged and as vicious as any debt-collector. Mia had asked me not to contact him, there was nothing he could do to stop us using the material she'd shot. I wasn't worried in any meaningful sense. I'd survived on the street and there were nastier pieces of work out there. I'd seen the damage they could inflict. But not on me. I had a protector: a woman with a Boudica complex. Where did she think we were going in her chariot of fire, wheels scything and heads flailing?

After our bit of music making we'd taken a taxi home in the early hours and she dropped me at the flat. She gave me a hug and thanked me for putting the evening together so well. She was going back to bed with her husband and it didn't seem quite right to kiss her then.

For some reason I felt sucked dry, as if I'd been asleep all night and woken to find the telltale puncture marks on my neck. Actually there were marks on my neck where that young dervish had goaded me on earlier in the day, but that was different. Had Mia seen them? I'd only seen them myself when I'd gone to the gents and the leer of the mirror had flung back the unwelcome portrait of a young dissolute, Dorian Gray deferring his evil hour. Luckily one of the Cherry Juice girls had been painting her face in the next door cubicle and happened to have some concealer which did the trick. Mia hadn't noticed when we were dancing; perhaps she hadn't even noticed when we were jamming. But the sweat and stress of the evening had definitely taken its toll, I had to shift before those penetrating eyes found me out under the streetlamp glare. A surge of panic propelled me out of the cab onto the pavement, from which safe distance I waved. As the taxi disappeared into the dawn I felt a pang that was more relief than longing, though I was developing something strangely akin to that too. At that moment I wanted to be on my own, even if it was borrowed space, borrowed time. She'd told me it would be a few days before she was ready to show me a rough cut. Plenty of time to think things over.

There were a thousand things we still hadn't said. A thousand tales to be told between the start and the finish of whatever we meant to each other. She'd stolen a place in my life and I wasn't sure what it was exactly. She had asked about my family only once, frowning at my bedside, wondering why she was shouldering the burden, and never since. Did she want to think of me as an immaculate conception? Her lost child? Would knowing where I came from make me somehow less significant in her perfect mind?

My mother was ten years her senior, the bearer of sons and bad tidings. My father was in Scotland, the property of another woman. Ma was now shacked up with a retired university lecturer and more interested in his grandchildren than my unfathomable unemployed status. That was how she saw it. She didn't follow my career because she didn't like social media and that was the only place where it truly existed. She didn't believe strumming a guitar was going to put a roof over my head and she was dead right. If I'd been my own son I'd have given myself a good talking to and withdrawn funding support. Which was exactly what she'd done. She had my mobile number but used it rarely, usually to let me know about births, deaths and marriages in the family. How was I to tell her about this woman who was not quite a surrogate mother, still less a lover? The absence of definition only made the idea of her more desirable. She was the only person I could have an adult conversation with. The only educated person I knew. The only person with the verbal tools to give me a definition for myself, writing her version even now as she worked out how to sell me, how to sell the music scene she'd stolen upon.

But how would my mother find the emotional tools to care about someone who was cheating on their husband in some obscure way in order to support me? What could they find to say to each other at all? Was she usurper? Mentor? Patron?

The terms of the debate seemed to have coarsened over time. In the good old days a patroness would have had a salon and a swarm of devoted young artists at her fingertips, whose creation in one's name was the biggest turn-on of all. It was a public, collective eros, a celebration of the artistic impulse, everybody high on finer things and surrounded by heavy brocade drapes. Nowadays being a patroness seemed to be all about money, politics and personal status. One thing was clear, those patronesses were out there, blaring their presence all over the web, hammering home their contributions to the cause of art, and this woman in my life was not. She was under wraps, shrouded in secrecy, behaving as if it was an illicit affair. So what did that make her?

If she'd been after me for sex, she might have been my cougar. There were plenty of my cruder friends who would have called her that anyway, but it hurt to think that might be how she'd appear in the eyes of the world. A cougar dressed up loud, gave you the eye, drank a few glasses more than she should in order to keep the conversation going, hung around for the action even as others more lucky were off home. She frequented specialist dating websites and danced in clubs bearing less-than-ambiguous names, with pimpled youths young enough to be her son. She fondled them in dark corners. She took them home for energetic, fleshly encounters. I found myself logging-off in a sweat. She wasn't like that. This was personal. Between us. Something had happened in the crystal air that night to recalibrate our worlds. A tenderness, wild inspiration, a yearning to heal something that was broken, an outpouring of generosity so oblique it was impossible to read or define. She was so far above cougar I was embarrassed at even googling the word. I deleted my search history, drew a red line under it. That wasn't it at all.

Still, I had to work out a few things. She was married, apparently happily and successfully, to her older man. Had she ever told me his name? I'd heard her calling *Stephen* on her mobile on more than one occasion. To me, she always referred to him as her husband. A status word, possessive, exclusive, keeping me at arm's length, just as the gold band on the fourth finger of her left hand both repelled and magnetised, branding her, making her his property. I'd touched it accidentally, the first time I took her money. It had been cold and hard in the night air, while her skin was fleetingly warm and soft in my calloused palm.

And the surname? Was it the same as that crazy

dancing girl who was now straddling the middle of my field of vision like an Egon Schiele forgery, that faintly lewd image I was spending so much of my time looking to the side of it was starting to feel like an acrylic jumper rubbing on cat's fur but would not be able to for much longer because... because... my rebel flesh was already stirring at the thought of what she'd done to me. God. My hand involuntarily went up to touch the bruise on my neck which was now throbbing as painfully as my erection. *God.*

Chancery. That was it. Lack of sleep made me fumble at the keyboard but there was his Wikipedia page. Stephen Chancery. Theatre and television director. A string of awards and glossy credits. Radical activist of the late seventies and eighties. Agitprop when it was still cool. Socialist playwright later moving into television actuality and hard-hitting docu-journalism, then arts and creative documentary. A daunting list of programmes, several published works, quotes from press and peers. An impressive career by any standards. A photo of a good-looking guy in his forties – ok, he was ten years greyer now – headphones slung round his neck, pointing intensely out of frame for the cameraman. Spouse: Mia Cowper. *She commanded this man, what was she doing?* People also search for: Kate Janes. Children: Harriet Chancery. Jack Chancery. Charlotte Cowper Chancery.

I'm Charlotte Chancery... Mia's daughter. It's what she said. Not what she did however. I flipped the screen shut to escape from them all, scrambled for the shower before I collapsed and ended up sleeping on the floor. It wouldn't have been the first time, and it certainly wasn't going to be the last the way things were heading. *I'd fucked her daughter!* To be more precise her daughter had fucked me, but that was just semantics. I'd be out on my ear the minute Mia found out, and what was to stop her finding out before she'd even imported that media onto her timeline? What was to stop this monstrous prodigy of hers blowing the whole thing wide open and taking to the skies with a ticket to Rio in her hand and a girl in her lap?

The hot water hit my head like a deluge of hot nails, but I needed the distraction. I sat in the shower basin for five minutes, head pounding, trying to unravel panic from probability. Somehow in between the rollercoaster of thoughts plunging through my mind I managed to apply shampoo and shower gel. Somehow I struggled my way dry with the help of a towel which bore the imprint of an unfamiliar shade of lipstick, and under the duvet which still bore the scent of my illicit encounters.

There is a point when you realise you are too tired to fall asleep. The vicious head massage I'd just received together with the invigorating circulatory workout and the waterfall of thoughts cascading through my head, conspired to keep me lying there, part crazed, part comatose. More than anything in the world at that moment I didn't want to lose the flat. It was the most pathetic, venal emotion I've ever suffered, but that was the fact. I suddenly realised what it was she'd given me, how bloody lucky I was, and how bloody uncomfortable I was likely to be soon. Practically weeping with self-pity, I vowed to shape up and stop abusing her trust and hospitality. I'd fallen headlong into a trap. Her daughter was not my friend, she was setting me up for a fall. I remembered with a stab of adrenaline the look on her face when she'd seen me lying on the spare bed in her parents' house. It was hostility not admiration. There was an institution to protect: the Chancery name. Her father and her mother together forever.

That, on the other hand, was the act of a thwarted twelve-year-old, not an independent creative professional with lusts and longings of her own. Nothing about our shared body language had told me she had an ulterior motive. Either she was a great actress or there had been something there, some spark we'd let loose between the music and the movement which existed despite the agenda, but which couldn't be repeated. A glorious one-off.

So what the hell had I been doing that whole evening in the club? Surfing the wave of my producer's goodwill and optimism, in love with my own ability to wrap the world around my little finger? It hadn't felt that way, if I was honest. I'd walked into that bar with my chin up and jaw clenched in order to stop my teeth from chattering. I felt like a horny little cheat, scared of stammering *I'm sorry* the moment she opened her mouth to me, scared of being found out *there's something you should know*, striding forward like a conquering hero on the offensive, because that was the only way not to be creeping through the back door, curling myself into a cowering mess and slipping effortlessly into the bottom of a pint glass. I could see it in her face. Not angry. Just relieved that I'd shown up. Of course I was going to show up, she wanted to make a star out of me. Only I knew what a deceiver's heart beat under my jacket. All I could give her at that moment was my best shot. I threw everything at the evening and the camera and didn't stop until we'd viewed that last frame. What did she get in return? My charisma. Whatever that is. But it showed up on the screen like a dream. As if someone had clicked the picture enhancement button marked *Supernova.*

Was I flirting with her? I suppose I was. She had a lovely mouth. Her daughter had it too, a kind of swell of the upper lip that looked as though a bee had stung there, made you want to touch it. I was never good at keeping my hands to myself. Helping myself to the sweetie jar when I had no right to touch her at all. Was it just to see the effect? There was an effect, whether she intended it or not, that faint explosion, a momentary collapse behind the eyes that said surrender, even when she was keeping me out with stern words. But why trespass there when it could only hurt her? Or me? Where the hell were the boundaries normal people set for themselves? I recalled a dog psychologist my mother had known who spoke of badly trained animals as having weak impulse control. That was me, a little cur with the same problem. Someone should just kick me where it hurt, attach me to a sled and make me run for twenty Siberian miles under the midnight sun. That should sort the problem.

And had I written about her in that song? Of course she was the woman in the silken dress, it's how I would always see her, detaching herself from the crowd in her sea-green evening gown in that single moment of hyper-reality. The rest I'd made up, a tangled skein of wool like the jacket her daughter draped around herself, a fabric compsed of fragments and colours. Part truth, part fiction. Inspiration born of a vague stirring in the gut and the first thing that dropped into your mind, a story woven from all the bits and pieces you gleaned from the surface of your life, thoughts that mulched around in the dark, all slung together around that riff that had kept you awake, the chorus that came to you on the way between one disastrous waking episode and the next. It always started with a germ, something that was uppermost in your mind, something that got twisted together, shaped and shaded into what was, in the end, just a story. Since that last night with Cleo, the girl who could never love me enough, I'd taken a step sideways. Songs would never be outpourings for one person alone, that made them too vulnerable, too short-lived, like evanescent butterflies with two days to mate and reproduce before drifting to sleep forever on the breeze. It seemed a waste. I wanted something more long-lasting. It had to be more coded, more filtered, more complex, one part message, three parts disguise.

Why did I persuade her to sing? To see if I could tempt her? Wanting to know if she was the star I'd made her in my mind? A backlit glimpse of the woman emerging through the smoke onto the full light of the stage? It had intrigued me, the notion that behind the lovely way she spoke might be music after all. Something in the way she'd talked about mine. Something that told me she was feeling it, not just thinking it. I had to know. And now I did. She had music inside her just like me, only she suppressed hers and I was powerless in the grip of mine.

When I finally lost consciousness, my dreams were queasy, operatic ramblings. I was in the thick of a crowd around the streets of Lincoln's Inn, borne along by people pressing around me, waving notebooks, tickets, flashing mobiles, snapping selfies. Perhaps they were fans turned out for my concert. I was lifted off the ground by the force of numbers, crowd-surfing my way to the entrance, with a sensation of constant falling. A fan-vaulted archway loomed ahead, a venerable building full of leaded lights, old as history. I was thrust forward like a battering-ram by hands I could not see, past faces and figures clothed in black, their faces deathly white, their eyes shadowy, towards the grand entrance and a blonde man in a tight suit, the manager I knew I should be avoiding but who seemed to be expecting our imminent collision with relish.

The walls leaned forward blackly to enclose us and I was in the dock with a noisy crowd baying for blood. A jury of the great and good clustered around a central table, Stephen Chancery among them, agreeing I should be detained for my own safety, no bail allowable in this instance. A veiled woman wept in the crowd, her head covered. She pulled off her wedding ring and threw it onto the polished wooden floor where a tousled child grovelled to pick it up, narrowly avoiding the kicks and scuffles of the tight-packed courtroom. As she did so, I realised that the honourable member closest to me was in fact a kangaroo. That explained a lot. The child held up the ring, placed it between her teeth and swallowed, giving me a triumphant look. Charlotte. The division bell started to ring for the vote. I reached out and silenced the unwelcome sound of my phone.

'I hope I'm not disturbing you?'

It was waking from one nightmare into another. 'Charlotte?'

'It's Mia.'

I was bolt upright in bed, heart lurching into overdrive. 'Sorry, Mia. What time is it?' How could I have forgotten her daughter hadn't taken my number, had no idea of my co-ordinates, she just knew where my front door was. So she said. I felt stalked and hassled, exhausted with the effort of keeping everything separate.

'Eleven, I'm just getting in the car. I'll bring you a coffee, I think we should talk through this artist management thing. It's not straightforward.'

And Tarzan to complete the tea party. How could he lay claim to my dreams when he'd never paid a penny towards my career? I imagined he was finding my ex too much of a handful and I was the nearest dumb animal to hand for punishment. But Mia was above all this. I didn't want to drag her into it.

She'd been listening to my silence. 'Are you ok?'

'Just thinking.'

'I'll see you shortly then.' She rang off, nothing about her producer's tone to tell me that we were anything but colleagues.

I'd run out of clean boxers, found myself ripping open another packet. It was time to get to the laundrette. Except I'd probably bump into the dancing girl and she'd tell me how much she'd enjoyed her heterosexual experiment, strictly in the cause of feminist science of course. She was probably even now dreaming up some androgynous piece of contemporary art fashioned from takeaway cartons and sex toys. We'd watch our dirty laundry together and speculate on the nature of the human orgasm. Had blind Tiresias been overselling when he declared the woman's experience to be ten times that of the man? She'd given me a pretty mindblowing experience so I hoped that straightforward penetration had done something for her. In the meantime I was lifting a clean shirt out of the cupboard and a pair of trousers her *mother* had bought for me out of friendship and, well, motherliness. It was a proper, incestuous little clusterfuck and no mistake.

I did my best impression of tidying up the flat in advance of our meeting, sweeping discarded clothing into the closet, throwing away extraneous bottles and coffee cups, straightening the bed. I even remembered to hook the lipstick-smeared towel out of the bathroom and replace it with a brand-new one from the linen-cupboard. What a queen, she'd provided everything for me. All I had to do was keep my head together, prop up the house of cards and I'd be fine. A squirt of bleach, a quick rub with kitchen cleaner, and she'd never know I wasn't the best trained house-sitter in west London.

The doorbell rang a few minutes after I'd sat down at my laptop to respond to the day's first batch of emails. One or two I studiously avoided opening, nothing else that looked too threatening. On Facebook, more feedback from the club night – great time, any chance of a slot next week kind of stuff – a couple of reviews, plenty of photos, fun links, hahas and hehes, all the usual social media fun of the fair. I glanced in the hall mirror and opened the door, trying to look focused and welcoming.

She looked radiant. I realised this with a start as I'd expected her to look how I felt, a bit puffy round the eyes and finding the world too bright for comfort. But no, she was effortlessly fresh and clear-skinned, hair curled and scented, including the cute strand that fell across her cheek, the merest touch of make-up that led you to believe that she wasn't wearing any, the effect softened by the swell of soft fleece around the neck and cuffs of an expensive-looking jacket. Immaculate: she didn't look any older than I did. Just richer.

'I don't think it's going to damage us too much,' was her opening gambit, handing me a large cappuccino with a peck on the cheek as she hung her jacket and perched on a stool at the kitchen bar. Damage I didn't like the sound of. Coffee put heart in a man. She crossed her slim legs and unlidded her own cup, sipping decorously and trying not to look down on me as I regained the workstation.

'Did you get his email then?' I ventured.

'I've made some notes. I think he's fishing. Tell me your side.'

'Not much to tell.' I could see by the tiny clench of her jaw that no messing was the best policy. 'I met him about five months ago, my ex-girlfriend Cleopatra introduced us. He was her manager at the time.'

She opened her tablet and tapped busily as I spoke. This wasn't the kind of interview I liked at all.

'And he became yours?'

'He promoted me for a couple of months. We didn't see eye to eye and we parted.'

'He says you assaulted him after a studio audition.'

'I told him some home truths about exploitation and he put his fist to my face one afternoon in Oxford Street.'

'You mean he hit you?'

I wanted to laugh, she looked so serious.

'D'you have any witnesses?'

'I hope not, it was fucking embarrassing.'

The notebook snapped shut, the only sign of vexation.

'Any sniff of a legal wrangle and the channel will just bury the pilot, you'll be lucky to see it on YouTube. Is that what you want?'

I shook my head. She drank her coffee, weighing me up. 'It doesn't sound as if the claim for physical damages will hold up. Did you hit him in self-defence?'

'He had me pinned to the pavement. I gave him a pretty fair kick in the groin as I recall.'

Her fingers went to work again. 'And there was no one else with you? No one saw you who might testify if it did come to court?'

My heart lunged unpleasantly. Of course there was someone. She glanced at me. 'Was there?'

'I called on my ex that evening, she helped clean me up a bit.'

She suppressed relief. 'That's good.'

Not for me. 'I'd rather not involve her.'

'Depends how dirty he wants to play. We're on cordial terms so far.'

'I'm in your hands.'

She looked me over, considering. Nodded. She wanted to trust me. There are so many kinds of love. I hadn't had this kind before.

'Did you sign a contract with him?'

'God, no.'

'Did he ever mention a contract?'

'Probably. At the beginning, when he wanted what I had.'

'Did he make bookings on your behalf?'

'Yes.'

'PR?'

'He introduced me to a photographer.'

'Engage in any activities that might incur expenses?'

'A recording session with a producer friend. Mostly he made me do the work and pick up the tab.'

'He was acting in good faith though?'

'In his own way.'

'Did you appear at all the concerts he booked for you?'

'Up to the point we split.'

I still had no idea how long a trail of unfulfilled commitments I'd left behind.

'Did you receive any remuneration from him for concerts or recordings?'

'We never got beyond the I.O.U. phase. I suppose he thought of it as re-investment in my development. It kept him in cigars for a few weeks.'

The notebook clicked shut again, strategy clear for the moment.

'I need you to call all the artists. Find out which of them he actually has signed. If there's any doubt I can't use their performance, the release forms alone won't hold up.'

A light sweat had broken out on my brow. The flat seemed overheated. The whole situation seemed overheated. Logically, I knew what she wanted me to do and why. My own interests were at stake. She was just speaking to me as a colleague but instinctively I wanted to pull back. It hadn't taken long for me to be hitting up against the limits of my professional capability, unable to find any distance. I'd never responded well to pressure. Some pathology going back to boyhood. Having a teacher for a father didn't help. Especially when he became an absentee from his own household, breaking all his own rules. Do as I say, not as I do. More importantly, I couldn't shake this growing sense of panic, it wasn't just Tarzan on my tail, I felt appropriated by her. It was the bitter downside of loving women, there was always a comeback. *Do this for me.* She was bossing me around. She owned my space. She had the right to use it whenever she wanted. She had the key to the front door. She was going to walk through it at the wrong time sooner or later. In her mind I had no life except what she projected onto me. She could catch me out at any point. I was holding the string to a net loaded with disappointment, ready to release its contents onto all our heads at the least convenient moment. There was no good ending possible to this story. *Honest men have nothing to fear.* But when was I ever honest? This was already shaping itself into a song.

I must have turned a bit pale, she was looking at me with second and third thoughts. 'Maybe it's quicker if you let me have their numbers. I'll just say I need some additional information, they'll understand that.' Her quick mind was already leaping ahead, assuming I was rejecting the idea, that I wasn't up to the task, that she had to protect me. Finally indignation at my own uselessness loosened my tongue. I was the bloody problem, not her, she was just asking for my help. We were supposed to be working together. It all tumbled out, not very elegant, but I was angry and needing to kick back at the misinformation she'd been fed.

'I know these guys, Mia. I track them for months before I even see them play. You develop an instinct for how musicians are going to run their lives, how they create, who they're likely to work with. I met Virginia at an open mic session when she was still at college. Dickon Brand is not going to be interested in someone like that, she's permanently too close to breakdown to make any money for him. It's too stressy, he can't be arsed. I don't believe he reps anyone you saw last night. He's trying to scare you off working with me because he's still angry, thinks I've pissed him about, whatever. Maybe I have, but it doesn't matter. He's nothing.'

She raised a delicately plucked eyebrow, replaced the lid on her coffee-cup and aimed it at the bin. She must have been wondering what she'd unleashed. I had plenty of bile where that came from if she cared to listen. 'Sam is a friend. I won't tell you some of the things he's said about Brand, they're too disgraceful. If I'd heard them first I'd have given him a wider berth myself.'

'You can tell them I need another short declaration for permission to use them in the show. That'll clear up any management issues. I'll email it to you.'

I mustered a weak smile. 'Leave me to it for a while, I'll text you with an update once I'm done. Some of those guys won't be awake for a couple of hours. Musicians aren't the most reliable morning people.'

The kitchen spotlight lit up her hair in a kind of halo and she contemplated me with the benefit of her superior insight. She'd decided to trust me to do it. Somewhere deep down she sensed I'd take the challenge because it was part of the price of success. Of my getting what I wanted. Maybe her too. She slid off the stool elegantly and retrieved her jacket.

'You're the anchor, it's how you spot and showcase talent that's interesting to an audience. What you bring to it over the next few weeks. It'll be great, don't worry.'

I wasn't convinced of her consistency at this point. Nor of my own power. Was that really what the broadcaster meeting had been about? The club night had worked but it still seemed more by luck than by judgement. What if that was the best we had? A few weeks was plenty of time to run out of steam. Best not go there. It had to work. I owed her.

We contemplated each other for a moment, searching for the right parting shot. I longed for her to say something beautiful. It was her belief in me that kept me hanging on. That was the drug I craved, uncut by business talk. I wanted it now, but she wasn't in the mood to fuel my addiction. Only that secret radiance of hers gave me hope. 'That was a serious meeting.'

'Oh yes, TV takes itself very seriously. It looks simple. Nothing's ever simple. I have a roomful of production files to prove it.'

'Don't you ever want to burn them all? Cut loose?'

She looked momentarily caught-out before brushing this aside with a half-laugh. 'No.'

Different generation. She was a serious individual with frivolous desires. There was too much at stake for her to act on them. I still thought I might make her try, though. Wondered if she would be the key that opened the door to my better self. I pushed a little further.

'I haven't even asked you how you slept.'

'Longer than you have, I expect.'

There was a tiny flicker in her eye as she said it. I wanted to ask her if her husband had been glad to have her back after such a long evening, but it felt impertinent. It had to stay professional for now.

'I'll call you as soon as I can. He might have fingered one or two but I hope they won't have been as dumb or as desperate as I was to make a deal with him.'

'We're having lunch together at one. Let me know what you can by then.'

I had to laugh. She was fearless. I was sure she'd have him wound around her little finger by two thirty regardless of my input. We hugged and she looked up into my face.

'As soon as this is sorted we'll arrange another filming date, are you ok with that?'

What a question. She could see that it was completely superfluous.

'Oh, before I go, I have something in the car I wonder if you could help me with?'

'Sure.'

She was already up the stone steps ahead of me, boot heels clicking hurriedly towards the car she'd left on hazard-lights. The wardens had left her alone, she'd been lucky. Again. She unlocked the car and the hatchback opened on a smart black guitar case wedged diagonally across the space.

'Could you take care of this for me please?'

'Whose is it?'

She gave a fidgety glance over her shoulder. 'Just lift it out for me would you? I really don't want to get a ticket now.'

As if that was anything to do with it. I tried to

look stern. 'I can't take this, Mia.'

She flushed, almost desperately. 'I think you'll need it over the next few months. Please.'

I solemnly did as I was told, shouldered the case and saw her into the car with a look that was probably unnecessarily elongated by stupifaction. *She'd bought me a guitar.* She slammed the door on me, looking slightly terrified at what she'd done, gunned the engine, swung the car around and tore off into the lunchtime traffic.

My hands trembled as I unlatched the case. It was a nice-quality, rigid case with a good finish, enough to make me a little nervous about what it contained. Inside was a Martin D-15M Burst. One of the most beautiful things I've seen in my life, deep red rosewood with the subtlest shading under the sun and a dark teardrop fingershield. It was mint new. It smelled of lacquer. Perhaps it was that made my eyes water. But my heart beat hard as I lifted that baby to my breast and touched the strings for the first time. This was not an instrument that you bought over the counter without having done your research. You had to know the breadth of your player a little. You had to have read at least a few guitar reviews to have made such a decision.

I wanted to call her but I knew it was no use. I wrote the song instead. It was everything and nothing that had been in my head before that moment. *Ars longa, vita brevis.* Probably the most significant thing I learnt from my father at any point in our shared life. Put more bluntly, I knew from long experience that songs were fragile creatures programmed for flight if you didn't nail them immediately after the moment of birth. So I imprisoned my moment of claustrophobia, swinging between the pressure of her longing and her daughter's sabotage and called it *The Gift*. I sent it bouncing off the walls in a cascading sequence of chords that flowed from brain to fretboard in the time it took for the kettle to boil.

In the time it took for the tea to brew and the toast to brown, there was the germ of a verse and a couple of thoughts at the chorus already on the page in my laptop before a gentle electronic trill hailed the arrival of a new message from someone called Roland: *Liking the new song. That is a beauty of a guitar, my my.*

I'd forgotten about the toast and Marmite completely, my scalp was prickling. No one knew about the guitar. It was Mia's secret. Was my upstairs neighbour now surveilling my every move with a glass tumbler to the floorboards? Jangled, I closed the chat window. It had to be someone I knew: the downside of being a promoter. Too many casual acquaintances with too much time on their hands, harbouring grudges against you for missing their moment of glory, their pub gig, their café slot, their open mic, their street happening, their flashmob, their bedroom concert. I had a hundred messages and invitations a week. I had far more online friends than I could remember, I could never be everywhere they wanted me to be.

Trying to blot out the intrusion I decided to get down to business and call the musicians who were key to whether I would sink or swim. Virginia picked up straight away. Sam took thirty minutes and four attempts to raise. After that it got more complicated. The call log, recorded on my mobile phone with their permission went something like this:

'Gin? How are you?'

'What's wrong?'

'Nothing at all hun, just wanted to thank you for a great slot the other day.'

'Oh. It didn't seem that great to me but ok, yeah.'

'Startling as ever.'

'What was startling, you knew the songs right?'

'Startling in a good way. Y'know, edgy, out there! Not your usual...'

'Oh. Thanks.'

'Anyone signed you for management yet?'

'I don't think I see myself as manageable in any meaningful sense.'

'Sure, right. Well we're just starting to edit so I'll let you know.'

'I never watch myself onscreen, it's usually so distressing.'

'Speak soon then...'

'Sam, my man, are you fine?'

'How's yourself TP?'

'Some beautiful songs last week, thanks so much again.'

'My pleasure, my pleasure. How's the show shaping up?'

'All good, hard at work already. Couple of deets I need to check with you please.'

'Sure, go ahead.'

'You've signed the release form with the producer?'

'Yeah, did that for the lady, yep.'

'Any management permission we need to check?'

'Who's that? Oh! Working directly with a booking

agent for most things. Still waiting for some Mister
Niceguy to take that load from me. It's gonna happen
soon, I know.'

'Anyone in the frame?'

'Had a couple meetings. Harper Muse. Bew
Bailey. They're considering my material.'

'Sure one of them'll go with your next EP,
hopefully this little TV airing'll do some good.'

'Exactly, exactly.'

'Not thinking about our friend DB then?'

(Throaty laughter)

'That c**t. He should keep his hands off young
flesh is all I know.'

'Thanks for that.'

'Good to hear you old friend...'

'Jewel.'

'Tom?'

'How you feeling today?'

'Yeah, good. It went ok don't you think?'

'I do! Our producer is very happy. D'you sign
that release form for her by the way?'

'That what? Oh, yeah, she gave me a bit of paper,
mhm. Did you?'

'Of course.' (Actually that wasn't true, strictly
speaking. I had it sitting in front of me on the desk at
that very moment.) 'Nothing else?'

'How d'you mean?'

'You didn't sign anything else?'

'What, with all those autograph-hunters storming
the stage?'

'I mean, bits of paper. Jewel.'

'You ok, Tom?'

Sigh. 'You know the guy I mean. The creep who

thinks he owns everyone in the club.'

'I'm a bit more choosy than you think. Can I call you later? I'm right in the middle of a Prokofiev sonata and it's feckin' hard...'

'Hi Eri. Thanks for patching me up.'

'Oo, you are most welcome gorgeous guy. You know you're going to have to stop playing around some time, why don't ya marry me? We can have a swarm of little cherry pies and live in the mountains in the sun.'

'Ahhh. I love happy endings.'

'Yeah, me too. Did you like the set?'

'Loved it!'

'Seen any clips from that camera guy?'

'Yup. Just calling about that. Who's your manager now? I might need to clear footage with them.'

'Wow, was it hot?'

'Absolutely. So?'

Pause. 'You know we parted company with Lou a couple of months back?'

'Sorry to hear it.'

'We've had a couple of meetings with Dickon Brand, d'you know him? He seems really nice. On the side of the artist, y'know?'

Longer pause. Mine this time. 'Can I give you some advice?'

'Sure, babe.'

'If you do decide to go with him, we might not be able to include your material in the show.'

'Aha?'

'He's been quite obstructive about one or two things.'

'I see.'

'Have a think and let me know when you've spoken to the girls, will you? Your set is really good. Could be your breakthrough moment.'

'Shit, this is really unwelcome news.'

'I know. Sorry.'

'Shit.'

'And keep it to yourselves please. Call me later.'

I didn't like to think of those girls on the cutting room floor, but they were as good as there unless I had assurances by that evening. As for the Dumb Waiters...

'Simon?'

'Ahhhhh!! Arghhh! Urgh!'

'Who's your manager you dumbf**k?'

'We're a co-operative! Ahhhgh!!'

'Ever heard of Dickon Brand?'

'Dickon whoooaahhhhgh?!'

'Are you signed with a manager?'

'No, you f**ker. F**k off, I'm getting... ahhhhh ahh!'

Happy to do as I was told, I was less sure about sharing my precious TV debut with these monsters. Maybe a brief clip of mayhem and dancing would do it. It was time to start thinking about slots for my next club night.

I dialled the number Mia had called me from earlier. A male voice answered, a rich, well-rounded baritone, RP. Friendly, casual. 'Yeah?'

I'd messed up. She'd had the phone she normally texted me from with her and I'd called the landline. I was speaking to her husband. The man who'd banned me from the house. No choice but to accelerate forward… 'Is Mia there?'

'She's out at the moment, can I take a message?'

…And over the cliff. 'I'll call back later. Thanks.'

I was off the phone. In freefall. My number was now stored in their phone memory and it was going to burn a hole in her little secret if we weren't careful.

I texted her. *4 out of 5. Cherry Juice girls have talked with him but not signed. Catch up later.* I got one word back: *Thanks.* Unreal. She'd be deep into a salade niçoise with that smooth-talking barbarian by now.

I left the flat with my dirty laundry and my phone. I wasn't sure when I was coming back. A new sim card might be sensible to have in reserve in case that number of mine was trashed irretrievably. I was oppressed by the feeling that I had to find somewhere else to stay. There was someone on my tail, the secret was starting to leak and it was only a couple of weeks old. How the hell was it all supposed to work? I weighed my options. I could use the cash she'd given me as deposit on a room somewhere but that would clean me out and I'd no address from which to sign on. I'd cleared a hundred from the Charlatan once the artists were settled and the club had taken their cut. That constituted a profit but it was still pretty meagre pickings as far as paying rent was concerned. Would Jewel take me on as a flatmate until I could sort something out? I didn't think she'd like the idea, it was crossing too many lines. And then there was the guitar… worth a cool fifteen hundred cash, probably. No, I couldn't go there. There least of all. I strode on, feeling trapped.

One block away there was a laundrette run by a sad-looking Iranian guy stuck at the back with the dry-cleaning fumes. Morose, but helpful with change for the machines. I didn't feel like hanging around anywhere for too long. Leaving my underwear alone to circulate, I took off down the Uxbridge Road in search of a place to hideaway and maybe make some calls. Between one of the international greengrocers and the Bush Hall I passed a phone repair shop. That cheap sim beckoned, my parachute in case of dire need. I was just handing over cash when an unmistakeable figure in gaudy woollen jacket walked past the shop door.

'Tom?'

So she did know my name, cheeky little witch. She was all over smiles, it was impossible to be unhappy at the sight of her. It was also impossible to avoid her.

'Did the show go well?'

'It did! Have a look...'

She tapped at her phone and thrust it into my hand. There she was on YouTube in a black dress, all sharp angles like her sculptures and looking like a star with her hair piled high and a mic to her mouth, words tumbling out of her like a prophet.

'Not bad!'

She re-pocketed the phone, proud and pleased as punch while I weighed her up.

'Is there anything you can't do?'

She shrugged carelessly. 'My keyhole surgery skills are poor in fact.'

'Seven hundred hits already. My, my.'

'I told them not to upload it actually.'

'If you've got it, flaunt it. But I don't think you need my advice do you?'

She was linking arms now, as we seemed to be

walking the same direction. Except we weren't, she'd just kidnapped me to her purpose. How was I to defend myself against this space-invader?

'So, neighbour. If you'd like to come round tonight for some drinking and a pretty unforgettable vegetarian thali at ours you'd be very welcome. Fancy it?'

I was caught between panic and pleasure, it seemed to be the tenor of our relationship. It must have shown in my face. She took out a pen, pushed up my sleeve and wrote her address on my arm along with a little dancing figure with its tongue out. Short of a physical tussle there was very little I could do about it. She'd tattooed me like one of her girlfriends and I'd have to keep my sleeve rolled down for days. She ignored the sigh escaping from my lips. 'There. Nine o'clock, bring your own liquid. Unless you want to drink from the tap.'

'I think we should talk.'

She eyed my neck mischievously, pursing *ouch* with her lips. 'Later? I'd love to see you. Bring your instrument.'

With that she was bowling down the street, the wind racing leaves through her hair.

11.

He was there before her, seated in the window busily poring over the menu. He had waited for her to arrive before ordering drinks. He was polite, unsmiling, immaculately dressed in a dark blue suit and white shirt, no tie, scarlet handkerchief poked jauntily in his top pocket like a discreet red rag to a bull. One of those handshakes that went on a little too long, as he weighed her up with his disconcerting, colourless eyes.

'Thanks for joining me at such short notice.'

'Pleasure.'

Mia handed her jacket to the restaurant manager.

'What would you like to drink, Dickon?'

'I'll take a San Pellegrino. Perhaps a glass of wine with the meal.'

It was the gracelessness that riled. He was like an armour-encased insect, not quite human. She'd have to work hard to find any chink at all. She ordered for them both and they contemplated each other across the elegant table linen.

'How's business?'

He wasn't expecting a direct question from her so early in the proceedings but barely a flicker betrayed him. She knew from her due diligence that despite his degree in economics and a spell at a major label doing artist PR, he was still at the start-up stage of a career in which he possibly needed her goodwill as much as she needed his.

'Fine. And yours? An award-winning company must have plenty of offers.'

He'd done his homework for which she was grateful, it gave her more space to hone her argument. 'Let's just say it opens doors. Our slate's full for the next two years.'

'If you're looking to do any synch deals nearer completion you know where to come. I'm working with a couple of boutique publishers and an excellent audio library I'd be happy to put you in touch with.'

Mia listened to his pitch and ordered salmon and salad. He went for the expensive blue *filet de boeuf*, rare, and a rather special bottle of Bordeaux. No doubt he'd sleep it off later in his Audi which he'd ostentatiously parked outside where she could see it, fretting periodically about passing traffic wardens, extolling the virtues of electronic payment. Everything about him bristled and barked *look at me*. He was a bundle of insecurities which untangled only very slowly as he worked his way through the red wine. They talked London life, property and profit margins. They talked access and air quality, fitness and the freelance economy. Only as their espressos arrived did he feel compelled to open the subject of music which must otherwise drift off the agenda altogether. She felt light and focused as he carved his way into the territory that he needed to dominate. It was business for him and a moderately dirty one at that, but she doubted whether it was his passion.

'Passion and clarity,' he said, spooning lime sorbet. 'That's what I bring to the table. My artists all understand that. I spend a lot of time working with them to develop a concept for what they want to achieve. Evolve a position in the market that's appropriate to their aims. It's a relationship, it takes time, like great sex it's something that's got to be done together.'

Mia sipped her strong coffee and eyed him sagely.

'Musicians do music. They're creatives not business people. Without a good manager they're not going to get any exposure let alone build a career. Look.' He flipped open his tablet and brought up a promotional picture of someone she was starting to recognise. 'This is a girl I've been developing for two years. She's kicking off a national tour next month to promote her début album. Star written all over her.'

Mia wondered whether Dickon was capable of great sex with anything or anybody as she scanned the sleekly but slightly clad, immaculately curled and curvaceous beauty on his screen.

'Cleopatra M. Have I seen her somewhere before?'

'I doubt it, I've stopped her playing small venues. If you've got that kind of class you've got to make audiences know what you're worth.'

'You were at the Charlatan club together the other night?'

Dickon scrolled through his publicity images thoughtfully. He didn't answer.

'What kind of music?'

'She's a baroque pop diva in the mould of Björk and Florence. Writes her own material though I've got her penning songs with some top international writers. She's smart. Totally committed. You should use her on your TV show. We could tie in dates, it could work well for both of us.'

He had it all clicking nicely into position just as the bill arrived. Mia keyed in her PIN number and waited for her receipt before responding.

'I'd be very happy to help you showcase her, Dickon, she'd bring a new dimension, some scale.'

'How I see it.'

'Let's take the heat out of the rest of the discussion too. We really have much more to gain from being friends over this. But I can't change what the channel has commissioned. They bought Tom Pavelin as front man and host, that's not negotiable. He's an essential element.'

'I could have found you better.'

'I'd very much like you to be involved but you have to get off his back and let him do his job, ok?'

It rankled, but he was not going to get a better or a quicker slot for his starlet. Mia shook hands with him and took his sampler. 'I'll look forward to listening, and to creating a show we can all be proud of.'

Declining his offer of a lift to the tube, she decided to walk the two miles home. It was a beautiful, cloud-racing day, cold, bright, exhilarating. Her thoughts came fast, furiously conflicting like everything tumbling before her in the windy street, a dank pigeon, feathers awry on its zigzag course, a plastic bag ballooning past her, a discarded coffee cup careening in circles, a rush of dry leaves blown from their walled corner in a percussive stutter.

She had a secret weapon in her pocket that had come to her unbidden and yet with a strange inevitability: the siren who had screwed up her protégé and lured him to the point of self-destruct. In the name of preserving his position and keeping the show on course Mia had made a deal that might do more damage than good, but it was a professional response to a situation which arguably had become too inflected with personal emotion to succeed without new input. If the girl was right for the show then she'd appear in it and he would find a way of dealing with his wounded vanity. If she was too big, or too pop, if she stretched the format too far, then Mia could always stall along with the rest of her kind: most producers spent their lives avoiding making decisions, it was so much easier never saying no. For now at least she had a position: they'd record Cleopatra as part of their schedule and if she became surplus to requirements in the edit, Mia would release Dickon the rights to the footage once the pilot was safely delivered to the broadcaster.

Impatient to hear the music, she strode faster, breathless by the time she reached home, her colour high as she mounted the steps to the front door. It was three-fifteen and Stephen was in the study, power-dozing at his desktop. She tapped delicately on the window and watched him unfurl from sleep. Habit made her rifle through her bag for they key even as his figure loomed behind the door glass to open for her, disguising sluggishness in a bright welcome.

'How was it? Sort him out?'

She hung up her jacket and kissed his warm face. 'After a fashion. We made a deal.'

'Good for you. I made a deal with a structural anomaly that's been bugging the hell out of me for the last week. Thank god for pragmatism.'

'Did you eat already?'

'I thought I'd wait for you.'

'Not today darling, it was a business lunch I'm afraid.'

'Hope the bugger paid.'

'The broadcaster paid. Indirectly anyway.'

In the kitchen she ground coffee and fixed her husband a sandwich while he ruminated on the complexities of telling the story of the surveillance society through the optic of Orwell's *1984*. It was an absolute gift and a total git in one breath. He'd had to pin the commissioning editor's nipples to the wall to get him to decide: drama-documentary inspired by the novel, hybrid biopic, or a new realisation of the story set in some fictional urban dystopia, not a million miles away from now, everyone ducking out of the way of the CCTV cameras and only able to communicate via social media with Google as the new big brother. He was pleased they'd gone for his fictionalised version, although he'd acquired an additional boss in the drama department as part of the process. At least the Beeb were still prepared to take a punt on him. He was very excited to be thinking about *character* not subject. Totally refreshing. And completely knackering.

'Brilliant you.' Mia watched him eat and talk, ruminative in both senses of the word. It wasn't new to her this feeling of standing outside his world, admiring but separate. It had to be that way of course for the moment, she had taken the step sideways herself. He had such certainty, she didn't know if she would ever match him for confidence of vision. She'd shared that vision for so long she'd almost thought of it as being her own. She'd identified with his creative thoughts, his analytical mind, his hacking of a path through the intellectual thicket, for so many years, she now found herself on the far side of the lake straining her eyes to make out whether it was really the same person with whom she'd spent nearly all of her adult life.

She knew in her heart the simple act of telling a story represented the high road, the road her husband had tried to lead her onto and still, so far, failed. She was still powering along the low road it seemed, snatching at reality, making pictures that might stay with the world or might not, moulding her own vision, fuelled by infatuation. It was, perhaps, a step-up from marketing and promotion. But as content it was infantile, disposable. It was not thought rendered into art. It was not immortal. It was not, in the end, anything Stephen thought worthy of her. Would she ever write? Was her husband's belief in her justified or was that only his infatuation?

Panic crept over her. Why could she not stop this mad downhill dash for the gate and realise she was already in was the place where the flowers grew? She was tumbling so hard it was inevitable a pothole would open up beneath her and she'd be slip-sliding into one of those underground caverns, like the disused mine where she'd once walked with Stephen, the path ribboning between silent birches, the collapsed tunnels only feet from her own. She'd been afraid of falling, held on the balance by a six-inch wide sheep track between imminent landslip above and cavernous oblivion below. What would it be like to lie, broken, on a stony underground floor, staring up at the circle of sky and know there was no way back? Would she, like Alice down the rabbit-hole, have to crawl her way past the tiniest of exits, glimpse the green beyond and know that there was never any way into the garden beyond?

The phone rang for Stephen, and she took refuge up in the attic which she'd appropriated as her workspace. She could have taken over Lottie's room with her laptop and few files, but it was too soon and it made her sad. She couldn't yet face the idea that her daughter wouldn't be home this weekend, wouldn't envelop her in those light, warm arms, wouldn't breathe her little animal greeting into Mia's cheek, wouldn't stretch out on the sofa with her head on her shoulder, just to be quiet together. She had taken her warmth away. She bestowed it on people who were strangers to her mother.

Instead she called up the images of the girl Cleopatra, someone else's daughter. Perhaps a few years older than Lottie. The two were forged from different elements. Her own dark-eyed girl was a lambent flame, alive and real. She was fierce and crazy, stubborn and tempestuous, she was fleet of foot, spontaneous, generous, a head full of hornets, a soul full of deep, deep mystery. She was a puzzle no one could solve, a torrent no one could quell. She was a star quite unlike the serpentine beauty burning off the screen.

Cleopatra was artificed. Mia considered the word

carefully, for it would have been inaccurate to say artificial. She had the art not to look self-conscious about the most self-conscious of poses. In another life, if the spin of the dice had gone another way, if the coin had turned its other face, she could have been a porn star. In the world of the pop diva the line had anyway been reduced to a few atoms distinction between skinflick and music promo. Cleopatra M, very much all mouth and no trousers at all, flaunted her long legs and played to the gallery whose souls she would steal and whose pockets she intended to empty. She gazed into the camera with eyes that were the colour of sin. Green like the eyes of Eve, green as the apple proffered for consumption. Green with the nonchalance of a cat who pinions its prey out of sight of the viewing eye. Green with the desire to become an obsession.

Mia watched her new video. In motion she was fluid, slow and deliberated, gathering each movement into her light before throwing it back so much brighter. She was as vivid as if she were there in the room, but cut to pieces, fragments, shards of crystal, diamond raindrops shot through with dazzle and sunshine, rendered composite and more powerful by the succession of moments that were so much greater than continuity of action.

What would she be like, live onstage, all the cubist layering removed, everything stripped back? Mia spent some time on the web searching for gig footage. Anything that had previously been online had apparently been removed by the user, censored by the hand of this highly controlling, perhaps more savvy than she had given him credit, manager. Dickon Brand had done a comprehensive job of presenting his artist the way he wanted. She was in a pre-launch state of virginity. She was intact and gorgeously unfathomable, inseparable from the marketing plan.

Mia pressed the CD sampler into her laptop drive and a deep, blues-soaked voice oozed out of the speaker system and sent a wave of gooseflesh up the back of her neck. Savage passion in the low notes giving way to seductive, heart-wrenching vulnerability in the high. Melodic lines that soared with consummate power: she really knew how to turn it on, become the touchpaper to everyone's fuse. Suddenly there was the feeling Mia had as a child when she'd thrown her head back on the garden swing, the strange swoop of head and stomach that came with her first hit of a joint, the lurch of the abdomen that came with teenage arousal. Lassooed tight and entangled like the nerves around a rogue wisdom tooth came the painful stab of recognition that this was what her poor boy had fallen for. He hadn't stood a chance.

There is a time in every story when a new element leaps into the frame, Mia remembered from countless late night conversations with Stephen. Sometimes it's an aspect of a character hitherto veiled from sight which suddenly reveals itself as the natural and logical place to go, that leads the story forward. Sometimes it's hidden from sight, with good reason, because it's a landmine that will blow a hole in the structure you've so painstakingly built and there will be no way for the story to survive it. Her feelings about Cleopatra were correspondingly ambivalent. Getting her for the show would be a huge leap forward. She would be a star, Mia would take personal credit for introducing her, a headliner to propel her programme format into the public eye, make the whole thing catch light and seal the commission. But would it lose her the anchor?

She was going to have to meet the girl, but she didn't want to do it through her manager. She'd have her work cut out circumventing him anyway. As she scoured the internet for a private contact number she felt increasingly like the online stalker she feared herself to be becoming. But there it was at last, tucked away on an ageing blog site too obscure to show higher than page ten of the search engine rankings. Clearly Dickon had missed a few tiny details, including one or two salacious selfies locked up amongst the billions of online images.

What was it they said? Anything you post on the internet is like taking your clothes off in public and shouting look at me, in perpetuity. Removing your footprint, eradicating the trail, masking your scent, let alone disappearing or becoming a private individual again, were all riddles that no one yet had the answer to. We were all still too much in love with ourselves, with the exposure, with the illusion of fame, to fear how our own visibility would be used against us. Orwell saw further, he saw the moment the teeth were bared once we were all sufficiently hooked on our technopiate, once the spying culture kicked in and mob rule succeeded to democratic representation. *If you want a vision of the future, imagine a boot stamping on a human face - forever.* The brutality that succeeds to loss of truth.

She dialled the number, apprehensive at what she might unleash, but following the logic she must. This was her chemistry experiment and if it was going to blow the roof off the lab, then she was not going to risk the accusation that she'd given a job to her favourite without seeing him for what he was, testing whether he measured up to the bigger context.

'Hello?'

'Hi, Cleopatra?'

'Yes?'

'This is Mia Cowper from Absolute Films, I'd like to talk to you about a project I'm developing.'

A fractional pause on the line. 'Just a second.'

The phone was covered. Whispers proceeded in the background and what sounded like the rustle of clothing, then she was back, apparently having moved into another space.

'That sounds interesting, what kind of a project?'

Her voice was gentler than Mia had expected. The power of marketing evaporated for the moment and they were just two strangers, a young woman and an older one who perhaps should know better, talking down the wire to each other. But she was not going to pitch her wares cold to a fledgling starlet, no matter how promising.

'We're piloting a music documentary series.' Of course, there were plenty of pranksters and time wasters, not to mention predators out there, she probably just wanted to know she wasn't going to be walking into a trap. Mia could hear her fingers tapping in the background.

'You'll see from our website, we do high end television and film.'

'I think I saw *Lovergirls*. Liked it quite a lot actually.'

'So glad.' Mia was relieved she was starting to open up.

'I met that girl who was in it in fact.'

'Oh yes?'

'She was at a party I went to a few weeks back. Looks a bit Italian? Or Turkish maybe?'

'She's half-Moroccan.'

'Delilah?'

'Dalila.'

'Yes! What a funny co-incidence. Her girlfriend's lovely too, you must know her, Cissi.'

The sudden affirmation that Lottie was out, and very much about with this girl she didn't quite like – somewhere deep down didn't feel was worthy of her daughter's love – knocked Mia momentarily off balance. 'Of course.'

'Listen, thank you so much for getting in touch. I'm a bit busy right now with the album launch and tour – d'you want to get hold of my management and see if we have any slots free next week?'

Mia's goodwill shut down instantly. 'I'm pretty tied into my production schedule as things stand. If you want to propose some dates you know where to find me.'

She hung up, irritated by the casualness of a girl who would stab anyone between the shoulders in her scrabble for the stratosphere. Yet more irritated that her daughter was hanging out with ruthless little posers, when she was worth so much more. Was this just a bad attack of mother jealousy? Or the first intimation of leakage?

In time-honoured fashion, she busied herself with production demands. She needed an editor to start shaping the project while they gathered live material. She needed Tom to come up with a list of bookings for the next club night, so she could select the acts that would give the piece balance. She needed Lars's availability to film footage around the city to show

how a promoter recruited and worked with new talent.

She made a selection of recent graduates she thought might be good for the show and started calling. An hour later she had four interviews lined up the following morning and a plan to start compiling the project file in the afternoon with the successful candidate, a week's editing spread over the month with the potential to work on the series further down the line.

Having re-established her inner calm, she picked up the phone to Tom. She was pleasantly surprised to hear his voice rather than the answerphone. She wondered if he'd been waiting for her call, but that would have been uncool of course. She could hear running water in the background as if he was washing the dishes as they spoke.

'How was it?'

'Let's just say I think we've reached an understanding.'

'He wouldn't know how to stand up to a woman like you.'

She laughed. 'I wasn't that rough.'

'Hope you messed him up just a little bit?'

Was he flirting with her? She was almost relieved. She'd had misgivings about the guitar, knew she'd been heavy-handed that morning. But he just wanted to be adored. It wasn't so much to ask, and maybe the easiest way to get what she needed.

'He'll walk again don't worry.'

She could hear him smiling. 'Mia, thank you.'

'Have you given it a test drive?'

'Are you kidding.'

'I hope it'll see you through the next stage of your

career.'

'That sounds like goodbye.'

'Think of it as my investment in your future.'

He thought this over. 'They call it a dreadnought, but that tells you nothing about its colour and range. It's stunning.'

'I look forward to hearing it.'

'There's another song.'

'Already, goodness.' She swallowed involuntarily, hoped he wouldn't hear it.

'Are we ok with the artists?'

'Yes, all fixed. I'd like to discuss who's up for the next session, d'you have time?'

The water stopped sloshing in the background. 'Sure. It might be easiest if I showed you some clips though.'

'It might.'

'You should come to mine?'

She started, hearing the possessive pronoun. His unconscious appropriation of what she'd given him. Sacrifice accepted then. One step deeper into the mire.

'I'll be starting the edit tomorrow.'

'You could do it here.'

'Let me get underway, then we'll see.'

'Come round now. I've got a pretty hot longlist.'

Stephen was just wrapping up for the day as she sprang downstairs, dressed to go out. She'd hoped to dash while he was still distracted and be back before he'd had more than his pre-supper whisky soda and half the bottle of red, but instead they came face to face in the stained-glass glow of the upper hallway, leaving her feeling caught out.

'Off again, darling?'

She hugged him warmly. 'Not for too long, just a quick planning meeting.'

He looked, for the first time she could remember since his mother died, sad. Did he sense her growing economy with the truth?

'Thought I'd be able to look after you a little bit, this evening.'

Mia knew what that meant but said nothing, just leaned into him a little and kissed his cheek. As she drew back, he eyed her, not quite approvingly.

'You're throwing yourself so hard into this project, look at you, you look about fourteen!'

Jailbait. He meant she was losing weight. She knew it. She knew the fire inside was eating her away. She knew her eyes burned brighter in their sockets. She knew her skin looked different. She knew all of this and her better half wanted to be saved, healed, made whole, yet she had no power to change course. She was bound for collision and she knew it would be bloody when it came. She had not guile enough to keep her feelings secret the way some did.

She remembered a Canadian colleague, a co-producer they'd worked with years ago who'd come into the office one day declaring that he was unable to work that week as he had to find a new apartment. He'd just filed for divorce. His wife, an air-hostess and the mother of their three-year-old son, had apparently been running a separate household in France with two older children and another husband who may or may not have been the father of his own. What stunned him was how she had run a double life for ten years and he had known nothing, absolutely *nothing* about it until the previous day when she'd unaccountably broken the news. How was it she had managed to deceive him so magnificently? He wanted to kill himself. But before that he wanted to kill her. He dreamt up extravagantly creative ways to bring about her demise in the hour they spent together in a downtown bar in Calgary before sending him on his way and setting about finding a new partner for the project. Nobody dared mention the three-year-old who had apparently been taken by his mother on the next flight to Paris, where he would be safe with her other man, should anything happen to her.

Stephen and Mia had both marvelled at the deception. How long had Stephen been able to keep his love quiet from Kate? Three months? Four? How long had it taken Mia to leave Ben, her boyfriend at the time? She'd cut loose even before Stephen had asked her. Utterly smitten, even five years into their relationship, with their own three-year-old, it was hard to imagine such a deadpan performance. Hard to imagine the physical deception. How was it that partners didn't intuit the shift in hormone activity, didn't detect the rise in adrenaline? Was fidelity so self-evident? Was trust so blind?

'I'll be back in time to eat with you, there's fresh pasta and some spinach in the fridge, we can knock up something together later.'

He waved her out of the door, trying to be good, giving her space. 'If I'm not too pissed by then.' His eye fell on the hall table scribble pad. 'Someone called for you earlier by the way, said he'd try again. Did he reach you on your mobile?'

With a sick start, Mia realised the cycle of deception was already in motion. She shrugged, she wasn't sure who it could have been, maybe the Comm

Ed, she'd check with them in the morning. It was a lie and she knew it. She wasn't sure if Stephen guessed. She could paper over the cracks but the truth was going to start leaking out, little by little, until the stream of half-truths became a deluge. Unless she stopped it.

'You called my home number!'

She had practically beaten down the door in her urgency to say this to the perpetrator, having driven well above the speed limit from Holland Park to Shepherd's Bush with a recklessness that shocked her.

'I just used the last number you'd called from.'

She was incandescent, there was a force-field at arm's length around her that would have thrown him across the room if he'd made contact.

'You didn't check?!'

'I'm sorry.'

It had clearly been an innocent mistake, so what was she doing? She was balled up like a child about to throw a tantrum. They eyed each other across the three foot space separating them, on the edge of hostility.

'I've put myself on the line to help you. I'm crossing the line now, you know that.'

She wasn't entirely making sense. He darted in while her guard was down, enclosing her in the sudden warmth of his arms. She breathed the scent of him, stunned into acquiescence, drifting on the floodtide between two lives, but it was not surrender she felt, just the momentary quelling of fear.

He sat her down on the sofa and gave her tea laden with sugar, there being, as usual, no milk. She sipped, and they contemplated each other for a while.

Finally he broke their silence.

'I don't want to get in the way of your marriage, Mia. Maybe we should wrap this up and leave it at that. You've been more than good to me. You've rescued me from the street, healed me, given me a roof over my head, you've given me a chance, paid me.'

Mia fought tears of burning humiliation.

'Maybe the guitar's too much? I should let you have it back. It's hardly been played, you'll be able to get a refund.'

That was impossible, as surely he knew. Inadmissible, it had to be about the work.

'I've never failed to deliver what I promised. We have a project to complete.'

She opened her bag and searched for a moment before handing him a key. 'This is yours. I shouldn't have kept it, that was inappropriate.'

His fingers brushed hers in acceptance. A resigning of space. She didn't own him.

'I'll continue to pay the rent until delivery of the pilot. If there's a series commissioned, you should be able to take over the lease from me with your salary, or to find something else if you prefer.'

'You know I'm not going to hold you to that.'

'Let's continue as planned for now, shall we?'

She struggled hard to keep her composure and he at least had the discretion to look the other way and set up the playlist for her. She pulled up a chair and sat by him, feeling a million miles distant from the task ahead.

'All of these people are available on the 7th. This is a friend of mine who's being considered by a couple of big labels at the moment. She's written songs for bigger artists, not big herself just yet…'

Mia watched the bubbly-haired blonde with her irresistible sunshine smile and nodded absently. 'Yes, she'll be great.'

A succession of artists followed which she had trouble distinguishing from each other and consigned to the reserve list, then a black singer with a gorgeous alto voice, accompanying herself on an ancient, wheezing organ, which Mia somehow found unbearably touching. The song made her cry a little. Tom put his arm around her fleetingly. 'Always gets me, that one.'

Mia nodded, faintly aware her mood had thawed, cueing up the next artist, a cabaret girl with a zither. She was a maybe, but not if Cleopatra was in the show. That was still a conversation for which she had to steel herself. Then there was a rock chick with a blue electric guitar who played onstage barefoot. There was Tigerlily, who apparently was always available. There was an acoustic group featuring banjos and double-basses, good-time Mumford derivatives. There was a Nordic a cappella group and a cellist-singer with a virtuoso harmonica player. There seemed no end to the new folk revolution. After the twentieth act, Mia felt her eyelids weighing heavy.

'I think we can fix our shortlist, here's mine,' she passed him her scrap of paper, 'Are there many more?'

'I've put our best foot forward. You can share a beer with me now if you like.'

It was expressed so matter-of-factly, almost proprietorially, that she accepted. The cold lager slipped down her parched throat, reviving and relaxing her in a single draught.

'You work hard at not earning a living, don't you?'

'It's a disability I've learned to cope with.'

'D'you think you'll be ok? Long term, I mean.'

'I think I'm almost grown-up enough to answer the question.'

'Just not tonight?'

'Tonight, I'm enjoying some quiet time with you.'

As she met his eye, she realised with a jolt how far she had become the object of his admiration. It was completely clear, as if it were written in phosphorescent paint on the floor between them. Neither would cross that invisible boundary into speech or action, but at that moment, his gaze told her all she needed. He knew she was giving up something precious to him, which he had no right to possess.

He lifted his guitar, tuned and stroked the strings. 'Want to hear?'

She nodded, looking away.

> *Draw down the blind*
> *Push away the day*
> *There's a woman straying through your mind*
> *And she just wants to play*
> *Oh you play*
> *How you play*
> *But the dark side*
> *Of this wild blue planet*
> *Ain't gonna turn your way*
>
> *You took the gift*
> *Tuned it to your heart*
> *There's a woman dancing on your floor*

And she just wants to play
Oh you play
How you play
But the dark side
Of this wild blue planet
Ain't gonna turn your way

As the music washed through her, she felt herself filling with light. It was for her, of course, just as the other had been. He played the song passionately, with a directness and devotion that she'd missed in public, the richness of the guitar sound that making him sound, finally, like the star she wanted him to be. His voice subsided almost to a whisper with the final chorus, letting the closing chords die away. He turned his dark green eyes on her with a look that made her shiver.

It was past nine. She could not stay with any decency and keep her promise to Stephen. 'I have to go. He's expecting me.'

There was a flicker of irony in his response. 'I should make a move as well.'

'Somewhere nice?'

'Drink with the neighbours. Not sure whether to expect Ann Summers or American Psycho.'

She laughed. 'I take it you're newly acquainted.'

'Barely acquainted in fact.'

She felt she must tell him now, or lose her courage. 'Tom. I've agreed to consider one of Brand's clients in return for his getting off your back and leaving us free editorial rein.'

'Which client.'

'I think you know who I mean.'

The chill between them was immediate and

palpable. 'If it's Cleopatra, then the answer's no. You'll have to take the scalpel to my sections tomorrow and I'll pay you back as and when I can. No, Mia.'

He was already receding, opting out, running from her. He yanked on his jacket savagely, mouth drawn into a pout.

'I haven't made up my mind. It might stretch things too far stylistically and I'm not sure she represents the kind of indie music we're exploring.'

'You're damn right.'

'Try to see it more neutrally, Dickon will keep his hands off everything we've done to date, that's progress. We've agreed a possible way forward.'

'It's a raid, don't trust him.'

'I might decide she isn't right for the show, but I need to take her seriously and record some footage first.'

'He'll be all over the thing. You don't know him.'

Outside, footsteps clattered softly down the steps. The doorbell rang.

'I'll leave you to your evening, Tom.' Turning to don her jacket, she missed the baleful look, the sudden pallor. 'I don't think you need overreact – you're the main draw, it's not about her.'

'Mia…' He would have stopped her, but she'd already opened the door.

Her daughter stood on the doorstep, part shivering against the cold, part with the anticipation of what was to come.

'Lottie?'

'Mum, are you sure you should be here.' She was into the room and flinging herself moodily onto the sofa before either could react.

Mia was so unprepared, she struggled at first to put the pieces together. Her current state of understanding was that Lottie had moved in with her half-sister in Tufnell Park. Mia had last seen her in Shoreditch, the other end of town from the family home. And of all the flats in west London she should turn up at the one Mia had illicitly rented for the one person who might count as an object of desire, the single apparent transgression of her twenty year marriage? She felt faint with the overwhelming sense of having been exposed by the person she loved most in the world. She'd been violated, spied upon, confounded. How had Lottie discovered him? Why was she even on speaking terms with him?

'I had no idea you knew each other.'

Her words tumbled like cripples into the room which had become as airless as a vacuum. Lottie eyed her, poker-faced, a hint of mischief. 'You could call us intimate strangers.' She glanced at Tom, who said nothing, though his eyes were burning. 'You were late, I thought I'd come and get you.'

'I thought it was an invitation not an order.'

There was violence in the room, a bizarre complicity Mia didn't understand, but she knew these two children could do damage, whether to each other or to her, she didn't wish to discover.

'I'm very glad you've met up, anyway. You're not at Hattie's?'

'It's a big city, I have my stop-offs.'

'Well, I'm sure that's wise.'

'My collaborators live in the next street. Funny, isn't it?'

Mia pictured them ranked on dining chairs plotting the overthrow of the monarchy; the destruction of the parliamentary system; the end of the civilised world.

'Your artist friends?'

'Artful dodgers!' She laughed prettily, but it made no impression on Tom, in whom the storm clouds were gathering. 'We're planning the next step in our bid for world domination.'

'Sounds ambitious, darling.'

'We're exploring music and space. I'm hoping to have a first conversation with our handsome wandering minstrel tonight.'

'You haven't asked me.' He was clearly livid, feeling invaded.

'Don't you think it would be cool?'

'I think you should show your mother some respect. And I think you should ask her if I'm available.'

Lottie frowned. She'd rallied well but he'd hit harder. Mia declined to get dragged into the crossfire. 'Why don't you explore the options, see how you both feel?'

It was an odd moment. If he'd been expecting her to assert prior claim over him then he'd be sadly disappointed. He glanced at her as if she'd cut him loose and sent him veering toward the rocks, while her daughter looked on, serene but inscrutable, combing her Lorelei locks. And now she was going to have to leave them together, despite his discomfort, despite her own confusion.

'I'll be in touch once we've got the edit underway, Tom. Have a good evening.' She blew a kiss and closed the door on them seated at opposite ends of the room, a study in communication breakdown. A tableau of alienation. A paradigm of lovers in separate spaces.

And could they be lovers? Impossible to fathom. Though she loved Lottie deeply, her daughter was beyond her control or her understanding, more beautiful and more androgynous each time they met. Her life had become as freewheeling as her poetry, all flux and flow, driven by soul-searing instincts, not unerring and certainly not unmanipulative.

Though she thought she'd dealt with the last ten minutes with equanimity, fear overtook her as she unlocked the car. Heart pounding, she got into the driver's seat and tried to calm her thoughts, reluctant to drive until she had made some sense of the situation.

Lottie's furious response to the interloper that first night, violent enough to precipitate her leaving home, now seemed as much to do with the girl's own unadmitted feelings as Mia's apparent misplaced desire. The atavism of the younger female carving out her rights to the virile flesh of the house. Biology drawing a red mist down over the visionary polemic of this most artful young female, who thought she was free to choose how and who to love. How maddening that one's body betrayed one in the end. A jumble of hormones and neurotransmitters conspiring to mess with one's freewill.

Lottie's current public version of herself made her the lover of a girl, an audacious piece of self-branding with which Mia continued to struggle, a relationship that seemed increasingly about surfaces, a fashionable partnering that had everything to do with sexual spontaneity and much less to do with love, let alone commitment. Was it hopelessly romantic, even old fashioned to expect that for her daughter? It clearly wasn't an exclusive relationship, this walking-out and sleeping-in with Dalila. What about her co-artist Roland? The intimacy between them murmured like the secret language of an underground stream, yet she wore the young man's adoration so carelessly, spinning him a thread of silk that bound him into the web at her command, along with all the others. For all Mia knew, Roland had a male lover with whom he traced the fires of the night. The entire erotic sweep of Lottie's social group was fluid, embracing ambiguity and multiplicity. She might be in love with any, or all of them. Did that give her the right to punish Tom for his audacity, heaving him in playful vengeance over the threshold of the sexually omnivorous world she inhabited?

In the end, all that mattered was that she knew her mother was spending time with him. Whether professionally or personally signified little. If Lottie chose to drop a casual comment – and it was hard to believe that she had no ulterior motive – then what would become of her marriage? What had become of it anyway, that she kept this box-within-a-box locked close, out of sight? Nothing had happened, and yet everything had happened: her emotions had been magnetised by this potential lover, forever pointing false. That is what he would remain to the end of time, more potent and more dangerous than any heady six-week fling locked away after use with the key flung into the lake. She had done nothing, yet how did she answer the pulsing of her blood? How did she assuage the images that came to her at night, waking, sleeping, conscious, unconscious? No logic could make it less than a betrayal. And once this betrayal was revealed, a worse was hiding in the wings ready for the jump scare, ready to pounce on the dying corpse of her relationship and rend the flesh from the bones.

Why do we learn to lie? Mia had stumbled across a radio documentary about the anatomy of untruth in European culture some years before and had been strangely haunted to realise that we lie from our earliest years. We interpret likely consequences and we adjust our versions at our own convenience. We lie to save our friends from trouble, our parents from hurt, to obscure our desires, to obtain rewards. We distinguish readily between good lies and bad lies. Between small and big. We learn to lie from the adults who should teach us never to lie. *I'm telling you this for your own good. I love you just the way you are. I never meant to hurt you. I will love you forever.*

Stephen looked up from his second bottle of Bardolino as she came downstairs into the basement. The ten o'clock news flickered unsettlingly across his face in a room that was otherwise in darkness. Inexpressibly weary, she sat by him, resting her head on his shoulder.

'Did you eat already?' She knew the answer already. The kitchen was undisturbed.

'No.'

His voice was faint, husky. He buried his face in her hair and breathed the cold night scent of her. She tried to tame her sense of foreboding. Her voice sounded too bright, brittle even, culpability streaming from her like static.

'Shall we fix something now? It's not too late.'

His response was delayed, like a bad piece of lip synch, the look came long before the words could.

'Honestly, I think I'm a bit past it.'

Mia retrieved a glass from the cupboard before kicking off her shoes and rejoining him. 'May I catch up with you a little, before we decide?'

He encircled her neck and drew her softly to him, planting a kiss on her forehead, oddly chaste. 'Always so elegant with your words, dear heart.'

Dear heart how like you this. Anne Boleyn lets the silk fall loosely from her shoulders and surrenders to her lover Thomas Wyatt her beauty in all its blinding delicacy. *Noli me tangere for Caesar's I am.* Most unfortunate of poets, to love the woman who had become the King's property.

12.

There's a kind of silence that's corrosive. The kind lovers fall into when things go wrong. The kind that forms acid in your gut and makes you want to damage things. The kind that happens when two people in the same room are furious about the same thing from completely different perspectives.

This girl didn't even respect the silence, she was leaping to the offensive before I could ask her to leave, taking me apart in the friendliest possible way, complete with the beautiful smile. 'It's pointless showing me the door. I should be showing it to you my *dear.*'

'Meaning what, exactly?'

'Meaning you are a kept man, here in your little bolt hole.'

My fingers longed to slap that perfect pale skin, but I kept it reigned in.

'You are full of it, aren't you.'

'And you're not? *Ask your mother if I'm available?* Very cute.'

'She's my employer! It's her service flat!'

'And what kind of services do you perform here?'

We were standing face to face like cats braced to fight, arched with antagonism. Her face flushed, her hand sprang forward and for one moment I thought she was going to take her nails to my face, but instead she grabbed my hair and pulled my face to hers, her mouth hard on mine. 'This?' She pulled my hand between her legs. 'This?'

There was no choice but to fight it out. Five minutes later we were re-arranging our clothes and trying to normalise the situation in the room.

'Isn't this a bit sick?'

Her face was suffused, softened by orgasm, her eyes darker than ever in the low light, but she could still pull that smile on me. 'Just testing.'

It's hard to feel truly angry with a brain drenched in oxytocin, but I was getting faster on the recovery. 'Testing *what*?!'

'I don't think you'd have reacted that way if you'd just been doing it with her.'

'Bloody hell!' It was like trying to stand up straight at midnight during a total eclipse of the moon on a lake covered in black ice.

She kissed my neck, apologetically. 'Have you ever?'

'What.'

'Slept with her?'

I pushed her away, starting to sweat with the effort of keeping her at bay.

'I don't think it would be very gallant of me to

answer on her behalf.'

She twinkled with merriment. 'That means yes?'

'No! Fuck. It means no.'

'But you'd like to?'

'Don't judge her by your standards, you have nothing in common that way.'

I sounded like a frosty old maid, but I couldn't help the way it came out. Mia was a complex woman with a subtly developed moral sense, and this mooncalf of hers was the most amoral person I had ever met.

'Don't be so cross. I'm just curious.'

'No, you're just destructive. Do you want to hurt her?'

'Of course not, she's my mum. I'd never hurt her. But I think she's getting in deeper than she means to. Deeper than she should. I can tell that and so can you.'

'Maybe it's a journey she needs to go on.'

'Then again, maybe she's travelled far enough. She's a company boss not some rookie promo director.'

'I'm aware of that.'

'She's not short of offers.'

'I'm aware of that too.'

'She's a prize-winning producer.'

Better and better. I had to face up to the fact that I'd not done all the homework on her that I might have. Due diligence wasn't my style. I'd been too used to the world coming to me, in dribs and drabs and deluges. Going with the flow. A drifter on life's tide. Open to the wide, wide sky that was bred into me, all that time kicking my heels and dreaming in the eastern flatlands. Living in the moment: I always had time to spend. Sometimes it was worthwhile, sometimes not. I couldn't help my own curiosity, that was the source of my creative power, to feed off what I found, where I found it. Was that my slack upbringing? Too much rope to hang myself with? Maybe I was, after all, pathologically lazy. So many people had told me I was beautiful, or shown me as much, that I believed it. Even when I'd tried to erase that beauty, it had resurfaced as soon as there was a new reflector. It was my fatal flaw: assuming life would give me an easy ride. I'd been hoodwinked by the fallacy that a fair face is a mirror of a fair soul. Now, I sensed the accusation of this young maverick that I was a vain and idle underachiever, riding on the backs of others' hard graft and superior ability.

'Besides, she's forty-six years old. Your own mum's age, come on.'

'That comment is beneath you.'

'You just don't like me telling it how it is.'

'Insufferable little witch.'

She kissed me again, this time I wriggled from her succubus clutches.

'I'm just trying to put things in perspective for you.' She pushed back her hair and tidied herself perfunctorily. 'If I ask nicely, will you bring your new guitar?'

She was giving me goosebumps, and not in a good way.

I decided to go with her in a spirit of damage limitation. Once we'd freshened ourselves up in the bathroom, no one would ever have known the combustible history of the past half hour. I drew the red curtains and left the lights on. We quit the flat together apparently the best of friends, except there was this unease grumbling away in my gut that told me I was moving onto the wrong side of the argument.

We walked a couple of blocks through the calm rumble of the traffic and the crisp night air, through the labyrinth of backstreets between Uxbridge and Goldhawk Road. The shared house looked a cut above the neighbouring peeling paintwork and rusty railings, nestled behind its screen of bamboo and winter flowering shrubs. The paintwork was fresh and clean, they were a bunch of painters after all. The large front bay window was creatively draped in something billowing and faintly shiny like a space-age party dress. A large black metal sculpture adorned the gravelled front patch. Charlotte tapped lightly on the window and the door was swung open by an angular flatmate in beatnik black. A swirl of abstract music and cannabis smoke gently followed her.

'You've been ages! Were you mugged?'

'Not that I noticed.'

'We were about to come looking.'

'Lucky you didn't,' she glanced at me, 'we'd have missed each other for sure.'

She peeled off her mess of wool and slung it onto the hall bench along with a pile of assorted outer garments, revealing the skimpy dress beneath. 'This is Amalia, Tom. She does abstract expressionism.'

'Hi.' She extended a horny, painter's hand, dark nailed with months of impossible to remove pigment. I must have been looking mean, the small talk dried on her lips and she was soon whispering behind her artisan's fingers to Charlotte as I preceded them into the main room. I heard the words 'He's cool, sweetie,' before losing them in the general hubbub.

It wasn't quite a party. More a happening. I thought of Andy Warhol, Lou Reed, Nico, The Factory in New York. Was it possible I'd been invited to a Velvet Underground theme night, only they'd forgotten to tell me? The music was ambient, minimal, the bass more a subsonic pressure in the chest than actual sound. Textured organ patterns repeated according to a random number generator which a bushy, bespectacled guy controlled from his laptop, plugged through half-a-dozen small speakers slung around the room. From the ceiling were festooned pieces of contorted metal which I had to duck my gangling frame under in order to avoid losing an eye. I went over for a snoop at the sound desk and introduced myself. He was Dirk, he was Dutch, he'd done the sound for Charlotte's installation. He was a cool guy, clearly more interested in waveforms than people. I left him in search of a corkscrew.

In my hand the bottle of red I'd picked up en route was becoming nicely mulled. It had seemed more couth to arrive at an artist's house with wine than toting a pack of beers. People were drinking beer, but it was arty beer in coloured bottles with names like Rembrandt and Durer. Someone was drinking homebrew out of a glass jar. Someone else was drinking what looked like absinthe out of a chemist's flask and not long for this day. Or maybe we weren't, depending on whether the kitchen knives were locked away. My earlier thoughts of Patrick Bateman resurfaced fleetingly. The young man with the green drink was almost albino. White blonde hair. White eyelashes, white eyebrows. Skin that hardly covered the skull beneath. Eyes not red like the laboratory rat but transparent.

'Are you an artist?' I asked him.

'I do image manipulation.'

'Photographic?'

'Kind of. I'm into disintegrating realities.' He was clearly serious about his research, his eyes seemingly focused in different directions. Following the right eye, I saw he was in fact watching a black and white film projected on a nearby wall, all fractured image and digital noise, admired and discussed by various members of the household, amongst them my hostess. Beyond them was the rear window, looking out over the ranked gardens of the houses in the neighbourhood. As I stepped forward I could clearly see that red flash of curtain down there in the gloom. *My flat.* I'd stepped into the spymaster's den it seemed.

'Tom?' she slipped her hand through my free arm. 'Let's get this open, shall we?' I turned from my acquaintance and headed for the kitchen, narrowly missing a low-flying object in the doorway, still wondering how I'd managed to let myself be persuaded. 'I don't know about you,' she said lightly, with that mischievous curl of the mouth that short-circuited all my good resolutions, 'but I've got the munchies.'

A broody girl with a shock of black hair and glittering eyes, who looked as if she'd take a taser to anyone who got too close, was at the kitchen bar doing intricate things with a vegetable knife. Before her, trays nested countless exquisitely filled dishes containing chutneys, salads, relishes, raitas, puris, bhajis, as many shades of dhal as there were guests, complete with folded spirals of chapatti. It was, to my mind, the finest work of art in the house. I looked at her in respect. 'Did you make all this?'

She nodded, not friendly. 'Cissi doesn't cook.' A glance at her companion, busy hunting for the corkscrew, told me there was evasion going on, that Charlotte was even a little uncomfortable. The girl reached out and took the bottle from her. 'It's a screw top, lover.'

She poured for us generously, slipping an arm around Charlotte's waist and letting it move softly to her velvet-encased hip, where I swear I'd left the fingerprints of my earlier misdemeanour crushed into that fabric. Clearly, they were an item. I was definitely an add-on. I wasn't even introduced. I hung around to see if I could make anything of it, but they scarcely exchanged a word with each other that wasn't about the food. I preferred the girl that violated me in my own home. This one seemed under a shadow. Third-wheeling was never my scene, I was too vain, too hungry, so I was glad when a nice-looking guy with a touch of Heathcliff about him joined the company. 'Shall I take those for you, Dal?'

'Yeah, thanks.'

They left in convoy, like the catering team, leaving us stranded. I still wasn't getting it. 'Really?'

'What?'

'Is she your lover?'

She blushed. Finally lost her *sang froid* and her Hepburn smile. 'Why do you want to know?'

'I'm curious about why you're harrassing me for sex every other day when you have a perfectly workable model here at home.'

She actually looked shocked. 'Are you jealous?'

'No. Just confused.'

'Would it confuse you if I said we were platonic lovers?'

'It doesn't look platonic.'

A flustered look passed across her face. I half-wanted to unsay what I'd just thrown at her but it was too late, I was going to get the full confession. Half of it anyway.

'Dalila had a shitty childhood. She was raped by a couple of cousins when she was just a kid. Her family blamed her. She left home at fourteen and earned money from sex. She's been in prison for drug dealing. She was lucky: she found a mentor, a volunteer who pretty much adopted her and got her head sorted out, helped her find a home when she was released. My parents 'discovered' her whilst trawling the west London estates looking for enough trouble to make into a documentary. There was this girl gang completely under her control, she didn't need to threaten anyone, she just had something. Charisma, maybe, intelligence. All those girls were completely obsessed with her, they'd do anything for her. They loved her. She protected them from the men.'

'What about you?'

'She's my muse.'

Seeing my doubtful look she searched for reasons I might understand. 'She became it, anyway. I was on location for a lot of the shoot, mum's intern carrying coffee for the cameraman, filling in the camera sheets, all that. It began as a kind of project, I'd sketch her after hours, while the crew was packing up. I'd never met anyone like her.'

'Bit different from your middle-class upbringing.'

That hit a nerve, but she pushed further outside

her comfort zone. 'Class is dead. The only things that matter now are knowledge and money.'

'Exactly. You have both.'

'It's a choice to live on the outside. To find diamonds in the dirt. It's what all artists have to do.'

Of course, it helped to know that your parental bank account might be there to bale you out if the going got really tough. I'd burnt my bridges long ago on that score, and the coffers had always been pretty empty except when the monthly benefit payment came in.

'Come on, you're doing it to punish your mother.'

'Meaning what!'

'Doing the thing you know will piss her off the most. We've all been there, you'll grow out of it.'

'Why should I punish her?'

'For loving me.'

'It's completely unconnected.'

'You've taken on a whole lot of psychic trauma just to prove your independence and it's fucking with your head and starting to mess up everyone else's.'

'You're wrong! I love her. Everyone loves her, you're just not looking the right way.'

'I'm getting no vibe, nothing tells me she flicks your switch, nothing.'

'Why should you care? If you can't see she's special, why should I break myself convincing you? She's starring in another film next month. In the meantime, I share her bed and have the pleasure of breathing the scent of her body and telling her stories through the night.'

'You're moving on.'

'Just like you?'

Something odd happened to the room at that

point. The atoms seemed to change and regroup as if someone had cast a dark little spell. It wasn't just that I'd been breathing the thick, sweet atmosphere of other people's joints for the past hour. It wasn't the accumulating effect of the subsonic bass, which seemed to have taken over my heartbeat and cancelled it out, like destructive wave interference. It wasn't even the energetic prelude to the evening and the lack of food. In my giddy brain I had the overwhelming sense that the meaning of the party had changed and thickened. Like some high priestess, Charlotte was already receding into the dim light of the hall among the crush of bodies. 'Hello, darling,' came her voice from what seemed the end of a long tunnel. Kisses were exchanged. From the density of the group, a woman I knew detached herself and came forward towards me into the light.

'Tom.'

Nothing had prepared me to meet her here. Nothing had prepared me for the way I found her. All those images in my mind that I'd spent months cutting to ribbons, feeding through my mental shredder, overlaying with images of new friends and contacts, new women, as many women as possible, as different from her as possible; all that time I'd tried to overwrite the disc, to forget that we were ever anything to each other; all that time I thought I'd succeeding in moving on out into the big city where it was possible to lose someone, and yet I'd moved nowhere. We were standing face-to-face at someone's party. It was an arty party, sure, she was an arty popstress putting herself about, there was always going to be a microchance she might turn up in the same room. In the event of such a coincidence I'd always planned simply to make for the door, slip out quietly with the minimum fuss. That was based on the assumption that she matched the residual images in my mind which were, despite everything, still there.

But she wasn't the same woman. It was as if she'd come in disguise, as if someone had devised a plan for her to slip under my radar, looking like someone else, or perhaps someone new. Not that she'd altered anything tangible about her appearance, her hair still curled to her shoulders and around her cheek; her eyes were still the colour of jade; her lips curled into the same smile; she had the same willowy figure, the same grace. But she had softened around the edges. She had lost that quicksilver, lightning punch, that dangerous spike. She flowed like a sleek, dark river in full flood, in a soft dress that clung to her curves. Her pregnancy was clear for all to see.

'You're looking well.' I had no idea where to begin, no clue what I was saying. The blood drained from my head. I felt distant, faint. I felt as if I was standing on the surface of the moon.

'You too. Heard about your TV break, well done, it sounds brilliant.'

'And you? Who should I congratulate?' I couldn't quite keep the edge of bitterness out of my voice. Karl Fleet? Tarzan?

'You can wish us well. I decided to keep it.'

That was clear enough, but who was *us*, her and the baby? Her and the unknown father? Suddenly nothing mattered very much. She was as much a foreign land to me as she'd ever been.

'I wish I understood you.'

'It was just the timing. It took a lot of thinking about. I guess I finally worked out what was important to me and in what order.'

I had no words. My mouth was dry, the taste of wormwood bitter.

She took my hand. I flinched but didn't snatch it away. 'Here…' She placed my palm against the swell of her belly and my brain did a somersault more violent than the elusive convulsion inside her. Was this what you did if you were expecting someone else's child? Suddenly I was shaking like a leaf, seeking confirmation in her eyes.

'She's yours.'

'She?'

'I lied about the clinic. None of that happened.'

'You *lied*?'

How was I to believe a word she said? Sure, there were ways of verifying what she said but how was I to trust her now? She'd kept this treasure locked away from me. She'd deliberately kept me as much in the dark as the foetus that we both touched, for reasons only she knew. I wanted to snatch my hand away but she held it against her body so that I'd have to fight her for it, and who could fight against this life inside her? Creation burned my hand like a fever, my hand touching her, touching the unborn child, my fingertips triangulating the extent of the known world. Then doubt choked me and sent me flying for the surface gasping, not yet a drowned man.

'You're still lying. I don't know what you want, Cleo, but I'm not there to be a substitute for Karl Fleet. Get him to be a man for you.'

'It's nothing to do with him.'

'I left you as good as unbuttoning his fly, that was all nothing, I imagined it?'

'He took me out to dinner to discuss the album

and told me how we were going to change the world. He signed me that night.'

'It's what you were always good at, selling people what they wanted.'

'It's the truth.'

I felt the cavern opening up its mouth to swallow me whole. 'Then *why* did you let me believe our child was dead? How could you do it?'

'I thought… I didn't want this to be the only thing holding us together.'

'You knew you were still pregnant that night and you said nothing to stop me leaving.'

'I would have lost the record deal.'

She might have looked softer, but she was steel at the core. The extent to which she could control her emotions frightened me. I did, finally, wrench myself away. I wanted to weep for her, for her damaged heart, but my own felt like a desert and no tears came.

Slowly, very softly, she took my hand again. 'I heard you'd been living on the streets.'

'Does it matter?'

'Yes.' It mattered to her that she'd caused me pain, I could see it in her look. Never usually lost for them, somehow neither of us could find the words. There was so much, and so little still to say. 'You disappeared, I couldn't reach you.'

'That was the idea.'

'Were you scared?'

The heat flowed from her belly into my hand, my body, my brain, like balm loosening my tongue so I could let it all go, all those sensations, terrors, the hallucinogenic poetry of my eighty-nine days on the street. Finally, she had to know what she'd done.

'Once or twice. Mainly it was just mind-numbing.

A total blank. Wave upon wave of headlights, footsteps, voices, incessant noise, everything in motion. What you never realise about a city is how much noise there is until you can't escape from it. After a few days your head's on fire with all the sound. You're staggering with fatigue until you learn to blank out. In the end you can sleep anywhere.'

I could see her eyes widening with the impact of what she'd done.

'The worst thing's the cold. Being cold to the bone. No amount of clothing is ever enough. You get crazy with it, you do anything to be a bit nearer to that shop door, that air vent, that coffee cup, you spend all your time trying not to be visible in stations, lobbies, supermarkets. It becomes a complete obsession during the day so that you can get through the night. I was on fire for the first week or two before I noticed. Anger is pure, but it doesn't last. After it left me, I didn't care about anything. I wanted to die.'

'But you had your music?'

'Sure. I played enough to make anyone sick of the sound of me. When my fingers weren't bleeding.'

She turned my hand in hers, contemplating, looking for scars maybe. 'And now you're here.'

'I got lucky. Someone liked my playing.'

'Is that who you were with at the club?'

'You were *there*?'

'With Dickon. I thought you might prefer to avoid him. You looked great, everything seemed to be going so well.'

'She's married.'

She bit her lip, maybe in chagrin, maybe in relief, who could tell.

'How is this all supposed to work, Cleo?'

'I'm going on tour next week for three months, launching the album. I've been in studio for the last three.'

'Just time to paint the nursery when you get back? Seriously, I've fucked with your future, you've fucked with my heart, it doesn't feel like a great way to get back together.'

'Come on tour with me.'

It was out of her mouth before she could stop it. Now she'd found me again, she wanted to keep me in the frame. I could also see this would trample my survival campaign into the dust. 'I'm sure Tarzan's already got your support booked. He's not going to let me anywhere near your gigs, you know that.'

'You could come along for the ride?' It was the assumption that I'd drop everything just to be hanging on her coat tails. Waiting for her in the dressing room, chatting to her fans in the bar.

'I don't think so. I've got a career to salvage. Three months out and you lose all your momentum.'

She bent her wistful look on me, but it was a fleeting moment, she wasn't making any assumptions. 'I've got an amazing touring team, don't worry. Lots of friends. And my family has been great.'

So that was all right then. Except nothing was all right. She'd opened up the can of worms and they were writhing. There was our private life splashed all over someone else's carpet.

Our tête-à-tête was abridged by Charlotte's arrival with another platter of thali.

'If music be the food of love, then let's hear it.' She offered us the tray, from which Cleo delicately plucked sustenance and glanced at me.

'This girl! I love her…' The girls kissed decorously but suggestively. 'She's *so* creative.'

'A bit too creative for my liking.'

'She moves like a fairytale.'

'Stings like a bee.'

Charlotte extricated herself from Cleo's fond embrace and headed for the adjoining room. 'Time for cabaret my sweetings?'

Something in the arch of her eyebrow as she turned from us, her lightness of step, had the whiff of setup. I watched her go, caught Cleo by the arm as she went to follow. 'How well d'you know each other?'

She threw me a glance, not altogether happy with the question. 'Friends of friends.'

'Since long?'

Her Mona Lisa smile told me she wasn't going to let herself be drawn easily. Girlfriend loyalty runs deeper than lovers' and her history with Charlotte clearly went back long enough for her to have something to defend.

'Long enough to know her family?'

'Cissi's a very private person.'

'Except when she's very public.'

'I've never met her family.'

'But you know I'm working for her mother.'

'No, she never told me.' I thought I caught a trace of that catlike glint I'd come to mistrust.

We rejoined the party, which appeared to have re-dressed itself as another party. We were still in the sixties it seemed, but the place had morphed into an action painting studio. Stripped to the waist, Heathcliff was now sticking sheets of white paper to the wooden floor, while Dalila and Amalia moved the furniture out of the firing line and a girl with an Indian flute cooed softly from one of the sofas. Charlotte was wriggling out of her dress on the sidelines. Nobody seemed surprised when Heathcliff started to apply paint the colour of red ochre to her sheer bodysuit. Joints were rolled, glasses recharged, talk deepened. When she'd been soaked from head to foot she began to dance to the hooting, unearthly sounds, moving in her drenched state around the paper arena, trailing red paint like blood as she went, looking like the miscarriage every mother feared. She looked like a piece of raw flesh ripped from the demon's womb. She was homunculus, monster, war victim, axe-murderer. Her body arched, leapt. Paint sprayed and dripped from her clothing onto the paper. Her feet smeared it into crazed patterns.

If Cleo was discomforted by the scene, she betrayed nothing. It was over in a few minutes. Charlotte made art the way she made love, with total abandon and reckless speed. When she was done, applause peppered the air for a moment, then the group clustered around Dalila who had filmed the sequence on someone's camera. They were a fine bunch of art school posers but it was hard not to get swept up in it. Gales of laughter wracked the group. They were as pleased as a bunch of schoolkids with a porn video.

'Oh…my…god!'

'Eww, lady in red…'

'Nah, red dwarf…'

'It's all a bit gooey…'

'I love what's on the paper, look at the art damn you!'

'She is the art, Roland!'

My ears pricked up. So this was Heathcliff. Roland. Sender of unwelcome messages. *Liking the new song.* Were they all in on the conspiracy?

'Let's make some more!' This came from Charlotte, who was peeling off her leotard before the paint dried it onto her body. My eye met Roland's for a moment as he helped ease the straps down over her shoulders revealing the naked, paint-streaked flesh beneath. She wriggled the rest of her kit off and stood in the middle of the group like a savage.

'Tom, what about you and Cleo making some music for the next piece?'

I felt almost hurt by her lack of shame. She really was something else. What would her mother think. Unstructured impro was not something I'd normally have anything to do with in any company, but Cleo was already singing softly next to my ear which kind of unhinged me. An hour ago, nothing would have been further from my mind than stroking my strings for a girl I used to want to call my own. The one who'd ruined me and cast me off and now had decided that salvage was a noble profession. And this other girl I'd been intimate with only two hours ago asking me so guilelessly in her stained birthday suit, what could I do? I grabbed my guitar and tuned it down to some modal chord that would take no effort at all from my uneasy fingers. Tapped the guitar body and sampled it with my looper pedal. Hit the strings and took a second sample. Set it all playing back and started softly plucking single strings. It was turning into one of those days without an end. A day that flows into the next day without trying.

Surreally, the room began to regroup yet again, while in the middle of it all I played a repeating pattern that could have housed almost any vocal, while Cleo, the girl who was apparently carrying my child, sat on a stool next to me and began to sing the notes of a song I knew, from what seemed a lifetime ago. The song she'd sung on the night I cut loose from her. The memorial she'd composed for her sister, its meaning now transformed by approaching motherhood.

> *Root in me*
> *Grow through me*
> *Breathe through me*
> *Sequoia*

Around us, the finished painting was carefully peeled from the floor by determined fingers, dragged to safety and rolled by the group like a groundsheet being packed away by a bunch of scouts. New paper got stuck down, new colour mixed, indigo, kingfisher, plastered over naked flesh, while Dalila recorded everything like the faithful acolyte I could now see she was. It looked like some odd initiation ritual mated with the joy and abandon of the colour-slinging Holi festival.

There's a strange kind of eros in accompanying intimate physical contact between others. A shared voyeurism in which I felt outwardly neutral, inwardly deeply immersed. The new action was conducted lying down, paint forms generated by the couple rolling gently into foetal or stretched positions, while the music flowed from the placement of limbs sliding slowly across each other and across paper, the interplay of curving arms, entwined legs, twisted torsos, arched necks. There was something beautiful about the intermingling of colour, the physical contact which was intimate yet curiously asexual. They were snails on the flirt, dolphins at play, twin embryos entwining each other in the womb in Technicolor explosion, both random and by design. The colour thrummed in my brain with the power of its physical presence. As I followed my synaesthesic urgings, Cleo's melody wove around my arpeggiation, becoming more abstract, more insistent, more hypnotic. It was the first time she had ever let me lead her in music, and as her chant subsided into murmurs, cries, the deepest notes of her register slowing, finally, to stasis, I wondered if she really might mean half of what she'd said to me this evening.

I flicked the looper pedal off and Dalila's viewing eye followed as the two protagonists of the drama were pulled to safety by friendly arms. Charlotte kissed her partner in grime delightedly and did a little dance for the camera. Dalila took twenty seconds of the come down and general reaction and then cut to black. She climbed up on a chair and refocused on the painting itself. Just ten seconds, as still as she could, then she was done. She was absorbed, committed, in that moment almost reverent.

Cleo touched my arm. 'Thank you.'

'What for?'

'For listening.'

'You don't understand, Cleo. I had to kick the habit of you to survive.'

'I do.' She opened her arms. Not like a superstar in the spotlight. Like a woman. 'If you want a DNA test I'll arrange it. Just call me.'

She went to join the others watching the playback.

I looked at the painting. Through my blurred vision it was complex and beautiful. It radiated energy in dimensions I felt were beyond those on the floor or in the room. I could see the waves made by Charlotte's hair across the page as she had tossed her head from side to side, the partial imprint of a hand laid delicately to rest and swept in an arc from head to shoulder, the line of her thigh against his, the outlines of two bodies fused and locked together as if in combat, simultaneously uncoupled, unhinged in wild bacchanalia. I drank it in, liberated in a way I couldn't begin to explain.

The party fragmented, artists departing to clean up, discarded clothing and towels bundled toward the washing machine, the floor rescued from party shoes and the unintended footprints that spread across the long-suffering floorboards like some guide to a bizarre new dance.

Oblivious to the figures in transit around me, I fell upon the congealed dhal and chapati discarded on a corner table. I couldn't recall the last time I'd eaten; it felt as if I'd been fasting for a week. Another thing street life had taught me was how to appreciate discards, how to eat from dustbins, how to survive on the edible cast-offs of humanity. I'd been used to hunger. I had to control the sudden urge to cram the remains of everything on the tray into my mouth, and what wouldn't fit there, into my pockets. It tasted amazing to my starved system, I could feel the cells in my body starting to regenerate as the biochemistry kicked in. Then I realised someone was watching. Dalila. I licked my fingers, slightly shame-faced at my feral raid, but saw in her eye a curious look of recognition. 'D'you want some more? I've got plenty out back.'

'I'm fine. It was fantastic, saved my life just then.'

She smiled, with a tenderness that made me start to understand the elusive quality that drew Charlotte. 'I love to cook. It makes me forget all those times I was really hungry. You know what I mean?'

'Hunger tells us we're alive.'

'Or controlled by our cravings. But you'd have to be a Buddhist to sort that one out.'

We exchanged smiles, hostilities thawing.

'I should go. Say thanks for me?'

Her eyes glinted mischievously for a moment. 'I'll tell her. She speaks very highly of you.'

I slipped out quietly, but my heart was in uproar and I was glad of the cold to knock some sense into me, the city mist shrugging its damp cloak around my fevered body. The density of humanity in the flat that had cocooned us all from the listless, unfriendly city streets in whose life we were but a minor irritant, was abruptly gone, part of my history. As I looked back, shadows moved to and fro across the bay window. Only the faintest ghost of a soundtrack betrayed any kind of activity within. At a house further along the street, a dog barked, incessantly, stupidly. As I passed by, I came face to face with a street fox darting out from the upended bin. Remnants strewed the gravelled path. It froze guiltily for a moment, its gold eyes regarding me before slinking into the shadows. We were two of a kind, snatching at destiny before the unknown put the boot in.

I was a father. I hardly needed a DNA match to tell me that this was the truth. I was shaking like a leaf when I reached my front door, the news finally kicking me in the guts. I felt like an earthquake in human form, bursting apart in the violent shift of emotional tectonic plates. Seeing her had been hard, knowing how bad she'd been was ten times worse. How would it be spending the rest of my life with this woman? Would she leave me on the sidelines, watching from the wings with the kid and the bottle while she stepped into the light ready to crowd surf her thousands of fans? Would she cry when they groped her, or would she lash out with her heels and goad them on?

I made tea, hot and sweet, no milk. There was never any milk, though there would be more than I could stomach soon. Would it change her, being a mother? She was more ambitious than Lady Macbeth. Would she dash her babe's brains out on the stone flagging rather than sacrifice her career?

Exhaustion clamped its hands over my eyes and shut out the winking light of the intruder alarm as I huddled under the duvet waiting for the warmth to calm my convulsive shivering.

For a long time I was trapped inside a sealed bag, desperately searching for an opening which was never precisely where I was looking. Then all at once the fabric gave way and I was shooting into the light, a great cry of joy bursting from my lips, lying with her on the cushioned deck of a galleon in full sail under the blinding sun, scudding and bumping across the waves. *Drink me* she said, offering her breast, and as I sucked her fiery sweetness her siren song tore at my heart like a madness. A huge breaker crashed over the deck and sent the hulk splintering into fragments and I was adrift on the rolling ocean like a piece of flotsam, shrunk to the size of an infant, bobbing crazily in the waves. She was unreachable, commanding the swirling waters. The churning sea enveloped me, dragged me down, spat me out again onto the shoreline where a myriad babies crawled up the foaming beach like newly hatched turtles. There was a distant roar in my ears. The ground was hard and I was lying face down on a pavement shivering amid a sea of cars. She walked slowly past, silhouetted against the coloured neon, carrying a newborn wrapped in animal skin, a tall, gaunt man with slicked hair and dark glasses at her side. I heard the words *All yours, Karl* before snapping awake.

Why was it that I couldn't stop shaking? Was this what malaria felt like? Shuddering and convulsing to an early grave? I reached out for my phone and searched her number. It rang out several times and then she answered.

'Hi.'

'Book the test.'

13.

A sliver of dull orange-black prised its way under her eyelids. Sleepless, her husband shifted onto his back with a sigh. 'Mia.'

She turned onto her side, ready to feel him pressed against her and to drift again into sleep.

'Mia?'

A flash of adrenaline roused her from wine-drenched slumber, heart pounding. 'You ok?'

He took a deep breath and exhaled slowly, reluctant to break the silence. 'You've got to get a grip.'

A sick feeling spread slowly across her abdomen. 'What?'

'I think you know.'

If it was going to break, then let it happen cleanly, openly. Not by hints and obfuscations. And preferably in the morning. 'I don't know. And I'm asleep.'

'I'm trying to cut you some slack, really I am.'

A flash of anger. 'What does *that* mean?' She struggled with the image of an animal straining at the leash. She rolled over to read his face. He was clearly in a more lucid state than she was. He'd been awake, figuring this out.

'If you don't run a company, you lose it.'

'We run the company together. Both of us.'

'Exactly.'

'We share the responsibility, just as we always have.'

'Yes.'

'One of us takes the management reins when the other is in the hot seat.'

'Look, we know all this, it's always happened as naturally as breathing. But I've got a script delivery next month, I have creative responsibilities. Ally's phoning me from the office every hour with questions and you're not there. You're never there.'

'I have a deadline too.' The words felt banal even as they came out of her mouth, like a whining child. She was deemed in absentia. AWOL. Carried away by this piece of trivia which her husband thought unworthy of her and neglecting her core business. That was what it came down to. It pained her that he had to struggle to criticise her. It pained her even more that he didn't understand that the creation had become all his responsibility, and the support structure all hers. 'I'll be delivering the pilot to the channel in a fortnight. I'm editing tomorrow but I'll catch up with Ally during the day.'

The special pleading nauseated her. She felt wrong-footed. Of course she should have been at the office handling the executive business. Ally was, after all, just the office manager, with no creative role. What flashed over her in a sudden rage was the assumption that she should be content to steer the ship while Stephen shored up their creative capital. After all, it wasn't her writing a series for the BBC. It never had been her. Nor would it ever be unless something changed. *When are you going to write that screenplay for me* suddenly revealed itself as the hollow dare it was. A shot across her bows, something never to be realised. There was never a time when she hadn't worked to support their partnership, never a time when she'd taken a moment to work out whether she had a creative bone in her body. The more successful their company had become, the more she had lost confidence in her ability to create. It was *he* who had shown her in a moment, how simple it was. A penniless musician. An idiot boy who had nothing she hadn't given him, who could do nothing but create. Unwittingly, he had conveyed the blindingly obvious: you simply had to want it. But to want it, you had to step off the treadmill. You had to lose everything. Stephen sighed and turned to slip an arm around her. She rolled away from him, tensing with anger. It shocked her that her body had turned rebel. Resentment streamed from her. 'You said you were glad I had my own project.'

'I know you're worth better.'

'The first chance I have of proving I can actually create something and you're on me like a ton of bricks telling me I'm wasting my time!'

'Mia, you know that's not it.'

'*What* is it?!'

'I'm not thrilled to be losing my wife to some

young turk whose crooning now seems to mean more to her than twenty years of marriage.'

It was out. He'd said it. In the silence that followed she could hear the gulp of saliva in her throat. Then the blood roaring in her ears. She thought she would faint. She wanted to vomit. She swung between the two sensations in horrible suspension.

'That's unfair.'

'How is any of this unfair on *you*? You pick him up off the street, clean him up fit for service and tuck him away in a nice little love nest up the road, how the hell is it unfair on *you*?!'

For a moment, she thought he would hit her, so visceral was the trembling energy in the body next to hers. A terrible laughter bubbled up in her throat. 'You're wrong.'

'I'm not wrong, there's a tenancy agreement in your desk drawer.'

'It's a temporary arrangement while we're working on the series.'

'We have offices in the West End, what's wrong with conducting your meetings there and keeping an eye on our business affairs at the same time? Why the secrecy?'

'If I'd been keeping secrets do you think I'd have left the drawer unlocked?'

'Perhaps you thought I wouldn't notice how you've changed.'

'How have I changed? I dare to step outside the charmed circle, do something of my own and suddenly I'm no longer the same woman?'

'Your body language is more eloquent than you realise.'

'For Christ's sake, Stephen, stop talking like a stage play. There's nothing going on!'

'I don't believe it's nothing.'

'You'd rather believe your own suspicions than take my word?'

'It's what I feel. I can't help that I'm a writer. I'm paid to read between the lines.'

'That doesn't mean you always get it right. No one's infallible.'

She felt oddly tender towards his resignation. She felt sorry for their wounded love. She knew she was riding on a knife edge. Technically, she was in the right, but emotionally? She knew he was not altogether in the wrong.

'Tell me you're not in love with him.'

'I'm not! He's never even touched me. Ok, that's not quite true, he kissed me on the day we got the commission, but that was just… Please. I'm forty-six, I have my pride.'

Stephen reached out and touched her searchingly.

'I think you're infatuated. Maybe you haven't admitted it to yourself but… Mia, I know you. I look in those eyes and it's like a clear stream.'

'So you can read me like a book? No, I don't care for that, it's a trope. You're a good enough writer not to deal in those.'

'You're luminous and fine. He couldn't possibly know all the things you are.'

'I don't think he's remotely capable of trying. Or interested.'

She saw the clouds pass overhead as he moved from fury to enquiry, still felt the sting of anger thrumming at her skin. 'You've created a fiction out of him and I won't be treated like a lovesick teenager.

I'm your wife and lover, your creative partner.'

They were silent for a while as he took time for her avowals to sink in. They'd never needed them before and there was a sense of something foreign in the air that still crackled between them.

'Why are you wasting your time on him?'

'Let me ask you some questions. When you first choose a documentary subject, something hooks you. Something passes between you that will transform your experience of the world. You've done it countless times. The last time you did it you won an award for it. You know there's some spark that makes you, the documentarist, catch light, otherwise you wouldn't start. You wouldn't bother telling the story. Sometimes it's puzzlement, sometimes revulsion, sometimes fascination, sometimes empathy. But there's always eros because your subject must become the one thing in the world your audience must want to watch, and you're the first one to do the watching. In a way you're watching yourself. So where's the difference between what you've spent your career doing, and what I'm in the process of doing right now?'

'He's using you.'

'Maybe I'm using him too. I've never made a documentary on my own before. It isn't noble, it isn't intellectual, it has no grand concept. In fact, it's downright simple: poor street musician attracts the notice of a TV producer and is catapulted onto the nation's screens where he wins their hearts.'

'I think you're getting your genres crossed. That's a neat little movie plot but the documentary needs him lying in the gutter dodging the kicks of passers-by, getting his guitar crushed under the wheels of a

London cab, being evicted, shooting up under the arches and eventually drowning in the Thames.'

She resisted the urge to clout him, though her fingers tingled. He was rubbishing her programme, didn't want to understand her journey.

'If you'd taken the trouble to spy a little further than my desk drawer, you'd see that it's a documentary about the new music scene, with our mutual friend as anchor and interviewer. He's working at the heart of something quite vibrant. When I saw him on the street I felt frightened for him. His music touched me. I need him to be special. Just as you needed Dalila to be special. You make your subject.'

'All very finely expressed darling, and if you tell yourself something long enough it also becomes a kind of truth. But forgive me: you don't rent a flat for someone if they're just your subject. You really don't.'

'You threw him out, he had nowhere to go.'

'Exactly. But you never asked yourself who else he knew, no, you made yourself the centre of the picture, the only person who could possibly rescue him. Mia, a documentarist follows her subject out on the streets, grubbing around in the hostels and church halls, finding out how they survive playing their music to unreceptive ears whatever the cost. She films them ripping off their friends and pilfering from their relatives, hiding from their dealers, sleeping their way to a record deal. She doesn't massage reality to fit her own fantasy. No matter how creative your documentary, you stay on the side of reality. You don't intervene. When you do, you've crossed the line into fiction.'

'That's fundamentalist. Old-fashioned.'

'You're peddling a fairytale.'

'Maybe. And maybe it'll be entertaining.'

'Fatally blurring the line between actuality and wish-fulfilment.'

'People want wish-fulfilment. The commissioners want it.'

They were both standing now, separated by the marriage bed, Mia shivering in her nightdress, Stephen reaching for his dressing gown.

'I hope he's good enough to carry the show. I'm happy to look at the rough cut if you'll allow me.'

'Maybe we should keep our talents separate on this one.'

'Not if it's going out under our company name.'

'I see. So now you have a veto on my output as well. I never thought you'd turn so controlling in middle age, Stephen.'

'Someone's got to be in control. You clearly aren't.'

'You don't trust my judgement.'

'Frankly, no.'

He picked up the phone. It took her a moment to realise he was searching the menu. A fraction of a second later she realised he'd dialled a number stored in the memory. She sprang forward to snatch the handset but Stephen was quicker. He slammed into the bathroom, locking the door. From outside, she could hear the conversation.

'If you lay a finger on my wife, I shall come round and personally castrate you. Is that clear? I know where you are. I'm on your case. I'm also the executive producer of your little endeavour so let's keep it sweet, shall we?'

She couldn't tell if there was an answer, or silence at the other end. After a few moments, her husband hung up the phone and returned to the bedroom. There were livid spots at his temple and brow, but his cheeks were flushed, his lips almost blue with the exertion. He replaced the handset icily onto its base. As he withdrew, she could see his hand was shaking.

'Very assertive.'

'Make sure he's at the edit tomorrow morning.'

'It'll be the afternoon. I'm interviewing beforehand.'

'I'll call David first thing. We need someone quick and good.'

'I'd prefer to talk to the music editors on my list first.'

'David's done opera. Live streaming. He did that prize-winning rock documentary a couple of years back.'

'I want new talent! Something off the wall.'

'You're as off the wall as it gets on this show. Have you got all your footage yet?'

'There's a gig night we need to shoot, then we'll have enough for the pilot.'

'Enough for seventy-five minutes?'

'Why?'

'In case the broadcaster doesn't take it and we want to put it out as a feature. Come on, Mia, you're not thinking like a producer at all, you're miles behind the curve.'

'It's my commission, you can't just take it over. The contract's in my name.'

'Then I may have to sue you for joint ownership.'

He opened the closet and took out pillows and duvet.

'I'll grab a couple of hours sleep downstairs. See you for coffee.'

She watched the door close, watched the wood vibrate and the atoms resettle, seemingly in slow-motion. The world had re-grouped its elements around her. She felt the heated pulse in her neck, the tremors convulsing her body, the dry-mouthed disbelief, with dispassion. She was physically present, and yet she was somewhere else. She felt as if she were disintegrating internally, that she had become a shell, that everything inside her had turned to ashes. Her meaning had drained away to nothing. She was nothing. All at once the room was quiet with a graveyard insistence, and his footsteps creaked away into the silence of the lower house.

She was drinking espresso to keep her eyes from closing on the third interview of the morning when Stephen came into the basement to help himself. There were brief, polite introductions, then she was left with her interviewee while Stephen read his emails at the big table and scanned the morning papers online. It was eleven-thirty. She had not slept, although she had lain for an hour or so beneath the cooling bedclothes, struggling to regain her body heat, shocked to the core and yet curiously relieved. It felt funereal in her head, as if someone close but unidentified had died. She had tried his number as soon as Stephen had left the room. A hostile call from a husband demanded an explanation at least. Unsurprisingly, he wasn't picking up. She sent him a text message. *I'm sorry you were disturbed in such an unpleasant manner. We're editing from one-thirty. You should be there.*

Now she was interviewing by mathematics, all personal response to her candidates seemingly out of reach. She had their CVs in a neat pile in front of her, she'd scanned their showreels in the grey moments before the dawn broke. It hadn't taken long. Susana, who filmed and edited music promos, was her front-runner, a dab-hand with digital effects, her style fluid, rhythmic, witty. Stephen clearly wasn't convinced. Film-school post-graduate Leon was working as a commercials editor to pay back his loan and came with a thicket of questions as dense as a Polish forest, which Mia had no inclination to answer. 'Do you think this kind of material is really up your street, Leon?' she heard herself asking.

'Honestly? No. Next time you make a feature film, please let me know.'

'We don't really make feature films, but thanks for coming. You can let yourself out, can't you?'

She wrapped up as swiftly as she decently could with crop-haired, bespectacled Ingrid whose art-films lacked the commercial edge she needed. She ought to have been intrigued for the sake of future development, but she felt blank. She could see no future for her company and felt the presence of her husband dismissing her choices even before she had a chance to consider them. She saw the young woman to the door and returned to await her final appointment.

'What time have you asked David?'

'Twelve-thirty for an early sandwich.'

By the wall clock it was eleven fifty-five. 'I'll have to join you at quarter-to, my next one is running behind.'

'Call it off.'

'What?'

'Cancel them. If they can't turn up on time, they're not under consideration.'

'Can you stop this, please?'

'It's more important that you're there to brief David with whatever is in your head.'

She watched him scrolling apparently absorbed, the lines on his face thrown into sharp relief by the burning laptop screen.

'I've made an appointment!'

'Don't waste your time, Mia. New talent has to be underpinned by experience. You've got your new talent onscreen, that was your choice.'

'The bullying tone doesn't suit you, I suggest you drop it and we try to adopt a more civilised discourse.'

'An award-winning producer doesn't bother waiting for a timewaster.'

'They're ten minutes late, for goodness sake!'

'It's a question of status.'

'I thought I knew you. I don't know you at all.'

'Just call them and let's have some more coffee.'

Bristling with irritation, she filled the cafetière, only because she was not sure she could speak in a straight line without a further dose of caffeine.

She let Stephen find out about David's travels in Ethiopia while she did her duty by the girl, an Oxford graduate and assistant editor in a Soho post-house eager to cut her teeth on music content. Couldn't wait to go down in the world, as David laughingly put it after she'd gone. David knew all about her, he'd been a guest lecturer on her film course. She was working with his mate in the West End. A nice girl but a lot to learn. Mia had heard such talk so many times she felt like gagging, but she kept a brave face and clung to her objective – there was a pilot to edit and she knew David could put it together in his sleep. She wasn't sure if the path of least resistance was the right one, but she knew she had a deadline.

He'd been the consulting editor on *Lovergirls*, but Stephen had known him almost as long as he'd known Mia. Back then they'd dubbed him, mischievously, the Buddha of Suburbia. He had graceful hands, the most agile thing about him, and an ever-expanding girth like some benign paraplegic. He took two sugars in his coffee and like any nocturnal nightclubbing teen had a weakness for sweets. Walking into his edit suite you might mistake him for a corner shopkeeper from the 1960s, the array of glass jars ranked around his Avid station filled with jelly beans, sherbert lemons, smarties. The jars were always full. It was rare to see him eat, his hands ever busy in the service of his timeline. Fleetingly, in the time it took to import another section of media or to call up some rushes, his hand would dip into one of the jars and scoop out a handful of consumables which would disappear quickly and fuel him for the next hour. He did not move from one end of a twelve-hour session to the other. He metabolised like a camel, drinking little except his recreational midnight whisky.

She had a painful and growing dread of exposure as she watched the two men cheerfully work their way through freshly delivered wraps. She had no appetite. She felt feverish, as if she were protecting a fresh wound in danger of infection. She had a horror of subjecting her protégé to their jibes. She had heard nothing and didn't even know if he still had the address, so she was not expecting him to grace them with his presence. He would surely keep a low profile. He was young, callow, entirely inexperienced in the politics of marriage. Why would he enter the lion's den?

But at one-forty, just as Mia was setting up her laptop to show David the footage, the doorbell rang and there he was at the basement door, with her husband letting him in. The room felt airless. She stood up to greet him and it was like looking at a ghost. Her first thought was that he'd taken drugs, but he greeted her politely and shook hands with David, quite lucid, just remote. They didn't touch, safer to remain at arm's length. His face was drawn, with a slightly cadaverous look about the mouth. She wanted to ask him if he was all right, but that was impossible. It dawned on her how far intimacy had coloured their normal discourse, tried to quell the irrational fear that she'd lost him. But she had lost him. He was a different person.

Stephen shot her a sidelong glance and took possession of the moment. 'Have a seat by David, mate.'

'Sure.'

Shame flashed over her, she was disgusted by her husband's fake chumminess. Tom took the coffee from him with nod and drank it off like a cup of hemlock. He was too tall for the chair he'd been given and sat hunched over his long legs, knee jogging incessantly, grappled to the screen as if it were his lifeline.

There they all sat around the dining table, while the two laptops chattered away sharing data, David's hands working, footage whirling in fast-forward as he logged each sequence into the project.

'Where did you shoot?' asked David, not interested.

Mia felt like her own interpreter. The words didn't seem hers at all. 'It's the Charlatan club in Shoreditch.'

'Looks fun.'

'It was.'

'So, Mia, how are we going to put this together?' It was her husband this time. Was the whole edit going to be an inquisition? For a moment she longed to snatch the laptop from the table and hurl it from the window. Better lose what she'd had than be pinned out on a board like a flayed rat. Then something in her changed gear with a kind of clunk. Everything in her cooled. She had a separate professional self that wouldn't allow all that effort to go to waste. She knew exactly what she wanted, she didn't care what anyone else thought, she would stay in control.

'I'll show you the trailer we shot, David, that's what the people at the channel liked and we need to keep that sense of flow even in long form.' She called up the file and hit play. 'The overall format is performance interspersed with interviews. We want to get a sense of the people who work and socialise there and how the microclimate functions.'

'And our red thread is our young musician here... who... guides us through the pleasure garden... interacting with the oddballs who inhabit it... he also sings... ok, got that.'

She was relieved at how much was already clear from the images on the screen. They told their own story. More importantly, she knew that Stephen was attentive, that he couldn't simply rubbish what she'd done. He kept his counsel and was silent, taking it all in. She glanced at him, watching the younger man at work. What was in his mind? How much of the subtext between them would he get?

They reviewed the footage, just as Mia and Tom had done for the hours after shooting, this time under scrutiny of a first audience, without the benefit of closeness and adrenaline. After the first hour, she wondered if Tom had fallen asleep, but he was just very still and contained, as tense as steel wire, clenched hands to his lips in that odd anti-prayer pose. It was as if he'd placed himself in a sealed box from which nothing could emanate. There might have been one looped, silent scream playing over in his mind, yet she couldn't read him. He had ceased to be porous. Whatever flow of feeling had been between them, it had switched off as suddenly as the Gulf Stream and she was now in Alaska.

Stephen, by contrast, was open, friendly, on his best behaviour. The exchange of the early hours might never have taken place. Gradually, though, she realised there was a drift, an undertow to the discussion that she didn't quite like.

'It's very engaging… what's the story?'

'The story is the music.'

'I think the story is the musician.'

'Ok, the musician then.'

'So what's his story?'

'He's… a promoter, mining for new voices among the clubland cacophony.'

'You're sure that's a story?'

'Yes.'

'He was on the streets.'

'That's outside the remit of the show.'

'I'm not so sure.'

'It's not what I sold.'

'It what makes him unique.'

'We can't shoot that, it's over.'

'Of course we can shoot it.'

'That's tasteless. It's not what I want.'

'Mia, don't be crazy, the story is what drove him onto the street and what saved him. It's a love story played out through the music scene.'

Now she really did want to seize her laptop and throw it overboard. They were being hijacked and exposed in the same breath. At that moment, something close to hatred for Stephen overwhelmed her. 'No.'

Tom glanced at her, finally emerging from his autism. 'I can see that working,' he said to Stephen. 'I'll lose some weight, grow a beard, avoid the shower for a while and you can shoot it last. I know some quiet places around town we can use.'

Stephen chuckled. 'There we go, great!'

'But it's not real.'

'None of it's real, Mia. The magic lantern. The thing that seduces us all.'

'It's a lie.'

'I think you're being a mite pretentious. The boy wants his moment of glory, we're going to make it pack some emotional punch is all.'

Mia regarded the three men who were so bizarrely closing ranks against her.

'Let's make a schedule for next week shall we?'

As the afternoon drained of light and the basement darkened and coalesced around the blue glow of their improvised workstation, so Mia's sense of ownership both of her programme and her protégé seeped away in the growing enthusiasm of her husband and his editor. Something shadowy at her back was urging her toward the open doors of the plane. Soon, it would not be long now, she would have to jump. She wondered what it would be like, freefalling. How many minutes would she have to think about the end that was inevitable, unavoidable, once that small step lifted her into the void?

Tom clearly didn't want to speak to her. Her husband had in his own immaculate way seduced him, very much in the way he had seduced all his subjects, ever since she had known him. He had that easy way of connecting. Of intuiting what his quarry meant in human terms, in the overall fabric of life. He had perspective. He had understanding. Identification. It was one of the qualities she had most admired in him, from the earliest moments of their relationship, and in this moment, the quality which made him most destructive. He had to be the leader. He had to own the project. He had to interpret reality. That was what made him a director, and a creator. It was what she'd always supported and served in him. But now he was working against her and it hurt her more than a bruised cheek or a black eye would have done.

They spoke on neutral subjects, Stephen cleverly using the technical detail to recruit his allegiance. The sound rushes from the resident recording system needed synching up to picture along with a corresponding discussion about cut points and working around performance glitches. Of course they would have to use camera sound for some sequences, not ideal, but they could rebalance it in the sound edit and in any case it added to the grainy immediacy of the whole. Stephen liked it more as he got used to it. Mia wasn't sure if there was an implied criticism. It had all come together so fast, of course she hadn't hired a sound recordist. She wondered if Stephen found it all too amateur for words. Tom gave nothing away. Out of the corner of her eye, she glimpsed the glassy intensity of his look, his deadpan responses, his eye glinting in the screenlight, barely visible beneath the tangle of hair that kept his face half-obscured. From time to time his phone would trill its presence and he would check it briefly, tap in a few words occasionally before returning it to his pocket. Most likely trying to fix up somewhere to live, another beat in his separation from her.

They had a rough-cut slung together by late in the evening and Stephen proposed they order a Thai meal to celebrate. 'I'm liking this, it's quite grabby isn't it?' he ventured by way of peace-offering, a compliment directed at them both. This was tacit praise of what she'd done and she knew he meant it generously, but his magnanimity only seemed to mark the extent to which he felt secure in his ownership of her, and her output.

Ill-at-ease, keen to escape the overheated adult ménage, Tom moved towards the door. 'Got to shoot off.'

'That's fine, we'll tidy up some of the rough edges and see you at the club on Friday?'

'Sure.'

'Don't forget: spurn the razor. I'll book a make-up artist for the rest. And bring your laundry bag.'

Mia escorted him to the door, a touch defiantly. 'If you want to talk about any of this, let me know,' she murmured.

Shaking hands seemed both superfluous and an embarrassing falsity. They stood apart for a moment, a strange little qualm in the space between them, then he was gone.

14.

I didn't ask for the hanged man, but there it was in the spread of her cards, the only one I was truly afraid of and she'd turned it over for me with one flick of her slender fingers. Twenty-four hours had made me fear the executioner so hard I'd finally locked the door of the flat and carried a change of clothes, laptop and guitars across town to sleep on Jewel's floor. I'd had to plead with her for a couple of nights' grace. She smelt danger coming. I told her my story and watched the assault of gravity on her face. She was Catholic, I didn't have to tell her what it signified. All she saw was the chasm opening irrevocably between us, the definitive closure of any possibility of ever consummating her unrequited love. I felt so shabby having to rely on her hospitality I nearly picked up my possessions and walked out again. But she was never going to let me go lightly and there were three flights of wrought-iron fire escape between me and blamelessness.

'It doesn't mean death, anyways, it means surrender.'

'It looks like the end to me.'

She turned her soulful grey eyes on me. 'No, no, you're being too masculine about this. It's about finding truth in a paradox. Look at the guy: he's letting go.'

'Hanging by his heels in a dark alley. Where I deserve to be.'

'It means reversal.'

'Mhm.'

'You turn the world on its head. It's a symbol of transformation.'

She was smiling, but her eyes were full of tears. That was the bit of the paradox I found hardest to take. We held hands for a while, quietly, while the traffic rushed past outside.

'You give up everything, you get it all back.'

'What about you, Jewel? What do you get?'

She shook her head and looked away. Whatever secrets she'd locked in her heart, she wasn't going to open them to me just then, if ever. 'Sleep well, yer leathcheann.' She kissed the top of my head and disappeared into the next room, closing the door firmly behind her.

The next I knew, she was standing over me with a cup of tea and it was already time to rise and shine. The sun was streaming in through the curtainless windows and giving her an auburn halo. I surfaced blearily from my sleeping bag. I'd already forgotten how hard a floor can be: living in Mia's flat had taught me to forget. Even in that brief time she'd softened me up. I'd been far too cosy for my own good. Perhaps it was as well to get some practice in dealing with discomfort before the shoot.

Two texts were waiting in my message box. One from Mia, trying to find out where we stood. I didn't answer it. One from Cleo giving me a time to meet her at a clinic somewhere near Tottenham Court Road. I'd been waiting for her message every hour since that dawn call of mine, but when it finally came it filled me with a stab of terror. Five days from now I would discover whether or not I was actually the father of her child. The beautiful day suffered a kick in the groin and suddenly looked as frowsy-round-the-edges as I felt. I spilled tea on the floor in my struggle with the unwelcome reality of taking responsibility, not just for myself but potentially three human-beings. How the hell was I ever going to manage it? People did it all the time, but I was in mortal fear of the change.

'There now!' Jewel was darting for a kitchen cloth and mopping up the mess. 'Were you very uncomfortable?'

'Slept like a prince.'

'Really?'

'No, not really.'

She gave me a sharp flick with the teatowel.

'Thanks for everything. You gem among women, you're looking lovely this morning, so y'are.'

I got a very old-fashioned look for my stumbling blarney. 'And you about to be a daddy, for shame!'

'For shame, indeed.'

It was all a shame, a lame apology for a scenario. I'd knocked up the bitch and was going to have to leave the white goddess alone here playing songs to the moon. What a travesty. I pictured myself in a year's time, sporting an untamed red beard and self-cropped hair (combed perhaps), check shirt and unbleached cotton jeans and plastic vegan shoes (she was a vegan, yes she was), a man-bag across one shoulder and a three-wheeler kid buggy out front (but only if the in-laws were paying). She'd be at my side in her rag-bag mummy-hipster gear, too Hoxton for words, our kid wrapped close to her in some gaudy papoose, still breast-feeding in public. She'd have short hair now because she was sick of the baby using it as a climbing rope. Probably no make-up so I'd be able to see all the hormone activity in her face, but I wouldn't notice. I'd be pumped full of the joys of fatherhood. We'd sit in a wholefood café talking non-stop about our offspring's miraculous qualities. The baby would already have sprouted its first teeth and be babbling obscenities, every cherished word a bid to enslave and hypnotise us to the cause of its survival. It would be wiping its breadsticks all over my jacket and drooling affectionately into my beard. Our friends would be almost exclusively the parents of our child's baby friends. People from the NCT. People from the local cafés and stalls. Volunteers at the Oxfam bookshop. We would have trouble gaining access to clubs and bars but we would brazen it out together and exhaust everyone's patience, including our own. All night we would sing baby songs to our kid, beautiful little pieces of nonsense with no artistic virtue whatever, useful only for drowning out the sound of teething. My guitar would have been wrecked and mangled by our little darling and I would have no heart to replace it. My woman's studio would be put into dry storage until all the tech had become too outdated to revive, or perhaps until it had become as retro as the analogue world was now. What would happen to our music? What was to become of us?

And if I thought she'd spent no time of her own mulling over the same, sad waste of time stretching before and after, then I barely knew this woman.

'Tom?'

Cleo was contemplating me with some concern in her face. She looked gentle. Harmless even. Of course I knew she was nothing of the kind. Unless… what scared me most of all was that she'd lost her claws and barbs and all that excitement between us was gone without our quite knowing where. We were sitting on opposite sides of a perfectly square glass coffee table, in a perfectly groomed waiting-room with walls as white as an asylum and opulent leather chairs. Between us lay copies of Vogue and Country Life. In my hand was a cup of bad coffee. In hers, a cup of camomile tea. For some reason I was dying for a cigarette. Something about the way she was weighing me up unconsciously as a potential life-partner, a perspective I'd never in a million years thought to cope with. She'd been my unattainable love, forever lost in the forest of my own yearnings, and now here we were on the fast track to stability. Or mutually assured destruction.

'Are you afraid?'

'Yes.'

'I'm not.' There was a flicker of the old dare in her face. 'We were on fire that night, weren't we?'

Those moments of ecstasy were probably what had kept me from ending it all when I'd been sleeping under the skies, drenched to the bone, heart-frozen and drowned in a sense of loss so profound I could never make her understand.

'It was lust.'

She looked disappointed, but she rallied quickly. 'White heat like that has to create something amazing doesn't it? What are you afraid of?'

So here we went with the full-on post-apocalypse rear-guard action. All her words of seduction to bring me to heel. I took a deep breath. 'Everything I don't know about you. Everything I don't trust. You say beautiful things but you don't mean them.'

Her smile curved into being, all glint and guile. Still with the power to make my guts turn over. Definitely in pursuit. She wanted to hold my hand but I retreated to the window and looked out at the rooftops of Fitzrovia, wishing myself at the top of the Telecom Tower with the disconsolate pigeons.

The soft undulation of her voice continued behind me. 'I sat looking at that thin blue line and it was like the end of the world. I wrote myself a business plan. All the rules of the game. How it would have to be. All the limitations that were suddenly there changing the life I thought I was going to have. I actually went ahead and booked a termination. Then I had this amazing dream. I saw her under a tree in a summer field full of flowers. She was so lovely I woke up crying. I knew I couldn't hurt her.'

'Of course she'll be a stunner. Like her mother.'

'She had your smile.'

'Let's not go there.'

A smart little nurse came out of one of the consulting rooms. All in white, perfectly matching the decor, perfectly manicured and coiffed, and perfectly reassuring.

'Cleopatra?'

The word sounded absurd in her mouth. She gave me a tight little smile and took Cleo into the room with her.

'D'you want me there too?' The ease with which the words fell out of my mouth appalled me. I was already behaving like the father.

Not that there was anything complicated. Just a tube of blood. It couldn't have been more simple. All the complicated stuff was going on inside her body. Cells dividing and multiplying with their own miraculous intent, like some weird little factory where everything was programmed to a gene map and no way of knowing the contents. The most colossal gamble any of us were capable of, no word on the odds, everybody happy to go into it blindly knowing nothing of the outcome, 353,000 times across the world every single day. The power of biology.

The nurse unstrapped her arm, withdrew the needle and pressed a wad of cotton wool over it along with a tiny strip of plaster. 'That's it. All done. I'll just label it up for you. You've got the address of the lab for sending the samples?'

'Yes. Thank you so much.'

'If you could leave your cheque with the receptionist before you go?'

'Of course.'

Cleo perched on a chair to complete the paperwork. She also had something for me. A little sampling pack. She sent me into the gents to wash my hands, rub the swab on the inside of my cheek for ten seconds and stick it back in the tube. Apparently there was enough DNA in whatever mouth goo I came up with to connect me genetically with the foetus. Or not.

When it was done and packaged up ready to send to the lab, I escorted her to the post office in Southampton Row, then back to her apartment via Clerkenwell and Old Street. It was still a beautiful day, just a little warped with the emotional pitch of things. She seemed serene. As if there was no room for doubt.

'So you're just doing this to prove it to me?' Something about the forensics seemed to make every fertile male a criminal.

'If you still think it's Karl Fleet's baby, nothing I say is going to convince you. I'll bring you the certificate once I receive it.'

'You're honestly telling me he never laid a finger on you?'

'I'm not sure you have the right to doubt me and possess me at the same time.'

'Maybe not.'

'There's a difference between performance and reality. You know perfectly well that our business needs us to sex things up but you can't conceive just by flirting, Tom.'

'You need a bodyguard.'

'Yes, I probably do.' Her eyes were at their most penetrating and catlike. 'If you come on tour with me you can guard me 24/7. That might be fun, don't you think?'

I'd walked into that one without even trying. 'Let's wait for the result.'

She didn't quite like this. 'So my judge and hangman: has anyone laid a finger on *you* recently?'

What was I to say? That I'd had multiple fingers laid upon me, mainly while I'd been fantasising about laying mine on somebody else's wife? 'Nothing serious,' I said.

I was gratified to see she was jealous. There was a tiny flare to her nostril as she tossed back her head in the sunshine. 'Men are such hypocrites.'

We'd arrived at the door to her apartment, but I wasn't sure I was ready to step inside just yet. The ghosts of that night four months ago were still roaring from the stairwell. There was a jumble of thoughts in my mind like so many cats fighting in a sack. Did she actually love me? Or was she just impressed at her own reproductive audacity? Her splendid conception at which I happened to be the key donor? If she had felt something real and tender for me, why weave such an intricate tissue of lies to keep me out of her life? If I was her bit of rough, her walk on the wild side, if I was so far beneath her ambitions, then why did she want me now?

She eyed me a little wistfully. 'Would you like to come up?'

'I'm not sure it's a good idea.'

'I can fix you a salad? I've got to rehearse later anyway.' She looked almost frail for a moment. 'I have a pre-tour gig at the Charlatan on Friday, will you be there?'

'I think your manager has done a little deal behind my back.'

'Really?'

'Don't pretend you don't know.'

I followed her up the stairway, impatience getting the better of me. The glorious flat was shining like a fanfare, fifty shades of gold bouncing off its immaculately designed surfaces, like an enchanted castle. The place dazzled me with its luxury, refinement and self-confidence. I sat in one of her opulent armchairs and watched her making green tea. Was she really offering me a part of this? Or would it all crumble to dust as soon as I asked the wrong question?

She came and sat near me, poured the delicate pale liquid into bone china cups that were translucent, like pulled teeth. It was now or forever hold my peace.

'You want to know what I think?'

'About what?'

'About you and Mr. Fleet.'

She flicked me a long-lashed glance that wasn't quite friendly. 'You're starting to sound not very polite, my lover.'

'I don't believe for a minute he never slept with you. You were together the night I left, you were together for weeks after that, maybe months, what do I know? You were pregnant, you didn't have to hold anything back. You threw everything you had into your performance. You bought yourself a record deal. You got him to sign you an advance to see you through the studio and out the other side. Your manager is more pimp than manager, but perhaps he's more sinned against than sinning and at least he gets a tour for his pains. As things went on, you thought: I could be Mrs. Fleet. He'll be delighted to be a father, it'll be his crowning achievement. No one will ever know about that night out back up against the wall amongst the crates and the trash cans. So you kept on servicing him, telling yourself it was all going your way, until the pregnancy began to show, then he wasn't so keen. In fact, he ran a mile. But the signatures are good for this album, and the next. Still enough to launch a career. And if the tour's good, a short break will whet the public's appetite for more. Nothing lost. Sexy mothers are fashionable. But what will it be like to raise a child as a single mother, all those long hours recording, performing, promoting? How can you be a shooting star and still the centre of that child's universe? No, it's impossible. You struggle through many sleepless nights, turning it over in your mind. Then fate offers you a solution. Something so magical, it must have been meant to happen. You meet a little pixie at one of your gigs. A gorgeous little punk poet. You get pretty close, pretty fast, maybe you write some songs together. She invites you over for a party and you meet up with your lost lover whom she's trying to prise apart from her mother… maybe it's just by accident, maybe by design. But you decide you still like the look of him. Even after the school of hard knocks, he's matured a little, one or two interesting scars. You'd still go out back with him. And in time, he might just grow into the fall-guy you need. You don't need him to earn, not yet, your contract's good for now, and your parents have money. You do need him to love you so hard that he can transfer that love onto the little piece of flesh that you've inadvertently produced together. It's just another fairytale of London town. What do you think? Am I getting close?'

Her hand was shaking as she put down the tea-cup. 'I think you should leave.'

She was crying now. Not the way she'd cried when she'd seduced me that night, then told me our relationship was over. No, these were big, bold tears that carved rivers down her cheeks, contorted her lovely features and made her look like every other jilted girl. She flung herself onto the sofa and wailed inconsolably. She'd lost the game.

I went over and touched her shoulder softly, it seemed sad to see her collapsed beneath her own house of cards. But she screamed at me to get out, so I retreated down the stairs, trying not to hear the wrenching sound of her sobs.

It took a few minutes for the shock to kick in, then I felt pretty shaky myself. I spent the next hour wandering the streets, feeling like a loose cannon, uncertain where the path of least damage lay, letting the geometry of the East End slow my thoughts. On the way back to Jewel's, I was drawn by the smell of fresh bagels and coffee at a music café in Exmouth Market, where I sat for a while, letting the sound drift over me, trying to unravel my dizzy brain. I couldn't decide whether I'd made the worst decision of my life or just had a narrow escape. Either way, it didn't feel great.

I decided to take my next dose of pain and dialled Mia's number. I'd brought trouble under her roof, but there was also a job to finish and she owed me money on completion, so it was in my interests to fall in with whoever was going to get the thing done fastest. Her husband, to be fair, was a pro. He'd made it clear he had no animus against me personally, he was just being territorial. Male to male, I respected his position. With a wife like his and a media reputation to defend, I'd probably have done the same. Except I had no prospect of ever finding that out. I didn't have the right background or education. I had no social caché whatever and I wasn't ruthless enough to acquire it by proxy. I was a pathological under-achiever, a coward. A fair-weather friend and lover.

Always taking the path of least resistance. Never facing up to the difficult stuff. Sniffing conflict, I'd run a mile. Whatever my attraction to Mia – the only adult who'd taken me seriously since I'd left home – Stephen Chancery had cauterised this vein of vanity as surely as if he'd held the hot iron to it. There wasn't the remotest chance of possessing her. I was going to have to find my own way of shaping a future.

'How do you feel about this stuff on the streets? Are you happy with it?' She sounded distant, as though it was a long-distance call from Timbuktu.

'If it makes sense of the show it's cool with me.'

She hesitated only a fraction. 'Ok, we'll shoot a couple of sequences just in case we need them. We'll base ourselves at the Charlatan and nip outside while we set up the evening session. Does that work?'

'Yes. It's fine.'

'Where are you now?'

'I'm in town.'

'Have you moved out of the flat?'

I pictured her ringing at the door and finding the place unoccupied. 'I need time to think. I'm staying at a friend's.'

I felt a moment's guilt washed away by the floodtide of relief. Her voice sounded smaller. I'd hurt her. But it couldn't go on. It was all too close for comfort now.

'Just let me know. I'll need to sublet it.'

'Sure.'

'One other thing. Dickon Brand wants me to confirm the headline slot for Cleopatra. Is this something we can work with?'

It was strange hearing her name in Mia's mouth.

Like a profanity. How was she to know how far I'd come in a short week?

'She'll put on a good show.'

'And how do you feel about it?'

Her considerateness was beginning to get under my skin. 'It's business, Mia. It'll make a great contrast with everything else we've got. She's about to launch big, so if you broadcast quick enough it should get a decent audience share.'

I could hear her thinking, trying to fathom the change.

'Ok, I'll get onto him and book it now.'

She was gone, with a suddenness that seemed to burn into the silence.

I thought it was just an overdose of adrenaline, but by the time I reached Jewel's that evening, I was shaking like a leaf and my skin ached as if I'd been beaten up in a dark alley. She pressed her cool white hand to my forehead, tut-tutting her way around the flat making tea and emptying her cupboards for paracetemol. 'You're as hot as hell. Into bed with you.'

She meant her own. She bundled me into an old dressing gown of hers – bright red with white hearts, very fetching – and under the duvet that was fragrant with vanilla shower gel and her own sweet yeasty scent. According to her I was dead to the world in seconds, lying sedately on my back like a knight on a tomb. I was so unconscious, I had no idea where she spent the night. Or the following one. It was a queen-sized bed, she could have slipped in beside me while I sweated my way through her teenage nightwear, but in retrospect I decided she'd probably chosen the sofa. She'd appear intermittently with pills, iced water, sweet tea, damp cloths. I opened my eyes at one point to find her sitting close and dabbing gently at my forehead. She started as if I'd caught her in some transgressive act.

'Jewel.'

'Yes, Tom.'

'I'm sorry to be so much trouble.'

'I don't mind.'

She could have followed with, 'What are friends for?' or something equally trite. But her gentle look spoke to me far more eloquently. She was doing it for love. A love I had no right to at all. I'd have liked to have kissed her then, but propriety and viral fatigue kept me prone.

'I'm going to write you a song.'

'You do that.' She looked quite merry at the idea. 'That should take you all of five minutes. Make sure to do it while you're asleep.'

'Don't mock the afflicted.'

'I'm off to college now. I have Prokofiev to attend to and he's much more challenging than you are. I'll leave you to your private purgatory and make us some chicken soup when I get back, how's that.'

'I love you.'

'I bet you say that to all the girls.'

'No.'

That was true, though I wasn't going to expect her to believe me. She scorched me with her scepticism and left me branded but with my sins expunged.

By the day of the shoot I was on my feet again but only just. Suitably etiolated, with a healthy growth of stubble and a clammily unbathed body wrapped in my best unlaundered jeans and sweater, I was a kilo or two the worse for the infection and had an artistically tubercular cough. It was drizzling lightly and the walk from the tube had taken it out of me. I could see the concern leap to attention in Mia's face as I approached the unit base, the little encampment of equipment and a handful of personnel, including our friend the cameraman, all sheltering under a barrage of outsize umbrellas. A couple of estate cars were parked on the coned-off single yellow line, from the boot of which I was issued with a cup of hot coffee and a dry towel. She was all in navy, slightly military, her hair swept up and tucked into a cap which I had to admit rather suited her. My eardrums throbbed, everything coming to me in snatches, like passing islands in an archipelago of action which I hadn't the energy to navigate in its entirety. It felt like I was doing the slow tour in a beat-up motorboat with a cupful of diesel on board.

Mia asked if I was ok and I replied in the affirmative although she clearly wanted me shut in a warm car without delay to fend off the damp. Her husband, clad like a communist biker, told me through the window that he couldn't have prepped me better himself. He clearly approved of my deteriorated state, but we were going to add some finishing touches apparently. In a surreal moment, I was introduced to his daughter who was doing make-up for them today and in she climbed. I could hear Stephen Chancery's instructions continuing outside.

'...A bit of subtle shadowing under the eyes, make it slightly grimier beneath the cheekbones, just where the stubble begins. We should have a look at his hands, too…'

She eyed me with that incorrigible directness that made my sweat glands go into overdrive. 'Not looking too hot today.'

'No.'

She pursed her lips and began to load her make-up brush from a palette of charcoal greys. 'Close your eyes for me.'

'Should I open my mouth?'

She applied shadow lightly, deftly, minded to rise above any lewdness. 'That won't be necessary.'

'Tell me, was it necessary to land your mother with a whole heap of heartache just to salve your family honour?'

'Don't talk, I need to do your cheeks.'

I shut up and made do with fixing her with my most bilious gaze. One hand disappeared out of sight and reappeared again shaking a little box. 'Like a mint, sweetie?'

She popped one onto her tongue and stuck it out at me like a tab of 'e'. My fingers twitched, but she had me pinned to the back seat. She slipped the box into my hand so I took the hint and helped myself.

'Where you staying?'

'Never you mind.'

'Want to drop round some time and get your stuff?'

'It isn't mine.'

'That's never stopped you before.'

There was a tussle as I reached abruptly for the car-door handle. She was too much. She'd always been too much.

'Ah-ah, let's keep it professional. It happened more by accident than design. I know you'd like me as

Mata Hari though.' She smiled beatifically and rearranged my hair to her liking. It was torture of a bizarrely refined nature. 'I can lend you a couple of suitcases if you need them. I'd like to move my things in.'

'Thought you were all set up with your arty friends?'

'Yes, but it's more private when you want to… you know.'

I tried not to raise an eyebrow. 'Wanting your own space with Dalila?'

She shrieked with delight. 'No, Roland!'

Roland? 'What, Heathcliff?'

Her laughter tinkled through the fuggy interior. I was beginning to feel light-headed. There were more turnarounds in this plot than a Brazilian soap-opera.

'He's my lover.'

'Since when, yesterday?'

'Couldn't you tell?'

'I thought you were just being artistic.'

'You know, being a threesome is quite tiring.'

'You don't say.'

She was applying rouge to my knuckles to make it look like chilblains. 'We've decided to try monogamy.'

'How progressive. And what does Dalila think?'

'She's still my muse.'

'Best of soulmates.'

'Exactly! I knew you'd understand. And anyway, it's more convincing now.'

My head was beginning to swim with the excess of heat, not to mention information. 'Convincing?'

She smirked in a way I distinctly mistrusted. 'Now I'm pregnant…' The hairs on the back of my neck stood on end and my head seemed to fill with expanding helium.

The next thing I knew I was lying on my back with my feet raised and what sounded like a major fire alarm going off in my head, looking into her screwed-up little face and the anxious voices of Mia and Stephen in altercation outside the open car door. Her mouth was moving. She had my hand in hers. It took a moment for her words to resolve themselves into anything I recognised. She was saying sorry. Sorry. 'It was just a tease. Can you hear me? Say something?'

I felt like Prometheus breaking his bondage on the mountainside, my body heaving itself of its own volition out of that car door and away from her. Stephen steadied me against the force of gravity that threatened to propel me headlong onto the pavement. But it was to Mia's horrified glance I appealed.

'Keep your crazy daughter away from me, otherwise I'm going to do something I might regret.'

'What's happened?'

'Ask her.'

She gave me a queasy look before clicking into producer mode. 'Have you fainted before?'

'No.'

'I should call a doctor.'

'Don't waste your money, Mia.'

'You're not well.'

'Just give me a few minutes, please.'

Tense, she watched me staggering up and down for a while to try and regain some sense of equilibrium. Now the crisis was over, Stephen had lost interest and was discussing shots with the cameraman. Charlotte rolled herself a cigarette and huddled, somewhat abashed, in the doorway of the club. The rain grew heavier. It was shaping up to be a great day.

Plying me with more pills and powders, and a cup of hot, sweet tea, Mia insisted that we shoot the exteriors as quickly as possible. A couple of lamps were hauled out of the back of Lars's camera car by a bedraggled assistant electrician. They crackled as the current was switched on. Lars shook his head, not keen. Stephen reasoned, urged. The rain bounced off the housing. I curled up on a pile of sleeping bags as instructed like a filthy alley cat haunting the stage door and did my best to ignore the rain spattering my ankles. It wasn't much less uncomfortable than real homelessness, just fake, but at least I didn't have to try too hard to look pissed off. Under the shelter of the largest umbrella, brandished by his long-suffering sidekick, Lars took some shots of me feigning sleep – I was still drowsy after the blackout and not sorry to lie down for a bit – followed by a walking sequence along the graffiti-layered brick wall that housed the Charlatan. We did four set-ups, the umbrella following the camera step-by-step along the way with me artistically exposed to the elements, the rain beautifully lit by tungsten, by which time I was soaked to the skin.

Mia called a pause. The equipment was duly derigged and re-stashed in its vehicle. She sent me inside the club to get changed with a bag of clothes and another towel, waiting outside the door of the gents herself to collect my sodden clothes, instructing her daughter to use the hand-dryer in the ladies to take some of the moisture out. Bearing a passing resemblance to Ophelia pulled from the brink, Charlotte wrinkled her delicate nose and obeyed.

When the rain eased, we were outside again for

some busking sequences in a nearby patch of scrubland masquerading as a garden, more often a hangout for the local junkies than a haven for toddlers.

Back in my glad rags, warm, distinctly less sodden, and high enough to create a force field, I unpacked my old guitar and they put me where they wanted me and lit the shot. They'd take the master first, then use the playback to get a second establisher and various close angles, profile headshot, hand shots. It was strange to be handling the beat-up instrument which had accompanied me through all those weeks of hardship and living rough. Something about the fretboard under my fingers brought it painfully, lividly back to life. It was an old friend which had seen me through times of betrayal and I clasped it to me one more time like a talisman.

'Assuming the weather holds up, as well as my voice, I'll do two different songs, ok?'

Mia nodded her approval. 'See how you feel. You've got a long day ahead, you don't want to burn yourself out.'

Still protective of me, as she had been all that time I was in the hospital. Intimations of loss clouded my vision momentarily. I would miss her when all this was done.

The sound recordist moved his boom into position. Mia stepped forward next to her husband.

'Stand by…'

'Camera ready.'

'Turnover…'

'Speed.'

'Sound rolling.'

'Mark it… and… action.'

'This is *Lovergirl*.'

The months kaleidoscoped into a quickening whirl of images, lifting me up and for that brief moment, outside myself. There was love, anger, adrenaline, gathering force in my mind, hitting me like a tidal wave which carried me through. This was the one. We were winning.

> *Can't see can't breathe can't die can't live*
> *You're onto me*
> *You're onto me*
> *You're sweet hard dark light*
> *Know how to feel right*
> *Into me*
> *You're into me*
> *Lovergirl*
> *Lovergirl*
> *Dance me to your backbeat*
> *Burn me with your black heat*
> *Against the wall for you*
> *I'll take it all for you*
> *Lovergirl*
> *Ah Lovergirl*

15.

There were, she realised later, so many versions of that day that could have taken place. So many options that would have led not to catastrophe but to an ordinary parting of the ways and to closure. There were always options. Her challenge, she knew, was dealing with the new reality, but behind her professional mask she was already retreating into an irrational state that made her afraid. The spark between them had gone, and with it, her ability to perceive the world as it was.

Late morning, the club was wearing its Cinderella best, a smeary, grey-around-the-gills, morning-after face. A mournful African cleaner was doing his best with the previous night's depredations, more bottles than Mia could possibly imagine being drunk on one evening, stacks of dirty plastic glasses containing half-consumed measures of noxious liquids, in some of which illicit cigarette-butts floated evilly, discarded paper napkins blotted with lipstick, occasional blue carrier bags screwed and knotted into a bundle concealing secrets and habits fit only for the trash. One of the barmen was rolling a new barrel across the floor ready for priming behind the bar, where the radio whined tinnily into the echoing space and a thin-faced blonde half-heartedly polished the counter. Everyone seemed hungover. No one wanted to speak.

They had set up their base-station in the back room, with the grudging approval of the barman. Playback of the exterior set-ups was satisfactory. Some of it even looked quite poetic out there in the rain, and she had no doubt the songs would offset the clubnight footage in a way that would impress the broadcaster. She had no argument with Stephen's judgement. It would all work out. Inside, she was numb. Nothing looked or felt the same. She was completely neutral as to whether the show was completed, delivered, accepted or refused. She couldn't remember what the office in Monmouth Street looked like and had no desire to go there and pick up the reins, not that day, nor that week. Perhaps she wouldn't return. She had no feelings about the future of her company. Its award-winning reputation seemed to belong to someone else. Her glance drifted away from the dingy room where they were all clustered. She had sent him to get washed and changed, she couldn't bear the smell of him any longer.

Earlier, she'd watched him lurch from her car with a feeling of surprise: a young vagrant caught stealing from her unlocked vehicle. He could have been anyone. She barely recognised him. What was it that had suddenly kicked off between him and Lottie?

'D'you know?' she asked her daughter.

'What?'

'In the car, I mean.'

An oppressive shadow crept over Lottie's brow. Mia knew that look of old: the time she'd upended a bag of flour over every surface in the kitchen to make snow. The day she'd confessed to letting a friend's brother finger her when they'd been playing in the basement. When she'd taken the scissors to the hair of the girl sitting in front of her in class. It was her goblin gene, recessive except in extremis. Was it becoming more dominant?

'I told him he'd impregnated me.'

Momentarily floored, Mia tried to read her daughter's face. 'And has he?'

She made an angry, laughing gesture of dismissal. 'He's probably spawned a whole tribe since you've known him. You have no idea!'

There was a bitterness in the back of Mia's throat. The spittle dried in her mouth. 'Tell me.'

'He'll fuck anything as long as it's female, just as long as he doesn't have to try too hard.'

'Has he hurt you?'

Lottie started to laugh in a way that quickly escalated and turned perilously close to tears. Mia grasped her by both arms, unable to bear it, needing to stop her. 'Lottie!'

'I'm impervious.'

'I don't think so.'

'I did it for someone else anyway.'

'Who?'

'Oh for god's sake, Mia, you're too *old* for this!'

As Mia searched her face her grip tightened, her

fingers leaving indentations on her daughter's flesh.

'It's not *me*! Don't be stupid!' Lottie shrugged her off, her face livid, her eyes black with malice. Mia released her grip, heart pounding, hardly knowing which way to look.

'Let's just say his past has finally caught up with him. You'll see.'

She turned and left the bar. Unwilling to engage in further histrionics, Mia watched her go, helplessly, feeling ashen and hollow. The ill-tempered, bleached-out day acquired a kind of leer, an air of menace.

When he appeared in the bar a short time later, all she could see was the loping gait of a chancer on the make, dressed in what she had spent time and money choosing for him, that deep blue jacket paired with designer jeans and an Italian shirt. He looked like a pretender. What had she been thinking of? If he was expecting her to comment on his transformation, then he would have been sadly disappointed. Her facial muscles seemed paralysed with indifference. The few words she was able to muster were matter-of-fact, and he seemed content to treat her simply as a colleague, with no hint that there had ever been a special understanding between them. Her heart was leaden with disappointment and the clear knowledge that she had ceased to be useful to him. Her husband had closed him down so effectively, she wondered what she had ever found to say to him.

The session proceeded like clockwork, without the need for intervention. She'd set it up well. Tom knew the routine and had his own line to Lars, who recorded his interviews with the artists playing that evening. They all seemed interchangeable in their varying levels of articulacy and their short attention spans. But he could still turn it on. Just not in her direction. She watched everything on the monitor, her attention drifting in and out of the talk. The Spanish-looking girl, whose edgy protest songs she remembered from her first visit to the club, spoke too fast and laughed too much for it to make much sense. The cello and harmonica duo they'd viewed on his laptop were whimsical in looks and words, but the fire was in the performance, not here. A bunch of handsome boys bristling with ridiculous instruments – double-bass minus one string, banjo, home-made drums – gave Tom a run for his money and threatened to take over the interview. Mia intervened graciously and asked them to tone it down, they'd get less than one minute of the show unfortunately.

Now a willowy girl with long blonde hair and a husky French accent who fancied herself as a chanteuse, sat on the red banquette. Mia watched Tom's body-language, listened to his soft-spoken, almost girlish banter, coaxing the story of the song out of her, and felt suddenly exhausted by the interchange. Hormones were squealing loud in the air around them. Impossible to think he might not end up in bed with the girl later on, what was to stop them? What was to stop him replicating the same pull, over and over for the next fifty years? It would go on as long as his libido held up. She had rescued him from the scrap heap and had made the grave mistake of thinking it earned her a special place in his heart, but he was moving on with such ease it crushed her that she had allowed herself to fall under his spell. Even now, as he was in the process of making himself homeless once more and saving her the trouble of being responsible for him, even now, he was lining up amorous possibilities, someone who would take him in for a while, someone who might have a friend with a room to rent, someone on whose generosity he could depend for a time before that friendship was also worn out. Like a rolling stone.

The day continued on its way, with the same routine, the same system of checks and balances she had known almost all her professional life. She was simply going through the motions. She wanted to get this one in the can and move on. But to where? For the first time in her life she couldn't see beyond the end of the day. And the day was brightening, thickening around her. As light drained from the spring afternoon and a cloudbank came in from the west bringing more rain, the brash neon and over-warm house lights turned the place into what she had always known it to be, a theatre of possibilities.

Sometime after five, at Stephen's insistence rather than his prompting, she was interviewing Tom from behind camera about his musical roots and his role in the new folk revival when the stage door creaked open, and a group of girls came into the lower bar, hauling instrument cases, shaking themselves dry like a bunch of unruly waterbirds, glad to escape the inhospitable weather. One of them, drawn by the brighter lights, approached their corner film set. Mia had her back to the entrance and her attention fixed on her laptop but she saw the change in his face. It was the same disappearance of blood from the head she'd observed in the last moments of her dying grandmother. The words dried on his lips.

'Hold it there for a moment,' said her husband, who'd been directing the sequence. Mia turned and saw the girl she recognised, shaking her hair out of a

Bardot beret and letting it tumble down her back against the flirt of her raincoat. Her brass buttons winked slyly in the artificial light. 'I hope I'm not interrupting?'

Lars raised his head from the view-finder. Stephen contemplated her with professional interest. Mia extended her hand. 'Cleopatra? We'll just be a few more minutes, perhaps we can get you something?' She exchanged glances with her daughter who was doodling disconsolately at her clipboard.

'Just a glass of water. Thanks.'

Even as she spoke, Mia realised with immediate certainty that this was different. Everything else was just sideshow. She could feel the electricity in the air. She could feel the room come to life. Tom was on his feet and moving. Not towards them but in the direction of the exit, as rapidly as the hardware would allow.

'I'm sorry, I need a break.'

And he was gone. Cleopatra watched him impassively, her eyes strangely bright. Mia called tea and headed to the stage door. The winding ribbon of Brick Lane at dusk with its oddly doleful air, punctuated by lone figures and occasional disembodied calls, stretched as far as the eye could see. She thought she heard footsteps further up the street where the light of an Asian supermarket spilled across the wet tarmac. But the shadows gathered beyond the glare and she couldn't be sure.

'Has he done a runner?' Her husband probed, at ease on his plastic chair, feet up on the stage where the girls were organising themselves.

'I've no idea.'

Stephen scanned the schedule cursorily. 'What do

we still need him for?'

'Ideally an interview with our headliner.'

'Who? the 'it' girl? Sure. Let them do the sound check and we'll see where we're up to. Is there tea?'

It maddened her how he slipped into ownership of every project. It was a peculiar myopia that she'd learned to accept until she'd tried to break the mould. Now it grated on her nerves. 'At the bar,' she almost snapped, and went to join the girls.

Steaming polystyrene cups were handed round, her daughter apparently holding court in the midst of the girlish banter, which for all its lip-pouting, strap-adjusting and instrument-tuning represented a production lull which made Mia's shoulder muscles harden. Cleopatra was on her phone, busily texting. A few moments later it was clear she'd been chasing her manager. Dickon strode in, helped himself to tea and started hustling. 'Where's the sound engineer?' He barked at the reluctant barman. 'We booked sound-check for five.'

Mia understood that Tom was supposed to be co-ordinating this, and since he was absent she left Dickon to liaise with the club staff, climbing the stairs to the balcony, from where she could observe the room without being disturbed.

Strangely, she felt as if she could have climbed onto the nearest banquette and fallen asleep. She yawned and leaned on her folded arms, gazing over the brass railing. Figures came and went in dumb-show. Dickon raised his voice. The barman picked up the phone. Two of the girls struck up an angular jazz impro on cello and cor anglais. Lottie's Petrushka moves drew laughter from the group. The lull deepened, grew oppressive.

Mia distantly watched her unit sound recordist being recruited by Dickon to set up mic stands. The microphones were apparently too valuable for anyone other than front-of-house to handle, the boxes kept locked, only the house sound engineer had the keys. He was on his way, just delayed. Dickon yelled. Nobody was much enjoying being bossed around. Cleo seemed to be in conversation with the Spanish girl, but her eyes kept straying to the door. Stephen and Lars were exchanging notes at the workstation, ignoring the proceedings and planning the evening's shot list.

Mia observed the flux and flow of the room from her bird's eye stance, with a growing sense that she must take the situation in hand. She should be driving this, but it was as if her will had been sucked out of her like bone-marrow. She felt weak, almost tearful at the idea, but something must happen. Long-bred habit forced her down into the throng.

She almost wept with relief to see the front-of-house engineer arriving. Long-haired and behatted, sleeveless under his raincoat, Jed was soaked up to the knee, taking it all in his stride. He ignored Dickon and shook Mia deliberately by the hand. His own bristled with rings. The one on his middle finger left its indent briefly on hers. It read 'Fuck 'em.' He smiled airily and the set-up got underway. The girls clambered variously onto the stage. Microphones were placed, tested, the sound balance was set.

'We'll do a couple of openings shall we? Test the extremes,' Cleo suggested to Jed in band-leader mode. There was an impromptu solo break from the accordionist that settled into a pushy little riff. The girl at the drum kit started footing it on the bass pedal, joined by cello and keyboard player. It was loud, bold and infectious. Still in her raincoat and mitts, Cleo stepped forward and clasped the mic, fixing the room and gathering herself like a puma before springing her beautiful, heartrending vocal, soaring over their heads like some unearthly call to worship.

You have no idea how this feels
The boulder on my desert floor
The siren screaming out for more
The nightmare beating down my door
You have no idea
Oooo lalalala
Oooo lalalala

And when the night comes down
When you ride me with your hair in flame
When you crush me with your frozen shame
When you cover me with blood and blame
You bring me down
So-lo lalalala
So low lalalala

I loved you dear such a clear line
But you acted in hate and I'm not fine
You shut your life down and you took mine
You left me to get out with no sign
I loved you
Now it's you lalalala
Only you lalalala

Mia watched her with conflicting emotions, a sense of exhilaration at being present at the birth of something new, and futility at finding herself outside and beyond it. Her daughter was right. She was too old for this. The first chorus told her she was in the presence of a girl who was already a star, it was only a question of putting the message out to enough people so that the whole thing blazed into 3D. She had no doubt the tour was going to be a success. And she had no doubt that the documentary would be remembered largely for Cleopatra's appearance in it.

The second song fragment was hushed, tense, spellbinding, an ode to abandoned love, with its unsettling harmonies and gently rolling percussion, like the tide coming in, slowly, inexorably. As the closing high note faded into silence, the girl's eyes reopened on the bar space and the hushed spell that had fallen was broken. A smattering of applause, the recommencement of chat.

'Bloody hell, Mia. Who is she?' murmured her husband. Lars, never one to miss his chance, had managed somehow to film the sequence, and he was still rolling as Mia gave Stephen the background, as far she knew it, but her eyes were on the stage door. Tom was standing there, the rain streaming from him, eyes blind with fire and his arms full of white roses, the symbol of his devotion and his suffering, the thorns pressing into his hands. He walked forward and laid them on the table in front of Cleopatra, as she stepped down from the stage into his arms and the room erupted into claps and whoops. It was as if everyone's best kept secret had come to light simultaneously. Tom held the girl close for a moment, then it was business as usual.

Much later that night, as she lay awake, she replayed

that scene and the others that followed over in her mind. She knew it was the last time she would see him. She also knew, in the end, that he had somehow outwitted her. She had underestimated him. She always had. Her sin was not that she had loved him but that she had never deemed him quite worthy of her love. She had never given him the grounds to make a move, and yet she felt a possessiveness of him which engulfed and stifled her now. She had a crystal-clear vision of his face at that moment, burning into the dark, imprinted on her eyelids: the faintly self-adulating smile of the unjust rewarded beyond their wildest deserts. On his arm hung a green-eyed beauty in a plum-coloured gown that swept the floor as if careless of what it might find there. A gown that elegantly clung to the ripeness of her belly and declared that she was both the property and the owner of the handsome young buck at her side. Had it been her own daughter she would have wept with joy to see something that looked so right standing before her. In reality, she felt the double loss of the young man to whom she was now nothing, a brief staging-post along the way in what was sure to be a tumultuous life, and the absence of an equivalent prospect for her radiant daughter whose lifeline seemed ever more tortuous and oblique.

The words he'd found were characteristically blunt. He'd told Mia they were having a child together. He would be going on tour with his girl in two weeks. He hoped they'd got all the material they needed for the documentary. He was looking forward to seeing it. Nothing more. What more was there to say? *Thanks for everything? For rescuing me when I was down? For believing in me? For offering me the status that brought her back to me?* He had thanked her, she knew it. But somehow she could only remember the one time. That night on the street when she had given him money.

If you love someone, set them free. She wanted to believe she had the strength and dignity to do this. She knew in her heart that it was the right thing. But there was so much more that was condemned to remain in her head about this person who had appropriated her peace and security. She thought she had admired and been attracted by his ability to live in the moment. Now she felt this was someone who trod so lightly on the earth that every relationship was contingent, contained the seed of its own extinction, whether the moment stretched to occupy a few minutes, a few days, a few years. With what variation in intensity would depend on the flash of fire that passed through him, the baffling chemistry that sustained his desire for however long. It was all instinct, intuition, right-side of the hemisphere.

She replayed again and again the moment she had understood that the girl was pregnant. There was fear in it and she approached with care at first, lest it overwhelm her, then ever more recklessly. Despite all she had said, despite convincing him of the contrary, lying to him in fact, she had kept the baby. Despite any misgivings about her future as an artist, despite any doubts about the partner with whom it had happened, she had given way to biology and accepted her destiny. Just as Mia had accepted hers and kept her own baby the first time. How different the second time had been. And how cruel. She realised with a struggle that the times had changed inexorably and she had changed with them. What she had learned painfully and alone was that she had been wrong. If she could have taken the decision again with the benefit of hindsight, wouldn't she have leapt at the chance? To be able to look now into the eyes of a beautiful young man who was flesh of her flesh?

What convulsed her was knowing that the girl in the plum-coloured gown would do something she had failed to do: face the odds that this precarious future would throw at her. She would struggle, but she would overcome. She had enough self-belief for that to happen. It was a kind of emancipation Mia had never attained. She had kept her first baby because she loved Stephen, not for herself. And she had killed her second because she feared for herself, not for her baby. Both times she had failed to love herself enough, to believe in her own strength enough. And now she had lost her substitute son, who was never any kind of son to her in reality, simply the focus of her obscurest desire, playing in her an echo of someone she might have become but now never would.

She felt increasingly, as she moved through the dumbshow of her life, watching her husband cutting her documentary together with such elegance and clarity, taking care that it would be up there with the best work they had done together, making it a joint endeavour they could both be proud of, that she had cheated him of the one piece of knowledge that would allow him to judge whether or not, in all the long years of their relationship, she had really loved him. It wasn't Tom, in the end. He was, perhaps, more symptom than pathology. It was as if she'd taken a brick out of the foundation of their relationship and the further they pushed into the future, the longer they were together, the more pressure the years exerted on this tiny absence. And now the building was so elaborately constructed there was no way ever to replace or repair what had been so fundamentally damaged.

Why, actually, had she done it? She knew still that it was the fear of never truly defining who she was. Uncertainty about ever finding the means of expressing herself. Why did that matter so very much? Why did her ego have the right to eclipse another's, insentient though it had been? She started to feel horror at herself, the monstrous selfishness and lack of humility, the idiotic lack of self-trust in what she might have achieved. Why could she not have understood that motherhood was only one aspect of who she was, and that there was plenty of time to become herself with any number of fellow travellers on board? Had she just been too young? At twenty-seven, she'd barely had time to emerge from her own musical vocation and grope around for others that might shape her future. But Cleopatra was the same age now as she had been, and clearly suffered no such uncertainty. Lottie, too, travelled her own bittersweet road with not a care for the possible obstacles in her way, she'd just take a boot to them and send them flying. Times had changed. Women were changing.

Stephen was yet again asking for her input, her comments on a sequence he had just threaded together with David. As she'd grown to expect from him, the editing style had become more elaborate, more about the artistry, the further involved he'd become. One part of her was mesmerised by his ability to enter a subject without becoming emotionally weighed down. His was the mark of a true documentarist, to be at once totally involved and simultaneously objective. Yet again, she was pulled into the uncomfortable process of scrutinising the one person she now would rather avoid looking at. It was a kind of punishment, she felt. Unspoken, but he'd made it her purgatorial fire, forcing her to go through the same story over and over until the myth was clear: boy suffering for his art on the street; boy taking club by storm with the power of his music and his power to bring the music of others to life; boy hooking girl star and ending up on his way to celebrity.

She had no quibble with the power of what he'd done. It was very similar to what she'd have done. But it was most definitely a standalone, with no chance of a spinoff. Stephen had deliberately sabotaged her format. He was unrepentant.

'Come on, the chances of a series from this are nil. Your star has already disappeared at the first whiff of a better offer. We'll take it to the channel next week and see what gives. It's a good piece of work, Mia, you did brilliantly. Now you can think about your own writing, we'll build your project into the development slate and get everything back on an even keel.'

That was it. He'd written the solution to the next phase of her life. Her bid to break the mould had failed, would always fail because the suggestions were never her own. Perhaps she didn't want to write a screenplay. Perhaps she couldn't. There were dark, lonely places calling to her and she didn't know how to explain her need for them.

The rejection of the pilot was still a shock. She

realised when she read the email from Jocelyn the commissioning editor that despite everything, especially despite its having been hijacked, she had believed in it, and in the power of Tom Pavelin. She had never expected it not to work. Stephen and she had delivered it personally and had a congenial, very friendly meeting, trailing the show with some highlights which the commissioning team had clearly loved. But in the cold light of day, a weel later, Jo wrote that though they'd really enjoyed the programme, in particular the stellar performance of Cleopatra Montagu whom they gathered was breaking big on her nationwide tour, music broadcast slots were highly competed for and they couldn't find the repeatable thirty-minute format they wanted, in addition to which they had some reservations about Tom Pavelin as a regular host.

Mia threw her mobile phone across the floor in vexation. She wasn't sure if she was angrier with the commissioners or with Stephen.

'We gave them the wrong thing! It wasn't what I sold them!'

'No, Mia, we gave them a great programme, given the limitations.'

'They'd rather have some stupid vlogger with five million subscribers.'

'Yes they would. Wouldn't you?'

'But he's better!'

'He's not big enough to sell advertising for them.'

'So frustrating!'

'They'll pay up to delivery, they'll just have to withhold the acceptance payment.'

'That's not the point.'

'Come on, you did well to get the commission in

the first place, it's just not how things run now.'

'It's such a waste of time.'

'Yes, but not the end of the world.'

But in a way, it was. Something inside her felt broken. She returned to the office to pick up the pieces with her long-suffering personal assistant, and to clear the embarrassment of emails. While Stephen completed his draft of the Orwell project, she overhauled their development slate, optioned a new biography at pre-publication stage and confirmed a business plan to release the music documentary with a fifty-percent profit share pledged to a charity for the homeless. On the surface she had reassumed her usual efficient producerly self. She was the same capable, cheerful professional her colleagues had always liked working with. Her brief sabbatical was put down to a personal project she'd been developing and now things started to move forward with one or two new ones, not necessarily previous front-runners, but still with the potential to come good. Underneath this veneer of active engagement, there was a growing chasm of alienation. She was going through the motions. In the evening she took to staying on late, after Ally had left the office, telling Stephen there was a lot to catch up with. Which indeed there was. She followed the Cleo Tour on social media and elsewhere on the web. The album reviews were almost universally favourable. Several were ecstatic. She certainly had the coverage, her manager was doing a good job. Fan videos started to appear, enthusiastic YouTubers capturing their favourite songs on their phones and tablets. Selected live appearances were captured for Vevo, edited with immaculate precision to focus on the intensity of her performance, backed by her bewitching band, giving their all to a room full of swaying phone-screens, lit up like candles in the dark. How beautiful it was. A modern fairytale indeed.

She turned to writing. Not a screenplay, that was somehow still too big a leap for her to make. She wrote poetry. Falteringly at first. Embarrassingly. She felt the spirit of what he had meant to her must somehow find its way onto the page to purge her inner chaos, so she worked at it while the city roared outside.

> *Strike your slender hand against the wall*
> *You, intoxicated, mad, appal*
> *The crowd now waiting for your fall*
> *Thown*
> *Out of furious brightness onto hard, cold stone*
> *What you want is what you cannot be*
> *Alone*
> *Faces you do not wish to see*
> *Clutch at the straws of your dignity*
> *Angled cheek against the night*
> *Blood seeps through sweat by neon light*
> *You, tensed and coiled to fight*
> *Loose, lank, unformed*
> *Nothing will come*
> *Of nothing*
>
> *You the beauteous one*
> *You drew them all on*
> *Dark star in their firmament*
> *What they took was not what you meant*
> *But the visions were real that burned in your mind*
> *Strike, strike again, strike blind*

The pictures of her that whirled through your head
While the flesh of the other roared take me to bed
And the baying for glory
That wasn't your story
Brought the night crashing in
The sky crushed your sweet skin
You were frozen in sin
And they won't let you in
Now the light's
Gone
Out

She found herself trembling when the final words clicked into position and she knew it was done. There was a sense of completeness and she thought, perhaps, if she could keep doing this, that somehow, her message would finally be understood. It took her some time to decide to send it to him. She read it over, ten times and more. Eventually, she put away the thought that he would dislike it. In the end it had to speak for itself, whether or not the recipient wished to hear.

She blocked it into the body of an email, which she began with a short message, glad that the tour was going so well, hoping that it wasn't too exhausting, wishing them luck with their upcoming dates. A superb exercise in neutral gear.

She closed down everything in the office and booked herself a taxi. It was past eleven-thirty and the tube would be overcrowded with youngsters jostling to get on the last trains home. She felt she'd had enough of the proximity of young flesh for a while. She was spent.

The house was dark except for the table lamp in

the hallway when she arrived. Stephen was not in his study, although the door was ajar and the PC on standby. Everything below was quiet. She crept softly up the stairs, trying to quell the rising tension, hoping that he was asleep. It was not that she was avoiding contact with him – she found his physical reappropriation of her understandable but unsettling – more that she wanted to be alone with her thoughts. She felt disconnected. She thought she would get better in time.

She undressed swiftly and covertly, avoiding the shower for fear of waking him. He'd been working hard on the screenplay. She'd read the first twenty pages and it was corruscating. She was proud of his intellect. She felt oddly tender towards his sleeping figure, arm curled around the spare pillow, his hair tousled, his breathing loud in the still room. Her husband. She slipped beneath the duvet next to him. He groaned softly and moved so that their bodies were touching but he didn't wake. Lulled by his warmth, she fell asleep.

Much too early she felt him pressing against her. It was dawn, and the birds knew it. There was something incongruous, even ridiculous in the urgency of his approach, but she was still drugged by sleep. In the recesses of her semi-conscious state she knew that her transgression was at least equal to his. Somewhere in the dark space of her mind stretched the starlit net of the poem she'd written. The first person she had sent it to was not her husband. Nor her lover. Nor anybody to her now.

With the morning news online and the reassuring ritual of coffee and fresh croissants from the French bakery round the corner, came a flicker of optimism.

Stephen was settled, looking forward to the writing day ahead. He knew it was progressing well. He was encouraging and supportive of her, grateful to know she was back in the driving seat. A strong marriage could withstand many knocks, what were the past few months measured against the long years they'd been together?

It was like watching a stage actor putting on greasepaint, her husband's gloss on her recent behaviour. Plastering the right flesh-tones over the pocked and wrinkled surface, a bold, ever-so-slightly arched brow, shadow and shading to give contour, a fullness to a mouth that perhaps was less generous than desired. Stephen was no stranger to the theatre, and onstage, his embodiment of Hera was a perfect replica of what should be. But if she put up her hand to those lips, the colour would smear and skid into a grimace revealing the pain beneath the mask.

She had never put herself inside Stephen's skin. She assumed his fight-back was grounded in a fiercely possessive love which he had fought for once before and had no intention of relinquishing to the first challenger. She used to think that he could read her like a book. She had opened herself to him when she was still young and he had taken possession without asking whether or how she might change, become more complex with time. It was so easy to think you were with someone and gradually, with acquired habit, only be with the body of shared knowledge, event, external force that encoded, represented them. How did one continue to love someone, body and soul? How must one continue to search for the core of meaning and intention?

They were sitting opposite each other at the

dining table, laptops facing, together and yet apart as so often. How easy to believe you were sharing a world, when you were drifting ever more rapidly out of each other's orbit. He was still scanning the headlines. She was still checking her messages. There was, of course, no reply to her email of the previous night. Perhaps she might have liked one, but she was not surprised at the silence. She was in error, attempting to extend this thread between herself and her former protegé, already stretched beyond breaking point.

And here, suddenly, was an article on her screen. Not a journal she normally read, but her trigger-finger search had led her here, and she was looking at a picture of Tom Pavelin with his arms laughingly around a moodily magnificent Cleopatra staring straight to camera. The geometry was telling. There was a long write-up about her début, her background, beliefs and aesthetics, the trials and treats of being pregnant on tour, introducing the man in her life. Between the kiss-and-tell lines blazed the overwhelming truth that this woman could dare to carry her personal life into the arena of pop stardom. If the reviews were anything to go by, it was a gamble she might just win. And he slotted so gracefully into her puzzle. Mia felt the door of eternity slammed shut against her. She was old news.

'Something good?' asked Stephen, finishing his coffee.

'Hm? Just coming up to speed with the day.'

He rose to give her a kiss. 'Better make a start. Unless you fancy another quick one?' A twinkle which almost worked, the winner's smile she had loved once. She shut her laptop and sprang up with a hair's breadth too much alacrity. 'What, up against the fridge, darling? You won't get your five pages done.'

He laughed at her serious face. 'Well, my oracle, how about dinner tonight? Luigi's, maybe?'

She worked up a smile. 'That sounds lovely.'

It was strange how the place beckoned to their subterranean misgivings. It used to be about work. Now it seemed to be about whether they were surviving as a couple.

Mia was quiet over her glass at first, but there was a pressure building inside her that the mellow wine finally brought to the surface. 'Stephen?'

'That sounds serious.' He wanted to keep it light, but he knew there were so many things left unsaid, he had to give them space. He poured a generous measure of the Barolo into the fine-stemmed glass and cupped it in his hand. Stage business. Something to pass the agonising seconds before the lost cue was remembered and delivered and the drama could continue.

'It's something that happened a long time ago.'

'Ok.'

'I'm sorry I've never told you this.'

A premonition made the glass grow heavy. 'Go on.' There was an edge in his voice he disliked but couldn't help.

'I got pregnant again when Lottie was still a baby. I had an abortion.'

The kick took his breath away. It was nothing like he'd been expecting. The woman he thought he knew was a complete enigma to him. She wasn't his at all. For almost the first time in his adult life he was lost for words.

'*Why?*'

'I didn't have the courage to go through it again.'

'Go through *what*?!'

She felt a still point expanding at her core, a terrible quietness that had nothing to do with the latent rage that was threatening to burst from him across the hushed interior of the restaurant.

'You're a man. How could you understand?'

'I'm your husband!'

'Exactly. And a writer. You would have found so many irrefutable arguments why I should continue along one path and not another.'

'You never asked me!'

'You persuaded me the first time against my better instincts.'

'Did I.'

'I was a kid. I'd done nothing, been nothing. I was your glorious girl, nothing more.'

'But you wouldn't have wished Lottie not to have a chance of life.'

'Of course not, that's asinine. Biology never presents you with that dilemma does it?' Her voice sounded chill in her ear. She felt hard and brittle. If he chose to hit her now, she felt she would tumble into fragments like a broken mirror. 'We've been lovers for nearly twenty years. It was a tiny cluster of cells, a potential life I decided not to continue.'

'You had no right, Mia.'

'It's my body, I have the right to self-determination. I was challenged enough hauling one child around the world and trying to make something of my own life. I never for a moment regretted having Lottie, you know that. She's my – our – greatest creation.'

He peered at her, still disbelieving, head in hands, hair awry. 'And how do you know what this tiny cluster of cells would have become?'

'I can't know, it's the same as if I'd had a miscarriage. It was too soon to know.'

'It might have been a boy.'

'Yes.'

'I'd have liked another boy.'

'So would I. Just not then.'

'D'you think it's why..? Were you damaged..?' he gestured weakly with his hand, unable to speak.

'I don't know.'

He reached out for the bottle savagely and refilled his glass before draining it. She watched, her face aflame and her eyes tearless as a statue's. She couldn't drink. Her mind was as clear as crystal. She was stripped clean of emotion.

'I can't un-hear this.'

'I know.'

She thought later that if she could have cried with him then, let it all out finally, perhaps they would have stood a chance of coming together, of healing each other before the bitterness set in, but they were in a public place. Glances were already slipping softly in their direction from one or two of the restaurant's discreet and wealthy clientele. They were known there, they couldn't make a scene, it would be bad for business, might even end up in the press. What they should have done is politely pay for their order, tell Luigi that something had come up and leave. Instead, Stephen ordered a second bottle and continued drinking. The silences between their hushed phrases were dangerous. Mia nursed her mineral water, stroked the condensation of her glass into crazy patterns, unseeing. She knew she was right. She had to be. After so much double-thinking on her part, she craved honesty. It cut her deep, not so much that she had wounded her husband, as that he judged her and could not help himself.

'You made me afraid to tell you.'

'That's ridiculous.'

'It's true.'

'Don't make this about me. You made a decision. You've lived with it for all these years. I have a way to go before I work out what it means. It's like finding out the person you've been closest to never gave themselves to you completely. It's a terrible betrayal.'

This, she knew, was untrue. She kicked back, hard and sharp. 'I shaped myself to your desire. You wore me to your image like a glacier.'

'That doesn't sound very sexy.'

She shook her head. He was shifting ground so fast she couldn't keep up. It felt as if they were speaking mutually incomprehensible languages. 'Perhaps I was just a projection of your longings. Perhaps you never saw me as I was.'

'Perhaps. And what did you see in me?'

'The key to unlock all the boxes I'd left behind in my life and make sense of what was in them. The key to unlock all the future boxes. I asked too much. When you delivered, I pushed back.'

'Too good at safe-cracking?'

Once, she would have smiled, but she was far away, looking down on the conversation from the dizzying pinnacle of her own separation.

'I think it's a choice. Either we internalise our lover's words and turn them into our own beliefs. Or we look for ways to shape our lovers into what we need them to be. Ultimately we're alone.'

'Tell me, Mia, is it because you no longer love me that you've finally found the courage to tell me all this?'

That was the hard ask. 'I'm sick of lies and half-truths. I don't believe love can continue in the same way for the entire duration of a relationship. People change. Love changes.'

Stephen growled the lines of an old song at her, screwing up his eyes to disguise hurt.

"*And then she turned homeward with one star awake...*"

'Don't let's do this here.'

"*Like the swan in the evening moves over the lake...*" What's the matter Mia, am I embarrassing you?'

There were tears running down his face now but she couldn't answer. She couldn't feel anything. There was a dark heart of anger building inside her like a thunderstorm and she needed to move to escape it. 'Let's go home,' she said.

Lottie was in the house when they got back. She'd come to collect the keys to the basement flat. Mia had promised to underwrite her first three month's rent as part of the handover and she rifled through the hall drawer in the half-dark while Stephen stumbled upstairs to bed, after having given his daughter a squeeze which was too long and too fervent not to arouse her suspicion.

'What is it?' She frowned after him.

'I think we drank a bit too much at Luigi's. You stopping over darling?' said Mia, kindly.

'If it's ok? I'll make an early start moving my things in the morning.'

'Sure. Just like old times.'

'Mum? What's up?'

Mia gave her a wan smile which she seemed to dredge from the depths of her distant memory. 'Just tired.'

Lottie hugged her. 'Goodnight then. Sorry to be such a pain.'

'You were never that.'

'Were?'

'Just bad grammar. Love you.'

'Love you.'

She watched her daughter climb the stairs. She waited quietly, she wasn't sure how long, until the house became quiet, then she climbed the stairs herself, all the way to the top floor.

She let herself in to the attic room which had become her sanctuary and closed the door behind her. She would not sleep. There was something pressing at the inside of her being which told her she would not be able to. She was as sober as she had ever been and she wanted to move. She wanted to express her anger at herself and at those who pushed her in ways she could not fathom. How had she become so weak?

Among the detritus of tech gear which she'd discarded years ago was a compact disc player. There was still a CD inside it, one she would no doubt remember if it would play at all. She expected the batteries to be long dead, but there was enough life left in them for her purposes. The track cued up.

A ghostly dervish flashed across the window pane then dissolved into the street lights beyond the glass. She barely recognised herself. Something less than mother, less than wife. Her hair flew wild, her body propelled by the relentless cacophony in her headphones, the soundtrack of her falling apart. In the room, the only noise was the stamp and shuffle of her bare feet against the floorboards. She danced.

ABOUT THE AUTHOR

As a writer and musician, Fiona Howe has long been fascinated by the interplay between words and music. Her professional background is in film and television. Having worked initially in production and script editing at the BBC and ITV, then as a screenplay writer for a number of European networks, she founded her own production company Scenario Films for whom she has produced, and composed the music for, an award-nominated trilogy of feature films: *Desire*, *Delight* and *Delirium*. A classical pianist and flautist with a BA in English Literature, she is also a singer-songwriter, having released her début album *Mermaid's Work* in 2016.

Printed in Poland
by Amazon Fulfillment
Poland Sp. z o.o., Wrocław